STRANGE BLOOD

STRANGE BLOOD

by

LINDSAY ASHFORD

HONNO MODERN FICTION

Published by Honno
'Ailsa Craig', Heol y Cawl, Dinas Powys
South Glamorgan, Wales, CF6 4AH

This is a work of fiction and no resemblance
to any actual individual or institution
is intended or implied.

ISBN 1 870206 69 X

Published with the financial support of the Welsh Books Council.

Cover design: Chris Lee Design
Cover image: Stone/Getty Images
Author photograph: Nicola Schumacher

Typeset and printed in Wales by
Dinefwr Press, Llandybïe.

For all those who have been wrongly accused

Acknowledgements

Thanks to my editor, Janet Thomas, whose help and advice was invaluable. Also to Nicola Craddock at Honno for her unwavering encouragement and support. Last, but not least, to Kevin for those long walks on the beach when everything fell into place.

Chapter 1

Delva Lobelo had never got used to going into the houses of the dead. Wheedling her way into the confidence of the bereaved, exploiting their grief, was not something she had ever felt good about. It was her job, of course, but not part of it she enjoyed. Last Thursday night the flock of professional vultures who thrived on every morsel of misery they could claw from a scene of death had gathered here. She wondered how they would take the news that she had been granted sole access.

She was early. Too early. Sitting in her car in the quiet cul-de-sac she glanced at the blue-and-white police tape stretching across the front garden. It was the only distinctive feature of this anonymous house on a sprawling estate so bland that strangers could drive around for hours without realising they had passed the same spot half a dozen times.

The white PVC windows were blinkered by hastily drawn curtains. Delva noticed that the ones in the living room overlapped at an untidy angle. That was not the way Tessa Ledbury would have drawn them, she was certain. The neat garden, the white, unscuffed front door – everything else spoke of a woman whose home had been the focus of her life. Even the football stickers and pennants in the upstairs bedroom window were arranged just so.

Delva scanned the houses on either side and turned to look at those further down the road. There was evidence of children in most of them; stickers or mobiles or miniature hammocks bulging with furry toys. But in the gardens, on the drives, there was nothing. It was a warm, sunny morning. Spring Bank Holiday week and half-term for the schools. Bikes and rollerblades and little feet should have been squashing the cherry blossom petals on the pavement. But the blossom lay in plump pink drifts where the breeze had blown it.

Wolverhampton woman stabbed to death . . .

The words of the headline she had read out on Friday's programme flashed through her mind again. There *had* to be more to it. Delva had reported from enough scenes of violent death to know what sort of reaction could be expected from the neighbours. And keeping kids indoors five days after the event was not something she had ever encountered, even in the sniffiest suburbs.

No, she thought, reaching into the glove compartment for her notebook, there was definitely something the police were holding back. Some gruesome detail had seeped along this self-respecting street like sewage from a cracked pipe. What was it these people knew that made them scared to let their children out of sight?

She glanced down at her skirt, rubbing at a mark she had suddenly noticed on the black fabric. She hated this suit. Her mother had once told her she looked like a skinny crow in black. And she was probably right, Delva thought, glancing at the sleeve of her jacket against the dark brown skin of her wrist.

The sound of a car made her look up and at the same moment she caught a flicker of movement from across the street. A curtain falling back. Someone had been watching her. Wondering what she was doing here.

The car drew to a halt behind hers and she watched in the mirror, waiting for the doors to open. Terry Bond got out of the driver's seat. He was the press office boss at West Midlands Police H.Q. in Birmingham and she had met him many times before. The man in the passenger seat was Detective Superintendent Steve Foy. For a minute or two the men stood glancing at each other over the roof of the car. Then one of the back doors opened and Delva caught a side view of a woman with black hair. For a split second she thought it was Megan Rhys. She had been half expecting her to be in on the interview. At the press conference on Friday Foy had mentioned the possibility of bringing in a profiler.

But as the woman turned face-on to the mirror Delva saw she looked nothing like Megan. Probably a plain clothes policewoman, Delva thought, watching her frown at Foy and give a quick shake of her head as she walked round to the back passenger door. Opening it she bent down, her head level with that of the other person inside the car. The husband. Delva could tell from the woman's posture and the way her head moved that she was trying to persuade him to come out. Richard Ledbury was obviously having second thoughts.

Delva sat rigid in her seat, not sure what to do. If she opened her door and got out now it might put him off completely. On the other hand she had often found that the sight of her face – a face from the television – had an unexpected effect on the bereaved. Many times she had gone to a house, steeling herself for a barrage of abuse, only to be invited in and plied with endless cups of tea while a shell-shocked relative poured their heart out. It was almost as if they were grateful that someone was taking an interest. Delva had never really understood it. She was sure that if anyone in her family met a tragic death a journalist would be the last person she would want to talk to.

She put out her hand to open the door but as she did so

she caught sight of Steve Foy coming towards the car. He tapped on the window. She pressed the button to open it and he leaned in, pursing his lips before whispering a suggestion.

'I think perhaps if *you* were to ask . . .' His words sent puffs of peppermint breath wafting into the car.

The slam of the door seemed to ricochet between the silent houses like a bullet. She followed Foy along the pavement. Standing on the podium at the press conference he had seemed taller. Skinny Crow meets Little Red Rooster, she thought, looking down at the carrot-coloured mop that had defied a liberal application of hair gel.

'Richard, this is Delva Lobelo . . .'

Delva tried a smile that was a mixture of friendliness and concern. She sometimes practised such faces in the mirror at home, although she would never have admitted it. It was one thing doing them in a mirror. Doing them in real life was incredibly difficult. The news editor had told her she looked too happy when she was was doing serious stories. Too bubbly, he'd said. And she had been made to feel so self-conscious that now, as she approached the poor, broken man huddled in the car, she felt as if her face were a grotesque mask.

In a smart guesthouse in Ballsbridge Doctor Megan Rhys was taking a shower. Over the course of the weekend her olive skin had turned nut brown in the unexpectedly hot Spring sunshine. On her back a pale cross marked the place where the straps of a red silk sundress had been. She reached for the shampoo, unaware that as she did so the contents of her handbag were being emptied onto the bed in her room. Patrick van Zeller grabbed the tiny silver mobile phone as it slid onto the rumpled sheets. With one eye on the bathroom door, he erased the messages without listening to them.

'Could you pass me a towel?' Megan called, her hand groping the empty rail. 'I think there's one on the back of the chair.'

Seeing her head emerge in a cloud of steam Patrick shoved the mobile back into the bag along with the lipsticks, pens and assorted junk.

If Megan had seen what he was doing she would have flipped. No doubt about it. But really, he thought as he grabbed the towel and whipped back the shower curtain, she ought to thank him for it.

'Don't s'pose we've got time for a quickie before breakfast?' he murmured, breathing in the coconut scent of her long black hair as he nibbled the wet skin of her shoulder.

'Patrick!'

'No, only joking,' he said, wrapping the towel around her. 'I've got one final treat lined up – we've just about got time before the flight.'

'Don't tell me,' she said, 'Coffee and cream cakes at Fitzer's? Lunch at Peacock Alley?' The tiny diamond stud in her nose glinted as she cocked her head.

'Not quite.' He grabbed her Rough Guide and flicked through the pages. 'There we are,' he said, handing it to her.

'Kilmainham Jail?' She stared at him, open-mouthed.

'Don't worry, you'll love it,' he said, snatching the book back. 'We're going to see an exhibition about the chap who invented hanging.'

'Are you mad?' Megan threw a pillow at him and he ducked.

'Well, that's not strictly true,' he said, throwing back the underwear she had laid out on the bed. 'He actually invented the modern method of hanging. Saved the poor buggers from choking to death.' He gave her a wicked grin.

'Come on,' he said, 'Don't want want to miss breakfast, do you?'

'This is . . . was . . . her on our wedding day.' Richard Ledbury handed Delva a large photograph in a heavy gilt frame.

'She's beautiful,' Delva said, trying to make her voice chatty and natural. It wasn't a lie. The face staring up at her would not have looked out of place on the cover of *Brides* magazine.

'It was our anniversary last Monday.' He took it back and stared out of the conservatory window. 'She bought me a sundial. Can you see it?'

Delva stood up and walked deliberately over to the window. There was a loud crackle as the cameraman pegged a blue filter across one of his lights. And he was humming. Humming, for God's sake! Delva couldn't believe they'd sent Barry Hudson to do this job. Of all the insensitive, wise-cracking jerks she had ever had the misfortune to work with, Barry had to be the absolute worst. He was taking forever to set up. And Richard Ledbury was a hair's breadth from cracking up again, she could tell.

'What a lovely garden,' she said, trying to lighten the atmosphere. As she spotted the pretty sundial in the middle of the manicured lawn a songthrush flew down and perched on its rim.

'Oh, look at that,' she said, thankful of a means of avoiding the inevitable platitude about his wife's gift.

He rose from the wicker armchair by instinct, but his glazed look seemed to melt momentarily when he saw the bird.

'I can understand why you wanted to do the interview in here,' she said, careful not to look at him directly. 'It's a lovely room. So peaceful.' Barry's humming was getting louder and she willed him with all her might to stop.

'Yes,' Richard said. 'Tessa spent a lot of time in here. It was her idea to build it. I tried to put her off but really I think it's the nicest room in the house.'

Delva heard the trembling in his voice as he spoke the last few words. She put out her hand to touch his shoulder and as she did so she noticed traces of fingerprint powder on the window frame a few inches from her face. Was this where the killer had got in? She cast a quick sideways glance at Richard Ledbury. If it was, he couldn't know, surely? Masking the movement by pretending to cough, she shifted her body so that her shoulder concealed the telltale grey residue.

'Right, Richard! If you'd like to make yourself comfy in that chair by the window we'll get the show on the road, shall we?' Barry strode across the room, a wide grin on his face, snapping down the conservatory blinds. Delva shot him a withering glance which he immediately mimicked, despite the fact Richard Ledbury was looking straight at him.

'I have to apologise for Barry,' Delva whispered, settling herself into a chair opposite Richard's. 'He's an excellent cameraman but his way of handling grief is to be very upbeat. Please try not to let him upset you.'

Richard nodded, lowering his head and squeezing his nose and chin between the palms of his hands. Delva bit her lip, making a silent prayer for the man to get through the next ten minutes without going to pieces.

Tears, yes. We don't mind a few tears.

A voice rang in Delva's ears. Des, the news editor, briefing her before she left the office this morning.

Quite effective really, long as it's not full-blown hysterics. You'll have to cut if he really blubs.

Sitting here now, looking at Richard Ledbury's face, the memory made her ashamed of her profession.

Barry leaned across and handed her the microphone. 'Now Richard,' she said gently, 'I'm just going to ask a couple of questions, that's all. I just want you to talk about Tessa, describe what sort of person she was. Don't worry if you have to stop. We can edit it afterwards. Barry's just going to take a soundcheck and then you tell me when you're ready to go.'

The lights went on. Richard flinched. Dazzled by the blue-white beam he looked like a frightened rabbit caught in headlights. This was the moment, Delva knew, when most people backed out. The lights brought it home in a stunning flash. This was television and *they* were going to be on it.

But as the camera rolled Richard Ledbury became a different person. Delva could hardly believe it. She was holding her breath, waiting for him to shake his head, put a hand up to the camera, break down. But he calmly described his wife, her beauty, what a wonderful mother she was to their three children, the fact that she was a Sunday school teacher; all without shedding a single tear.

When she asked him if he would like to make a direct appeal to people watching, he looked straight into the camera and delivered a perfect fifteen-second soundbite. He sat patiently while Barry took cutaways of his hands clasped together in his lap and even agreed to filming a second set-up in the garden, walking up to the sundial and looking at it with just the right expression on his face.

The only other time Delva had seen such a flawless performance was when she had interviewed a student who had apparently been first at the scene when a women was stabbed to death in a multi-storey carpark. He had described in a calm, even voice how he had held the woman's hand

and cradled her in his arms as she lay dying. Delva could still remember his face. It had been just as calm and devoid of emotion as he stood in court the day the judge sent him down for life.

But Richard Ledbury was no such devious actor, Delva was convinced, although she would have found it difficult to explain why. It had nothing to do with the fact that the police had already ruled him out. It was more a kind of sixth sense she had developed through interviewing so many people. Like a tiny lie-detector wired into her brain.

What she had just witnessed was the courageous act of a man who, in the midst of almost overwhelming grief, had pulled out all the stops in honour of the woman he had loved. Somehow he had held himself together in the firm belief that this appeal would help the police track down her killer. Delva had gone along with it because she had to. In her experience these appeals rarely achieved anything other than upping the viewing figures for the evening news.

Delva shook Richard Ledbury's hand and watched as the policewoman walked with him down the drive to the car. 'He was great,' she said, in answer to Detective Superintendent Foy's questioning look. 'Don't know how the hell he did it. Deserves a medal, poor man.'

Foy grunted something she couldn't hear and pulled a slip of paper from his pocket. 'These are the numbers to give out on air, okay? The incident room's at Tipton Street nick.'

'Right.' Delva tucked the paper into her bag. 'What about a profile? Any chance of getting something on tonight's programme?'

'Afraid not,' Foy said, 'We've been trying all weekend to get hold of Dr Rhys. Evidently she's gone walkabout in Dublin. Due back tonight.'

'Oh.' Delva frowned. Des was going to be disappointed. He had been counting on a studio interview to follow Richard Ledbury's appeal.

'Off the record,' Foy lowered his voice, 'I didn't used to have a lot of time for profilers.' He sniffed and glanced around the door at the waiting car. 'I mean, what the hell's the use of knowing the bugger you're after had a hard time from his mum and left school with no qualifications?' He shrugged. 'Anyway, I went on one of her courses at Heartland University a couple of months back. Pretty impressive, isn't she?'

Delva nodded. She had the distinct impression he had been about to add 'for a woman', but had checked himself just in time.

On the plane Megan stared at her mobile, puzzled. She had fished it out to switch off when the pre-flight blurb reminded her, but the screen's blank face told her she didn't need to. Odd, she thought. She could have sworn she'd turned it back on when they arrived at Shannon Airport on Thursday afternoon. Had it been off all week-end? She frowned as the plane began to move forward and turned to Patrick, but his eyes were closed. She groaned. Only he could manage to fall asleep on a flight that was less than an hour long.

She settled back in her seat, her dark brown, kohl-rimmed eyes lingering on him. His chest rose and fell in a steady rhythm, his blond wavy hair sliding forward over his eyes. He looked really young when he was sleeping. The corners of her mouth turned up in a bittersweet smile. They made an odd couple. Welsh-Indian and Irish-Dutch. Sometimes she tortured herself, imagining what a child of theirs might have looked like.

Never in her life had she been so happy and so miserable

at the same time. Up until last week it had been their secret. Or so she'd thought. It had been difficult these past few months, pretending nothing was going on. Watching the students flirting with him in the coffee lounge, unaware that he was fresh out of bed with their Head of Department. But if they'd fooled the students they hadn't fooled the staff. She flushed, remembering the look on her secretary's face as she'd wished Megan a good holiday. The invoice for the airline tickets had given her away. A slip of paper with Patrick's name alongside her own, left face up on her desk. She cursed herself for being so stupid.

It would be easier now he was moving to Liverpool. He would hardly have to come to Heartland at all apart from the odd visit to the library. She hoped that for the office gossips, out of sight would be out of mind.

As they walked across the tarmac at Birmingham International she flicked her mobile back on. It rang out immediately. 'Damn!' She frowned as she pressed it to her ear. 'Three voice messages.'

Patrick's eyes flicked to her face as they stepped onto a moving walkway. He said nothing.

'They're all from Steve Foy.' She bit her lip, the line between her eyebrows deepening.

'Who?'

'Detective Superintendent from Wolverhampton nick.' She paused to pull her passport from her bag, punching out numbers as soon as they were waved through. 'Remember the course we ran on serial sex offenders last term?' She looked at Patrick, the phone clamped to her ear. He nodded, still not quite with it. 'He was on it,'

'The mouthy one with red hair?

She nodded. 'Messages sounded a bit frantic.'

'Wonder what he wants?'

As she waited for Steve Foy to pick up she caught a flash

of something like panic in Patrick's eyes. But her attention was distracted by the sight of a headline on a board outside a newsagent's kiosk: **PRAYERS FOR MUM KILLED IN 'FRENZIED' KNIFE ATTACK.**

For once, Foy was short and to the point. While she listened she walked across to the kiosk and bought a paper. As she pressed the 'End Call' button Patrick emerged from the gents' toilet.

'What was it?'

Megan handed him the newspaper.

It was nearly eight o'clock when Steve Foy arrived at Megan's house. Patrick had gone to clear the last of the stuff from his flat and wouldn't be back until much later. She was glad. She didn't want Foy to know she was having a relationship with the PhD student he'd sat alongside at the sex offenders course.

'On your own?' he said when she showed him into the living room. He raised an enquiring eyebrow.

'Were you expecting someone else?' She looked at him, unblinking.

He looked away. 'Have you eaten?'

'Er . . . I had a snack on the plane.'

'Good,' he said, dropping a pile of photographs onto the coffee table. 'Because you won't want anything after you've seen *these*.'

Chapter 2

'As you can see', Foy said, handing Megan another photograph, 'it's definitely not your run-of-the-mill domestic
stabbing.'

Megan had to force herself to study the picture. The first
few had been inoffensive enough, straightforward establishing shots of the house, its position in the cul-de-sac, the
layout of the back garden. But now he had moved on to
shots of the body *in situ*.

The photographer had begun this sequence with a close-
up of Tessa Ledbury's upper body. Had she not known,
Megan would have been unable to tell that the body was
female, so mutilated was the flesh. The whole area of the
breasts was punctured and slashed with stab wounds.

With a barely perceptible sigh Megan laid the photograph down and put out her hand for the next one. The
evidence of vicious, uncontrolled stabbing had turned her
stomach, but at least she had been expecting it. The report
in the *Evening Mail* had made it pretty clear that this was
not a quick, 'clean' killing. But what she saw next shocked
her. Tessa Ledbury's face stared out of the picture, mouth
gaping and folds of white fabric protruding from her lips.
But it was not the gag that caught Megan's attention. The
hair had been scraped back from the woman's face with
what looked like a pair of tights. In the middle of her forehead, stretching from the hairline to the bridge of the nose,
was a five-pointed star. Its lines were so thin that at first

glance Megan thought it had been drawn on with a pen. But as she lifted the photograph closer to her face she could see that it was dark red.

'A knife?' she said in a whisper, to herself rather than to Foy.

Foy nodded. 'Looks that way. The whole thing was done in one continuous stroke.' He bent closer to Megan, peering at the image in the photograph. 'He started at the hairline and cut down diagonally.' Foy's stubby finger moved along the pentagram, pausing over Tessa Ledbury's right eyebrow. 'Then he went up to the left side of the forehead, across to the right, down to the left eyebrow and back up to the hairline.'

Megan stared wordlessly at this sick piece of art. The first thing that struck her was that it had been done *post mortem.* That much was obvious from the lack of bleeding from the incised lines. She looked at Foy. He had held back some of the details of the case at her own request. She had not wanted to be swayed by any theory, any suspect the police already had in mind. As he handed her the next picture she wondered what other macabre acts she was about to witness

Now she saw that Tessa Ledbury was completely naked. A wide shot showed her lying on a double bed, her arms protruding from her sides at right angles to her body and her legs wide apart. There were blood spatters on her neck, her arms, her abdomen and her thighs.

Megan put the photo on the table. 'Any ejaculant on the body?'

'No. In fact there's no evidence of any sexual activity at all.'

'Hmm.' Megan stared intently at the image. 'I think she's been displayed.'

Foy frowned. 'What do you mean?'

'It looks as if the body's been arranged in a way that's deliberately humiliating; arms wide open, legs apart.' She brought the photograph closer to her face. 'Then there's the cutting, the slicing.'

Foy raised his eyebrows. 'Go on.'

'Ever heard of picquerism?'

He shook his head.

'It's what's termed a secondary sexual mechanism. The high number of stab wounds could mean the killer got a sexual thrill from the act of stabbing or cutting flesh, rather than performing the sex act itself.' Megan sat back in her armchair. Her shoulders ached from being hunched up over the photos. 'It's the same with the arrangement of the body,' she said. 'It could indicate that the killer was prolonging his sexual dominance of the victim by posing her after death. If that's the case he wouldn't have an orgasm either in or on the victim – he'd save that until later when he's well away from the crime scene, in a safe place.'

Foy said nothing for a moment. He stared at the pile of photographs, rubbing his chin. 'What about the star?' he said suddenly. 'I mean, okay, the guy gets off on mutilating a woman, that much I accept, but a five-pointed star – a pentagram – there has to be some significance in that, don't you think?'

'You mean the occult,' Megan said, 'black magic, that sort of thing?'

Foy folded his arms and pursed his lips. 'It's not just me. One of my team was heavily involved in a child abuse case up north where occult practices were suspected. She's a bit of an expert on it now. Her name's Kate O'Leary. Anyway, soon as she saw the body she said, "You know what we've got here, don't you Guv?"'

Megan sifted through the remaining crime scene pictures. 'Was there anything left in the bedroom or at the house?

Anything that might be connected with a black magic ritual?'

Foy shook his head. 'Not unless we've missed something, no. The SOCOs only finished this morning but if they'd found anything like that I'd have heard by now.'

Megan nodded slowly. 'Well, in that case I'd be very wary of going down that path,' she said. 'That star or pentagram or whatever you want to call it could easily be the work of an experienced sex killer who's deliberately trying to confuse you.'

'Okay.' Foy reached for the close-up of the stab wounds and held it out. 'Let's set aside the pentagram for the moment,' he said. 'Let's concentrate on these.' He tapped the photo with his fingernail. 'According to the pathologist's report she was stabbed thirty-five times. Five of the wounds penetrated the heart and twelve perforated the lung. Any one of those could have been fatal. The rest vary in depth. Some are so deep they've actually damaged the skin on her back. Others are superficial, pricking-type injuries.' He looked up, his eyebrows knitted.

'Like I said,' Megan replied, 'This could be a guy who is turned on by penetration with a knife instead of a penis.'

'Yes, I know,' Foy nodded, 'but isn't what we're looking at here a classic case of overkill?'

Megan raised her eyebrows, challenging him to go on.

'Which suggests,' he said in a tone she had often heard him use during her seminars, 'that Tessa Ledbury almost certainly knew her killer.'

Megan listened patiently while Foy regurgitated chunks of the numerous books by FBI profilers he had acquired since attending Megan's course. 'That's the rule of thumb for overkill, isn't it?' he said. 'If a victim is stabbed more than twenty times it's something personal. She knew the guy who did it.'

'So you're telling me that if you come across a corpse who's been stabbed nineteen times you'll automatically rule out the wife or the husband?' Megan stared at him. 'Come on, Steve, you know that's complete crap.'

'Oh, so you're saying the entire Behavioural Science division at Quantico are talking through their arses, are you?' His face had gone very pink.

'No, Steve, that's not what I'm saying at all,' Megan sighed. 'What I'm saying is that it's not very helpful to tout some finite number of stab wounds when you're trying to work out who's responsible for a murder. I agree with you about the overkill thing, actually.'

He looked at her, a confused expression on his face.

'I think this attack *was* personal. But the level of forensic awareness makes me doubt that it was a straightforward crime of passion. To leave no trace of himself after such a frenzied attack would have required a lot of planning, which suggests Tessa didn't know him but *he* knew *her*.

'What do you mean?'

'I think there's a good chance that the killer knew the victim without her even realising it.' She turned to the photographs again, selecting one of the establishing shots of Tessa Ledbury's house. 'You said there was no sign of a break-in,' she said, 'and it happened sometime after she'd dropped her kids off at school. In the morning. In broad daylight. I presume no-one was seen calling at the house?'

He shook his head. 'Well,' she said, 'on what you've given me so far, I'd say this could be the work of an experienced burglar and sex attacker who's progressed to murder. Someone who chooses a victim, maybe stalks her for a while, and gets into the house when he's sure she's alone. Like I said, he knows her but she doesn't necessarily know him.'

'Right,' Foy said, nodding slowly. 'She represents someone he wants to kill but can't for some reason. And he hates this woman so much he stabs her again and again; completely loses control . . .' He looked at her. 'I want you to come and brief the team.'

Megan smiled, glad to see his face had returned to its normal colour. 'Okay, but first I need to know more about Tessa Ledbury. What was she like?'

Foy opened his briefcase. He unzipped a pocket in the lid and pulled out another photograph, handing it to Megan. It showed a smiling woman in a garden, standing with her arm around the shoulder of a girl who looked about seven years old. The child had the same blonde curly hair as her mother.

'She was thirty-six,' Foy began, 'Five foot five, weighed nine and a half stone . . .'

'No, Steve,' Megan cut in, 'I mean what was she *really* like? As a person?'

'Well, she was a housewife with three kids,' he faltered. 'Not a lot else really. Oh yeah, she was a Sunday School teacher at St. Paul's church in Pendleton.'

'And that's all you know?'

'Well, that's basically it, yes,' Foy said defensively. 'We've spoken to neighbours, friends at the church, other mothers from the school her kids went to. It was the same story from all of them. Devoted wife, mother, church member . . .'

'You said on the phone there was no hint of any affair, but are you sure there's no-one who might have had a grudge against her? I mean, we've both been making the assumption that the killer's a man, but it could just have easily have been a woman.

Foy took the photograph from her outstretched hand and stared at it. 'A jealous wife, you mean?'

'Possibly.' Megan's eyes narrowed. 'For all we know, she could've been a closet lesbian murdered by an over-possessive girlfriend.'

'Oh, come on!' Foy's eyebrows arched. 'I mean, statistically, it's likely to be a man.'

'I was being sarcastic, Steve. My point is I need to know a lot more details – if only to rule things out. I mean, apart from doing the housework and looking after the kids, how did she fill her days? Was she a member of any clubs or sports centres? Were there any particular places she went shopping? Did they have a dog, and if so, where did she take it for walks? Any details of that kind might lead to the killer.'

'Okay. I mean yes, we're already looking into all those things . . .'

'And I'll need to look at the house,' Megan said quickly. 'I'm not trying to suggest your lot have missed anything. I just think it'd help me get a better picture of her.'

'Sure. Could you meet me there at about nine-thirty tomorrow morning?'

'With a bit of re-arrangement of lectures, yes, I should think so. Can I keep these?' Megan nodded at the photographs. 'I'll have another look through them tonight and read the pathologist's report.'

'Right'. Foy stood up and put on his jacket. 'Oh, I didn't tell you about the appeal,' he said, feeling in his pocket and pulling out a video cassette.

Megan took the tape and slotted it into her machine. 'The husband?' she asked as an image flickered onto the screen.

'Yes. Poor sod found her after the school phoned him at work. No-one had turned up to collect the kids.'

They watched the video in silence.

'What's his alibi?', Megan asked as she rewound the tape.

'He was in meetings all day. They had to call him out of one to fetch the children.'

'Where is he now?'

'Staying at his mother's.'

'Lucky he's got one,' Megan said, pressing 'Eject'. 'He's certainly going to need her with three kids to bring up on his own.'

Delva Lobelo was waiting for the microwave. Chicken in Black Bean Sauce with Egg Fried Rice. For One. She perched on the kitchen table, a glass of chilled white wine in her hand, and tossed the empty box into the bin. Her aim was perfect but instead of slithering down the box stuck out. The bin was too full. She swore loudly. It could wait until tomorrow to be emptied.

She had just changed her clothes for the second time that day. The gloomy black suit was hanging in the wardrobe at work. Clad now in jeans and a T-shirt, with her feet stuck into a pair of old espadrilles, she was finally beginning to relax.

The phone rang just as the microwave pinged and Delva ignored it, reaching across to liberate the steaming food. After five rings the answering machine cut in. Delva picked up a knife to rip open the sachets of food but stopped when she heard the voice.

'Delva, it's Megan Rhys. I've just been talking to Steve Foy from Wolverhampton police . . .'

Delva dropped the knife and bounded across to the phone. 'Hi Megan. Sorry about the answerphone – I was just getting something out of the microwave.'

'Oh, sorry,' Megan said, 'I'll phone you back later, shall I?'

'No, it's okay. What's happened? Is it about the stabbing?'

'Yes. I've just been watching the interview you did with the victim's husband and there are a couple of things I wanted to ask you, but it's not urgent – honestly, I'll call you back.'

'Well why don't you pop round?' Delva asked. 'I've just opened a bottle of wine . . .'

Half an hour later Megan was sitting on the huge squashy sofa in Delva's living room.

'There you go.' Delva handed her a glass of wine. 'I'd offer you some food but I've just eaten the last thing in the fridge!' She gave Megan a rueful grin.

'It's okay, really,' Megan said, smiling in spite of herself. 'I couldn't have eaten anything anyway. Crime scene photographs, you know . . .'

'Ugh, I can imagine.' Delva pulled a face. 'When did Steve Foy get hold of you? He said something about you being in Dublin . . .'

'Yes, I didn't get the message till the plane landed. Anyway, he came round to the house and he brought a recording of the interview.' Megan took a sip of wine and laid the glass down on the coffee table. 'What was he like, this Richard Ledbury?'

'Well,' Delva said, folding her long legs underneath her in the armchair opposite, 'He was a complete mess at first. I didn't even think we were going to get him out of the car. He'd been very much against the idea of being interviewed anyway, and it was only when Terry Bond – you know, the press officer from West Mids HQ?' She paused and Megan nodded. 'It was only when he suggested a pooled interview that Richard agreed,' Delva went on. 'I was the one they chose to do it and the agreement was that the other channels would get to use the footage. Anyway, Richard insisted we do the interview at his house. When Terry Bond told me I thought it was a really bad idea. I mean, we'd offered him a studio at BTV or one of the interview rooms at Tipton Street nick. We even offered to go to his mother's house,' she leaned across to top up Megan's glass, 'But he wouldn't budge. The police said it would be okay because the SOCOs had finished, but I was sure he'd crack up when it came to the interview.'

'But he didn't?'

'No, that was the amazing thing. He was the original one-take wonder.'

Megan took another mouthful of wine. 'When you were talking to him did you get the impression there was any kind of trouble in the marriage?' She looked at the glass in her hand, rolling the stem between her finger and thumb. 'I mean, before the interview started, did he say anything that made you think that stuff about how wonderful his wife was might be a bit bogus?'

Delva thought for a moment. 'He didn't say a lot beforehand,' she said. 'It was like treading on eggshells. I was just making small talk, really.' She frowned and looked at the carpet, running the images of the morning through her head. 'He showed me a wedding photo and pointed out a sundial that she'd bought him as a present. He said it was their wedding anniversary last week.'

'Last week?' Megan's eyebrows furrowed.

'Yes. Why? Do you think it's significant?'

'It could be.' Megan looked at Delva. 'Birthdays, anniversaries, Christmas, New Year, you know what it's like – people take stock, don't they?'

Delva nodded slowly.

'If Tessa Ledbury had been having an affair,' Megan said, 'She might have decided on their wedding anniversary that she couldn't go on pretending any more. Perhaps she told Richard.'

'But he can't have done it!' Delva protested, 'I mean, physically, it couldn't have been him. He left the house at ten past eight and she was still alive at ten to nine. Loads of people saw her when she dropped her kids at school . . .'

'I know, I know,' Megan said. 'I'm not saying that. What I meant was she might have decided to end her affair. To save her marriage.'

'Oh, I see!' Delva said. 'You think the lover did it?'

'Well, that's the point. I don't even know if there was a lover. The police certainly don't think there was. But it could have been the sort of affair she wouldn't even tell her best friend about. That's why I wondered if you'd picked anything up from Richard's behaviour.'

'Hmm, yes, I see.' Delva sat back in her chair, rubbing her chin. 'Honestly though, Megan, if there was anything I must have missed it. I got the impression he was very much in love with her.'

'Haven't you ever found, though,' Megan said, putting down her empty glass, thinking out loud, 'that in marriages that seem really shaky the wife or husband can go completely over-the-top in terms of grief when the partner dies?'

'Yes, I suppose that does sometimes happen,' Delva said. 'In fact my parents were a bit like that. Always at each other's throats, but when Dad died Mum was inconsolable.'

'Well I'm not saying Richard Ledbury necessarily comes into that category, but it's something I need to rule out before I can stick my neck out with a profile.' Megan looked at Delva. 'Off the record,' she said, 'I'm not convinced Tessa was murdered by anyone who had a close relationship with her.'

Delva raised her eyebrows. 'So you think it was a stranger? Someone who broke into the house?'

'Like I said, this is all off the record, but yes, I think it could have been someone who knew of her but didn't actually know her, if you see what I mean. Someone who knew where she lived and knew she was alone in the house at that particular time.'

'What did he do to her, Megan?' Delva's eyes were full of foreboding. 'I know he stabbed her. But there was something else, wasn't there? The atmosphere in that road this morning when I was sitting outside in the car, it was just weird, as if people were afraid to come out of their houses.'

Megan looked away and Delva knew that she was working out what to say. They had only really got to know each
other in the past few months. Not very long, really, she
reflected. Megan must be wondering if she could trust her.

'Let's just say he used the knife for something else.
Something very sick that had nothing to do with actually
killing her.'

Delva drew in her breath, her mind suddenly filled with
a host of terrifying possibilities. 'Do you think he'll strike
again?'

'If it's a stranger killing, I'm afraid he almost certainly
will,' Megan said.

*It felt strangely satisfying, lying in bed, remembering the smell of
her perfume. Remembering how it had felt to kill her. Beyond
the window the night sky was punctured with starlight. The
connection was amusing. A signature as clear as day for those
with eyes to see it. But they were blind and stupid. That much
was obvious. Real intelligence was, after all, a star quality possessed
only by the chosen few.*

Chapter 3

When Megan got home the answerphone was flashing. The message was from her sister, asking how she'd got on in Dublin. Megan dialled the number and slid her arms out of her coat as she waited for it to answer.

'Ceri, it's me . . . Yes, I got back ages ago but it's been a bit hectic since . . . Yes, I know, I've had the guy in charge of the inquiry over here, actually. Listen, I'm coming over to Wolverhampton tomorrow – can I call and see you in the afternoon? . . . Yes, okay. Give the kids a kiss from me . . . 'Bye.'

Megan wondered what Ceri would say when she told her about Patrick. She was sure her sister had guessed that the trip to Dublin was more than just another academic conference.

A couple of weeks ago Ceri had asked Megan outright if she was seeing someone. 'Your eyes are all sparkly,' she had said in a knowing voice. 'Who is he, then?'

Megan had laughed it off, saying that what Tony had done was enough to put her off men for life. But Ceri was having none of it. 'Come on, Meg,' she'd said, 'just because you married a complete bastard doesn't mean you have to spend the rest of your life paying for it!'

She was right, of course. The irony was that for the past few months Megan had actually allowed herself to believe it. She glanced at the clock on the wall. Twenty past ten. She wondered how much longer Patrick was going to be.

A little voice was nagging away at the back of her mind. *'Why should he come back?'* it said, *'What future does he have with you?*

Megan had told Patrick about her inability to have children before they had started sleeping together. But the fact that he never seemed to want to talk about it was beginning to get to her.

It was half past eleven when she heard the sound of his key in the lock. She was still dressed, sitting in her study reading the pathologist's report. Patrick came padding up the stairs.

'In here!' she called.

He poked his head round the door and cocked it sideways to read what was printed on the spiral bound file in her hand. 'A little light bedtime reading?' His pale eyebrows arched and he grinned, walking across to her chair. He spun it back round to face the desk and started massaging her shoulders. She groaned and arched her back.

'Come on,' he said, 'I'll run us a bath.'

As steam billowed across the room he lit candles and poured geranium oil into a little terracotta burner. She stared at him in the flickering, hazy light, wondering what he was thinking. She had seen a new side of him in Dublin. It had been their first proper holiday together and he had been in his element, showing her the sights and introducing her to all his Irish relatives. There had been two little cousins, boys aged nine and seven, and she had stood watching him play football with them in the park. There had been a wistful look in his eyes when they came away but when she had asked him about it he had put his fingers on her lips as if he was afraid she might break the spell.

Trying to put it out of her mind, Megan climbed into the

bath and lay back against Patrick's chest. He smeared oil across her shoulders and squeezed the skin silently. The only sound came from the occasional car in the street below. She forced her mind back to the meeting with Steve Foy. She knew Patrick would not ask her about it. Even though she was no longer his supervisor there were times when he held back, unsure of his ground.

'Patrick,' she said slowly, her eyes half-closed, 'when you were working in Holland did you ever come across a case of picquerism?'

'Pick-what?' he said, taking his hands away.

'Picquerism. It's when someone gets a sexual thrill from cutting flesh. Keppel wrote about it – you know, the profiler from Washington State?'

'Oh, yes, I think I do vaguely remember something . . . the Clairemont killer, wasn't he into that sort of thing?'

'That's right.' Megan shifted her position, sending a surge of water towards the taps. 'I just wondered if you'd ever come across anything like that.'

'Can't say I have, really. I mean, it all depends on interpretation, doesn't it? How do you distinguish between someone who goes apeshit with a knife because they're pissed or in a jealous rage and someone who does it for kicks? Unless they tell you, that is . . .'

'I know.' She leaned her head back against his chest. 'The thing is, there was no ejaculant and in the photographs Steve Foy showed me some of the stab wounds looked quite superficial. That's a feature of picquerism. You get shallow, incised wounds as well as the deeper ones that actually kill. And in this case he hung around long enough to carve a pattern on her head as well.'

'You what?' Patrick sat upright, making the water slap the sides of the bath.

'He carved a five-pointed star onto her forehead.' Megan

eased herself into a standing position and stepped onto the cork mat, reaching for a towel. 'According to the pathologist's report it was done with something thin and sharp.' She looked at Patrick, whose face had taken on an expression of horrified fascination. 'It would have to have been something double-edged, because it was done in one continuous line, like this.' She ran her fingernail across her forehead the way Foy had demonstrated with the photograph.'

'Something like a stiletto knife, then,' Patrick said slowly, 'or a dagger.'

'Yes,' Megan said, 'or even a blade he's customised himself. Anyway it was a different knife from the one he stabbed her with. The pathologist reckons that would have been too blunt by the time she was dead.'

'So why a star?' Patrick asked. 'A *five*-pointed star, did you say?'

'That's right.' Megan wrapped the towel around her and perched on the edge of the rattan chair next to the bath.

'Sounds a bit occultish, that, doesn't it? You know, pentagrams and all that?'

'Hmm.' Megan smiled. 'I was wondering if you were going to pick up on that. One of Foy's team suggested it too, evidently. But there was nothing else to suggest black magic. It could be something the killer did deliberately to mislead the police.'

'Yes,' Patrick said, sliding back down to submerge his shoulders in the water. 'It's the kind of thing you can imagine some twisted bastard cooking up, isn't it? I mean, some of the stuff prisoners tell me when I'm interviewing them, books they're reading, that sort of thing . . .' He reached for the shampoo and poured the green liquid into his hand. 'They're into all the literature on profiling, you know. They must come out of jail with all sorts of ideas . . .'

Megan nodded. 'That's another thing I was thinking

about – prison, I mean. The level of forensic awareness suggests that whoever did this has probably been inside at least once already. Either that or he's had a near miss with the police.'

'No prints?' Shampoo floated onto Patrick's eyebrows as he tipped his lathered head backwards into the water.

Megan shook her head. 'He must have been wearing gloves the whole time. I think they would have to have been those thin latex ones – the kind surgeons wear. I don't see how he could have done something as intricate as that pentagram in ordinary gloves.'

'Well you can get those from loads of places,' Patrick said. 'I think they even sell them in chemist shops.'

'Hmm, I didn't think of that.' Megan stared at the dripping candles on the window ledge. 'I was making a list of work-places where someone would have access to gloves like that, but yes, he probably just walked into a chemist and bought them.' She shivered and drew the towel up around her shoulders. 'He used a gag, too, but I don't think that's going to lead us very far. It was one of those white dish-cloths, the kind you find in thousands of houses, not to mention schools, factories, restaurants . . . the list is endless.'

'Did Steve Foy say whether there'd been any rapes in the area lately – anything that might be linked?

'It depends how wide an area you take into account,' Megan said. 'I mean, if you take the whole of Wolverhampton there are dozens of sex offenders on the books. It'll take a while for Foy's lot to check them all out. But Pendleton's not actually in Wolverhampton. It's about ten miles out – one of those big greenfield estates. According to Foy the only sexual offences they've had so far this year are a serial flasher and some guy who allegedly raped his fourteen-year-old cousin and got her pregnant.'

'And they've been eliminated?' Patrick pulled out the bathplug and reached for a towel.

Megan nodded. 'The flasher's on remand in Winson Green and the other bloke was in hospital on the day of the murder because the girl's brothers beat him up.'

'Sounds like a delightful place.'

'Well it's not as bad as some of the estates in Birmingham,' Megan said. 'My sister nearly bought a house there once.'

'Bet you're glad she changed her mind, then, eh?' Patrick buried his head in the towel and rubbed his wet hair, not noticing how Megan's face had clouded.

'By the way,' he said, his voice muffled, 'when am I going to get to meet these relatives of yours?'

Later, when they lay in bed, Patrick reached out for her in the darkness. His hand caressed her face, lingering over the tiny jewelled stud in her nose. 'You know,' he said with a soft chuckle, 'I've been sharing a bed with you three or four times a week for the past five months and I've never seen you take this out . . .'

'Oh I do when you're not around', Megan whispered back. 'I leave it on the bedside table next to the glass with my false teeth in . . .'

Patrick grabbed her and started tickling her until she begged him to stop. 'Come here, you disgusting woman,' he laughed, sliding his hands around her waist and up towards her breasts. She flinched suddenly and he pulled back.

'What is it?'

'I'm sorry, Patrick. I . . . I just can't, that's all.'

'Hey, it's alright . . . it's no problem.'

'It's not that I don't want to,' Megan said, stroking his arm, 'I mean, you're going off to Liverpool in the morning and it's going to be ages before we're together again, but . . .'

'Is it the photographs?'

'Sort of.' She sighed. 'I just can't get them out of my head.' How could she explain that it was not just the gory images Foy had left behind? That the snap of Tessa Ledbury with her daughter had triggered a far more personal pain? She felt confused and guilty. How could her own sense of loss possibly be more disturbing than what she had seen in the last few hours?

'I used to get that.' Patrick stroked her arm. 'Whenever you close your eyes you see them, don't you?'

'Yes,' she mumbled, unable to tell him what was really on her mind. 'You'd think I'd be used to it by now, wouldn't you?'

'I don't think I ever got used to it.' Patrick rolled onto his back, staring at the shadows on the ceiling. 'I suppose I just drifted into doing what all cops do. Medics as well, come to that,' he said. 'I took refuge in sick humour. It's terrible, I know, but that's what we all did.'

Megan bit her lip. 'I can't imagine ever being able to do that,' she said. 'Maybe it's different when you're surrounded by people who're all seeing the same type of thing. I think what I've started doing is even worse, though.'

'What do you mean?'

'Oh, take no notice of me,' she said, 'I'm just becoming a bit too cynical for my own good, that's all.' She raised herself on one elbow and leaned across to touch his hair. 'Patrick,' she said softly, 'would you just hold me?'

It was still dark when the radio alarm by Delva Lobelo's bed crackled into life. She sat bolt upright in bed and stared at the glowing numbers of the digital display. Four fifteen. For a moment she blinked at it, confused. Then she slid her legs out from under the duvet and reached for the gold-embroidered red kimono draped across the ottoman at the end of the bed.

Delva hated the early shift. It messed her body clock around. Often she would try to take a nap in the afternoons to catch up on her sleep but it was fatal. She would wake a few hours later when it was still light and fly into a blind panic because she thought it was morning and she had overslept.

Right now she felt particularly groggy. She had been dreaming about Richard Ledbury. It had been a disturbing, sexual dream and now she was awake she felt weighed down by guilt. She got ready as quickly as she could, not bothering with make-up or breakfast. She would feel better when she got to work. There would be people to talk to, bulletins to prepare. And bright lights to chase away the lingering shadows of the night.

The duty engineer was already in when Delva walked into the newsroom. Her heart sank when she saw who it was. George Leith was a monosyllabic anorak who preferred machines to people. He grunted something at her, picked up his coffee and disappeared into the transmission area.

'Don't mind me, I'm just the invisible woman,' Delva muttered to herself as she sat down at the newsdesk. There was a note from the late sub reminding her to check the police voicebank for any update on the murder appeal. 'As if I needed reminding', she thought, as her mind played back images from last night's dream.

There was nothing new on the taped message from Terry Bond. Delva felt a tinge of disappointment. Richard Ledbury's bravura performance had come to nothing, then.

She thought about him again when she was getting ready for the first bulletin. Staring into the mirror she dabbed foundation onto her cheeks, frowning at the puffiness under her eyes. Nightmares always had this effect on her. 'Who are you trying to kid?' she said to her reflection.

What she had dreamed of doing with Richard Ledbury hardly counted as a nightmare.

She searched through her make-up box for the brightest lipstick she could find. If she could draw attention to her mouth she might be able to get away with her baggy eyes. Des, the news editor, always watched the early bulletins and made a point of slagging off any newsreader whose appearance was less than perfect.

By the time she had read her fourth bulletin she was ravenous. It was nearly nine-o'clock and the newsroom was beginning to come to life. Delva grabbed her bag and made for the door. Going for a fry-up was the only redeeming feature of the early shift. Normally she avoided the BTV canteen like the plague, but breakfast was the one dish they seemed to be able to get right.

'Delva!' George Leith had finally broken his silence.

Oh no, he wants to have breakfast with me, Delva thought as she glanced over her shoulder.

But George merely grunted, 'For you!' and cocked his head at the telephone, stalking off in the opposite direction as she came towards him. She picked up the receiver, feeling her stomach rumble.

'Hello?'

'Is that Delva Lobelo?' It was a woman's voice. There was something strange about it. Something slightly threatening. Delva was immediately on her guard.

'Yes,' she said. 'How can I help you?' She suspected it was one of the stable of cranks who regularly plagued the BTV newsreaders. But she didn't recognise the voice.

'I've got a story to sell.' The voice took on an even harder edge. 'It's about that woman who was stabbed. Tessa. I know something about her. Something the police don't know.'

Delva took a deep breath and glanced around the news-room. Des's chair was still empty. She was going to have to deal with this herself. 'Er, have you contacted the police incident room? I can give you the number if you like.'

'No. I don't want the police involved.' The woman paused and Delva heard a crackle and a mumbling as if the receiver had been covered over. 'Listen,' the voice rang out clearly now, 'Tessa and me go back a long way and I've got pictures to prove it. I'm offering you the story first 'cos I'm a fan of BTV. If you want it, meet me at the café at Pendleton precinct at half past eleven. If you don't show up I'll sell it to the *News of the World*.'

There was a click and then the dialling tone. Delva hit 1471 but was not in the least surprised to hear that the number had been witheld. She stood for a moment with the phone in her hand, wondering what to make of the bizarre call. She would tell Des about it when he arrived. He could decide whether to take it seriously. She doubted whether he would, but even if he did, she reasoned, they had until eleven-thirty to decide what to do. She walked resolutely towards the door. Whatever happened, she was not going to let it spoil her breakfast.

Megan and Patrick had said their goodbyes early. He had a train to catch and she had to go into the office to reorganise her lectures before driving to Wolverhampton.

There was a pile of post in her pigeonhole and she dropped it on her desk, sifting through the envelopes in search of anything that might be urgent. Her hand froze when she spotted the insignia of the Vice-Chancellor of the university. She ripped the letter open and stared at the two short paragraphs summoning her to a meeting the follow-ing Monday.

'Shit!' She stuffed the letter into a drawer, away from

prying eyes. This could mean only one thing. Someone had said something about Patrick. And she was in for a roasting.

She glanced around her office. At the books she had written; the photos of all the lifers she had interviewed; the framed press cuttings of cases she had helped to solve. How could she have been so stupid? Risked all this for . . . what? Love? Yes, Patrick said he loved her. And she loved him. But that wouldn't count for anything with the Vice-Chancellor. Would he believe her when she explained that the relationship had started only *after* Patrick had switched supervisors?

The words 'Head of the Department of Investigative Psychology, Heartland University' jumped out from the notepaper in front of her. She took a deep breath, reminding herself that, technically, she had done nothing wrong. Nothing to be ashamed of.

She suspected that the motive behind this was petty jealousy. One of her colleagues – all of whom were male – wanted her out. Wanted her job. All of them were nice to her on the surface, of course. Not one had given her grounds for suspicion up to now. She grunted and rose to her feet. Striding down the corridor she knocked sharply at the last door on the left.

Christopher Jessop looked up, startled, as she came through the door. His shaved head glistened in the sunshine and there was a hint of something in his large green eyes that reminded her of a guilty schoolboy caught smoking behind the bike sheds. Could he be the one?

Five years older than Megan, Jessop was a recent addition to the department, having moved from Manchester at the start of this academic year. At his interview he had told her he'd been frustrated at the lack of opportunity for promotion at his old department.

'Chris, I have to go to Wolverhampton in half an hour,' she said. 'It's the woman who was stabbed last week.'

He nodded. 'Oh – lucky you!'

Was he being sarcastic, she wondered? 'Would you mind covering my lectures?' She was asking nicely, although she didn't have to. As his boss she was at liberty to give orders.

'No problem.' He gave her a broad smile. 'Will it be okay if I give them some of the stuff I was planning to do later on this term?'

'Of course, you go ahead,' she smiled back, determined not to show any sign of the upset the Vice-Chancellor's letter had caused her. 'Remind me I'm doing your slots when they come up.'

She turned on her heel, pulling the door shut behind her. As she made her way out of the building she couldn't help picturing Jessop sitting in her desk. She was just going to have to fight her corner, the way she'd fought for every-thing she'd achieved in her career so far. *And she was damned if she was going to let him or anyone else take it away from her.*

'We had quite a few calls last night,' Steve Foy said as he unlocked the door of the Ledburys' house. 'The usual nutters, of course, but one or two useful ones as well.'

'What did they they say?' Megan followed him along the hall, glancing at the photographs of babies and children lining the walls.

'Well, we've got a better idea of Tessa's movements on the morning she died.' He walked into the kitchen, pulling out a chair for Megan before sitting down himself. 'She went straight to Pendleton shopping precinct after she'd dropped the kids at school. The receptionist at the medical centre remembers her calling for a prescription. After that she went to the chemist's and then to a newsagent to buy a birthday card. She can't have been back home much before ten o'clock.'

'What was the prescription for?'

'Contraceptive pills. She'd been taking them since the youngest child was born.'

'And is that what she got at the chemist's?'

Foy nodded.

'How old is the youngest child?'

'Three and a half. Why do you ask?'

'Is he or she at full-time school or nursery?'

'It's a he. Henry. He's in the nursery class of the primary school.'

'Right,' Megan nodded, 'So he's not there all day?'

'No. She used to pick him up at 11.30.' Foy folded his arms across his chest 'She was due to pick him up the day she was murdered – that's how the alarm was raised.'

Megan traced the pattern of the wood grain on the table with her finger. 'Was the child looked after by anyone else?'

'No.' Foy had a puzzled look on his face. 'D'you think that's significant?'

'Well, I suppose it explains why she had such a limited social life,' Megan replied. 'After dropping them off at school she'd have, what, just over two hours to herself before having to pick up the little one again?'

Foy nodded.

'No wonder she didn't have time for much else apart from the church, then. You said her only close friends were from St Paul's?'

'Yes.' Foy sniffed. 'Even so, you'd expect her to be close to some of the other mums from the school, wouldn't you? Or a neighbour?'

'But she wasn't.' Megan frowned. 'Bit of a loner, really, then?'

Foy shrugged.

'What about a computer? Was she one of those people who spend a lot of time in chatrooms?'

'I doubt it,' Foy said. 'There was no computer in the house and her husband said it had been taken away for repair a few weeks back.'

'So –' Megan looked at her notes. 'On the morning she died she picked up her packets of pills from the chemists. Anything else?'

He shook his head.

'What about the birthday card you mentioned?' Megan asked. 'Any idea who it was for?'

'Her eldest daughter. She was eight on Saturday.'

'God, those poor kids!' Megan glanced around the kitchen. One wall was covered with bright paintings and collages, obviously brought home from school. She looked away. This was going to be even more harrowing than she had imagined. She was going to have to do a better job of detaching her emotions if she was to be of any help at all in this inquiry.

'Can I start with the garden?' The chair scraped loudly as she stood up. 'I want to see how he might have got in.'

Foy led her out through the conservatory. 'As you can see,' he said, following the yellow gravel pathway through the flower beds, 'it's completely enclosed.'

Megan glanced at the high wood-panelled fence that surrounded the garden. The Ledburys had obviously taken a lot of trouble to conceal its prison-like starkness with climbing plants and fast-growing evergreens. There were no established trees, though. Nothing that would support a man's weight. The houses were too new for that.

'The SOCOs found some rope fibres on that post.' Foy pointed to a section of the fence halfway down the garden. 'There's an alley on the other side separating it from the house next door. Looks like he climbed up and dropped straight over the side.'

'Wouldn't the neighbours have spotted him?' Megan

shaded her eyes and peered upwards. 'Their bedroom window looks right over this garden.'

'House is empty.'

'Hmm.' Megan scanned the garden. 'Any footprints?'

'A toe section of a pair of bog-standard Hi-Tech trainers where he landed. Not enough to work out the size.'

'What about the fibres?'

Foy shrugged. 'We're still waiting for them to be analysed, but the SOCOs weren't very optimistic.'

Megan walked back towards the conservatory. 'So how did he get into the house? Was this door unlocked?'

'Well, it was when our lot arrived,' he said. 'According to Richard, Tessa spent a lot of time in the garden. With that fence she probably didn't bother too much about securing the back of the house.'

Megan stepped back into the conservatory. 'What's this part of the estate like, Steve? I know some areas are a bit rough, but I got the impression this cul-de-sac was more upmarket.'

'Well I suppose it is still one of the better addresses, yes, ' Foy said. 'There are a few Asian families in the road but they're everywhere in Wolverhampton, now aren't they?'

Megan stopped in her tracks. 'You what?' she said, fixing him with an icy stare.

'Er . . . I . . . I mean they . . .' Foy blinked at her in confusion.

'I was born in India, Steve,' she cut in with measured scorn. 'My grandmother was Asian.'

'I . . . I'm sorry, I didn't mean . . . I didn't realise . . .' His grovelling was cut short by the warble of his mobile phone. Turning away, he retreated to the far end of the garden.

Megan was in the conservatory examining the Ledburys' wedding photo when he came back. She heard his footsteps on the gravel but she didn't look up.

'That was the incident room,' he said. 'Tessa Ledbury made a phone call a few minutes before she died.'

Megan spun round, her mind switching up a gear. 'Who to?'

'The couple from the church I was telling you about – Bob and Jenny Spelman. They were members of a Bible study group Tessa held here on Tuesdays. Kate O'Leary's just been talking to the husband.'

'And?' Megan's mind was racing.

'He says Tessa called at quarter past ten on Thursday morning. He was out but he got back a few minutes later. He dialled 1471 and tried to ring her back but there was no reply.'

'How come you've only just found this out?'

'He and his wife went away for the Bank Holiday. They left on Thursday afternoon and they only got back this morning. They didn't know Tessa was dead until they saw it on the TV news.'

'And this Bob Spelman,' Megan frowned, 'does he check out?'

'You mean could he be in the frame?'

Megan nodded. 'For all we know he could have phoned his own number from here to give himself an alibi.'

'Well, obviously we'll be sending someone to interview him properly,' Foy said. 'Evidently he's a driving instructor and he says he was out giving a lesson when Tessa phoned, so it shouldn't be difficult to check.'

'Well, if he's telling the truth it's looking even more likely that she was followed back from the shopping precinct, isn't it?' Megan looked at Foy, who returned her gaze with one of polite anticipation. He was obviously trying to make up for his racist *faux pas*.

'You say she wouldn't have been home much before ten,' she went on, 'and this Spelman chap says she was dead by, what, half-past?'

'About a quarter to eleven, he says. He's not certain exactly what time but we can find out from BT.'

'Well I think it's too much of a coincidence that she was killed so soon after arriving home.' Megan replaced the photograph she had been holding and looked at her watch. 'Anyway,' she said, 'I think you'd better show me the rest of the house.'

The master bedroom was the only room in the house that bore witness to the brutality enacted five days earlier. The double bed had been stripped and the mattress taken away for analysis. There were spatters and smears of dried blood on the pale pink carpet and the top drawer of a chest of drawers had been pulled out. Various items of underwear protruded from it as if someone had been searching for something in a hurry.

'Is that where the tights came from?' Megan asked, remembering the makeshift hairband in the crime scene photographs.

'Yes. He didn't touch anything else, though. Didn't take anything, I mean.'

'No souvenirs?'

'Doesn't look like it.'

'Hmm, that could be significant.'

Foy looked at her.

'Well, if it was a stranger killing there's a good chance he'd be trophy-taker,' she explained. 'Killers like that some-times fuel their fantasies with something belonging to their victims.'

Foy shrugged. 'So no trophies means it's someone she knew?'

'I didn't say that, Steve.' Megan frowned. 'I'm just trying to weigh up all the possibilities. So, come on, talk me through it.'

'Well,' he began, 'She had to have been in the bedroom when he attacked her. There are no bloodstains or signs of a struggle anywhere else in the house. She was probably making the bed or something and he crept up behind her. There were hardly any defence wounds, so he must have overpowered her and got her down on the bed before she had time to react.'

'What about her clothes?' Megan asked. 'In the photographs she was naked.'

'He took her clothes off after he'd killed her,' Foy said. 'There was a blouse, jeans, knickers and a bra on the floor beside the bed and they were all bloodstained. The blouse and the bra were cut to ribbons.'

'That has to be significant,' Megan said. 'Why would he bother taking her clothes off after the event if it was a straightforward crime of passion? It must have been part of the horrific effect he wanted to create.' She glanced around the room. 'What about shoes?'

'She wasn't wearing any, I don't think,' Foy replied. 'There's a rack of them downstairs by the front door. She probably took them off when she got in and went upstairs barefoot.'

'Well, we need to know which pair she was wearing that morning. I want to know exactly what she looked like when she was out.' Megan thought for a minute, staring at the bloodstains on the carpet. 'How do you reckon he got out of the house without leaving blood anywhere else.'

'Ah, well, when I said there was no blood in the rest of the house I should have mentioned that there was a trace on the bathroom door handle,' Foy said. 'I'll show you.'

In the bathroom Foy pointed out how the killer could have cleaned himself up under the shower without leaving any forensic evidence of his own identity behind. Megan glanced around the small, immaculately-decorated room. The colour of the soap and the toilet paper matched the paintwork and the shell stencil on the walls was echoed on the laundry basket, the toothbrush holder and even the pedal bin.

'Presumably the towels have been taken away by the SOCOs,' Megan said.

Foy glanced at the notes in the folder he was carrying. 'A towel was taken away, yes.'

'Just one?'

He nodded. 'Yes.' He read from the inventory: 'One blue hand towel with shell motif.'

Megan flipped open the laundry basket. 'Were there any towels in here?'

'No,' Foy said. 'Just clothes. SOCOs took them all. There were towels in the airing cupboard down there.' He pointed back down the landing. 'They've all been taken away for forensic analysis.'

'I don't think you'll find anything there either,' Megan said quietly.

Foy looked at her, puzzled.

'Where's the bathtowel?' Megan asked simply.

Foy shrugged. 'I don't follow.'

'From what I've seen Tessa Ledbury was very house-proud. She had matching everything. The bathroom's very small, I grant you, but I find it hard to believe there weren't at least two towels in here . . .'

'Oh, I see what you're getting at.' The lines on Foy's forehead suddenly disappeared.

'In fact, taking the towel might have served a dual purpose,' Megan went on. 'Not only does he have a trophy to fuel his fantasies, he also takes any forensic evidence from his own body away with him.'

The sudden, loud ring of the doorbell made them both jump.

'That'll be Dave and Kate,' Foy said. 'Shall we talk in the conservatory?'

'You actually want me to go and meet her?' Delva stood open-mouthed in front of the news editor's desk. 'Des, are you winding me up?'

'No,' he said, unwrapping a sandwich and swallowing a huge mouthful before looking up at her, 'It could be important. You're off shift in a couple of hours anyway. Liz can do the lunchtime bully – you look a bit knackered, anyway.'

'Well thanks a bunch,' Delva muttered, 'Nice to know I'm appreciated, I must say.'

'Oh come on, Delva. It's not the sort of thing many people could handle. I'm sending you because I know I can trust you to handle it right, okay?'

'Hmm, I suppose so.'

'One thing, though,' Des took another bite. 'Take some-one with you, just in case it's a nutter. Get them to arrive at the café at the same time as you but don't acknowlege them in any way. All right?'

Delva wandered back to her desk and sat for a while staring at the phone. Suddenly she had an idea.

Detective Sergeant Dave Todd was hanging on Megan's every word, but D.S. Kate O'Leary was taking some con-vincing. She had argued fiercely when Megan had pointed out the shortcomings of the occult theory and although she had now started scribbling notes, the look on her face made it clear that she did not set much store by the profile.

'We're talking about a watcher,' Megan was saying, 'some-one who picks out women who have particular significance for him, probably because of their physical appearance, and he'll stalk them.'

'What sort of age would he be?' Dave Todd asked.

'Probably mid-thirties. Possibly even older. We're not dealing with a beginner here. I think whoever did this has killed before.'

'Why do you say that?' Kate O'Leary looked up, biting the end of her pencil.

'Because of the length of time he spent with the victim after death,' Megan said, 'A novice killer would want to get away as quickly as possible. The things he did to the body *post mortem* represent a behavioural pattern that he has refined over time.' She looked at each of them in turn, holding Kate O'Leary's eye. 'What you and the rest of the team should be looking for is a man with form for related sexual offences and probably for burglary as well.'

'Why burglary?' Dave Todd was writing as he spoke.

'Because unless Tessa let him in, we're talking about a man who breaks into someone's house in broad daylight and is confident enough to hang around for at least half an hour after he's killed. He's going to be of above-average intelligence and experienced at getting into other people's homes without drawing attention to himself. His forensic awareness and the fact that we've seen nothing of this nature in the Wolverhampton area before suggests that he might have done time. You should check all recent releases of sex offenders from prisons nationwide.'

'Right,' Foy leaned forward in his seat, rapping his pen on the table. 'We want something on *Crimewatch*. Dave – get on to it, will you? Tell them were doing a reconstruction tomorrow morning.' He turned to Kate O'Leary. 'BTV and the Beeb need to get camera crews along to that, okay?' Kate nodded. 'Megan,' he went on, without pausing for breath, 'How d'you fancy keeping me company on prime time TV?'

Megan stared at him in disbelief. The man's even more of an egomaniac than I realised, she thought. He's actually getting off on the idea of his face on national TV. He doesn't really *care* about finding Tessa's killer – all he cares about is what this case is going to do for *him*. She opened her mouth to say something but the sudden trill of her mobile phone cut her short. 'Excuse me.' Megan fished the phone out of her bag.

'Megan?' Something in the tone of Delva's voice made Megan move quickly out of the room.

'Yes?' She was in the conservatory now, out of earshot of the police officers. 'Delva, what is it?'

'It's about Tessa Ledbury. There's something you should know.'

It was tempting to linger in the precinct. The people were like extras in a film, their voices blurring into a hum of nothing, their clothes making splashes of colour against the dull, grey buildings. But not all were extras. One would have a starring role. Get their name in the newspapers. Their face on TV. But not now. Time was running out. Duty called. And none of the extras were quite right. By this time tomorrow, though. By this time tomorrow the director's cut would be made and another star would be born.

Chapter 4

Megan glanced at her watch as she fastened her seat belt. Half past eleven, Delva had said. She was not convinced that the rendezvous in the café was going to have any bearing on the murder inquiry but she planned to do a little research of her own on the way.

The journey from Tessa Ledbury's house to Pendleton shopping precinct took only twelve minutes. As Megan pulled into the carpark she caught sight of children running around in a school playground beyond the boundary fence. She hadn't realised how close the school was to the shops. Reaching for her notebook she flipped through until she found the right page. There it was: Tessa seen at school 8.50 a.m. Megan walked to the school gates and made a note of the time. Then she crossed the road to the precinct, scanning the buildings.

The Spring sunshine did nothing to soften the look of the place. The stark angles of the functional 'seventies architecture were broken here and there by unhealthy-looking shrubs. The odd shop sign aspired to something a little more artistic but the overall effect was depressing. Even the benches were made of concrete. This was a place you would visit for convenience, not from choice, Megan thought.

Beyond the shops was a stretch of greyish-looking water with a few ducks pecking at its litter-strewn banks. The view beyond this artificial lake was obscured by landscaped hillocks, but she knew that Pendleton College was just a short distance away. Ceri had just started working there as a part-time lecturer and Megan wondered whether her sister ever came across to the precinct to shop. The thought of it made her stomach churn.

On the near bank of the lake stood the medical centre, a squat building with walls the colour of salmon paste. The way in was through a set of double doors and Megan could smell the patients before she actually saw them. The waiting room was packed and the air was tainted with sweat and the odour of smokers. For a moment Megan was reminded of her father. He had smoked heavily right up to the day he died and even when he hadn't had a cigarette she could always tell which room he was in from the smell which seemed to ooze out from under the door.

In the stark light of the waiting room she was aware of half a dozen pairs of eyes looking her up and down. She glanced round and heads turned swiftly back to magazines or contemplation of the floor. Was this where Tessa's killer had first spotted her?

Megan checked the time. It had taken just five minutes to get from the school gates to the medical centre. Tessa would have been one of the first there last Thursday morning. There couldn't have been more than a handful of people in the waiting room then and it wouldn't have taken more than a minute or two for the receptionist to find the prescription and hand it over. No, Megan thought, the killer would have needed longer to select Tessa, to observe her and decide to stalk her. If that had happened here it would have to have to have been on some other day.

She pushed her way back through the doors, glad to be in the fresh air. The chemist's shop was about a hundred yards away on the short side of the L-shaped shopping area. As Megan walked towards it she caught sight of a cross made of some white, crystalline substance which glinted in the sunlight. It was on the side of a building further along the lake and Megan realised it must be St. Paul's, the church where Tessa had been a Sunday school teacher. She made a mental note to take a look at it later.

There were several people waiting to collect prescriptions from the pharmacy and Megan timed a man who arrived just after she did. She wandered around the shop while she was waiting and after a couple of minutes found a display containing rubber gloves. There they were, second from the bottom: *Marigold Ultra Thin*, £1.99 for eight pairs. She unhooked a packet and took them to the till.

Allowing another ten minutes for walking to the newsagent and choosing a card, Megan calculated that Tessa could have been back home as early as nine- twenty-five. She wrote it down and checked the notes she had made about Tessa's last phone call. Steve Foy hadn't said where the Spelmans lived or what time Bob Spelman had picked up his learner driver. She thought about it for a moment. If the Spelmans went to the same church as Tessa there was a good chance they also lived on the Pendleton estate. It suddenly occurred to Megan that Tessa could have been murdered within a matter of minutes, left for a period of time and her corpse mutilated later. In which case Bob Spelman was going to have to come up with a pretty comprehensive account of his movements on the morning Tessa died.

Megan sat down on one of the cold, hard benches. It was still too early to go to the café. She watched people pushing trolleys through the automatic doors of the supermarket in front of her. A brightly-coloured cardboard sign caught her eye. It offered free home delivery for goods totalling twenty-five pounds or more. Megan scribbled down the name of the store. If Tessa had ever used the home delivery service the drivers would have to be interviewed.

Opposite the supermarket was a shop selling electrical goods. She wrote down 'Television, Washing Machine, Dishwasher, Cooker' and wracked her brains to think of any other large piece of equipment Tessa might have had delivered to the house.

She glanced again at the people coming out of the supermarket. There were women pushing toddlers in buggies; elderly couples; middle-aged women; a gaggle of young girls who could be students. Megan frowned in concentration. What sort of women would be shopping alone between nine and ten on a weekday morning? It would be someone who wasn't at work. Someone whose children were in school. Whose husband would probably be at work. *Think like the killer.* She bit her lip as the words flashed through her mind. Yes, she reflected, that period straight after nine o'clock was an ideal time to stalk a woman. To follow her to a home that would probably be empty.

Then something else occurred to her, quite out of the blue. The fathers at the school. Someone who had dropped his children off at the same time as Tessa could have waited in the carpark and followed her home. She wondered if Steve Foy had considered that when he sent his team to question people at the school.

She pulled out her mobile phone.

'Hello, Steve, I'm still at Pendleton precinct . . .'

His reaction to her suggestion was one of indignation. Checking the fathers had been his top priority once Richard Ledbury was out of the frame and yes, he was certain no-one had been overlooked. He was a little less abrupt when she mentioned the supermarket delivery service and the electrical shop. He also accepted her point about the possibility of Tessa arriving home earlier than he had estimated.

'Bob Spelman's on his way to the station now,' he said. 'He does live near the Ledburys, actually, so I'll make sure he's got an alibi for the whole morning.'

'Right,' she said, 'If I think of anything else I'll call you.'

'Okay,' he replied. 'If you can't get hold of me try Dave Todd. He's still at Tessa's house – should be there most of the afternoon.'

A few minutes later she put her phone and notebook away and headed for the café. It was the only eating place in the precinct and the owner had obviously gone to some trouble to soften the uninviting look of the shop unit that housed it. Red and white checked curtains on brass rails screened the windows to shoulder height and the name *Pendleton Pantry* was inscribed on the glass in gold lettering which made the plastic fascias of the shops on either side look very tacky by comparison.

Before she reached the door Megan caught sight of Delva's head. It was turned away from the window but Megan immediately recognised the intricately braided hairstyle. They had agreed not to acknowledge one another and Megan went straight to the self-service counter without looking round.

She ordered a ham roll and a cappuccino and sat down two tables away from Delva. There were about a dozen other people in the café but it was a big room and not too noisy. Megan didn't think she would have much trouble eavesdropping when Delva's informer arrived.

Delva had her head buried in a magazine. She was obviously hoping nobody would recognise her. Megan glanced at the other tables, wondering if the woman had already arrived and was checking to see if Delva was really alone. But the customers were all in pairs or groups, a mixture of pensioners, students and mothers with small children. There was no-one that fitted the image Delva's words had conjured in Megan's mind.

Megan wished she had bought a paper when she was in the newsagent's. She studied the Toulouse Lautrec posters on the walls and read the baguette fillings listed on a blackboard above the servery. Two plump women who looked like sisters were chatting by the till. Behind them a man was slitting french sticks and smearing the insides with margarine. One of the women looked at Delva and turned to whisper something to the man. Megan noticed they were both wearing the same thin rubber gloves she had just bought at the chemist's.

At that moment the door opened and a tall, scrawny-looking woman with long, blonde hair made straight for Delva's table. Megan bit into her ham roll and stared at the chequered tablecloth, listening. The coffee machine roared suddenly into life and for a few crucial seconds she was unable to hear a word. Stealing a quick glance she saw that the woman was showing Delva a photograph.

'That's her, see?' The voice emerged, harsh and rasping as the noise of the coffee machine subsided. There was a strong Wolverhampton accent. 'That was at a party a couple of years ago. See the bloke next to her?' There was a pause. Megan resisted the temptation to look up again. 'That's Raven. He's got his hand on her knee, look.'

'Raven? Is that his name?' Delva's voice had its usual calm, controlled tone but there was a hint of disdain, giving the impression that she wasn't taking the woman seriously.

'I'm not telling you that unless you pay me,' the woman hissed.

'Can you prove they were having an affair?' Delva sounded even more sceptical now.

'Oh, yes.' Megan could hear the greed in the woman's voice. 'I've got other pictures. Much more graphic than this. But like I said, you've got to pay for 'em.'

'Listen,' Delva's voice dropped and Megan strained to hear. 'We don't usually pay for stories. The most we ever offer is a fifty quid tip-off fee.'

'Get lost! Do you know how much the *News of the World* would pay for something like this?'

'I think any newspaper would tell you that you're on very dodgy ground.' Megan heard the threatening undertone in Delva's voice. 'What you're doing is witholding information from the police. Don't you realise that's an offence?'

There was a loud scraping noise and Megan glanced up from her contemplation of the tablecloth. The woman had stood up but her way was blocked by the man who had been buttering the baguettes.

'Excuse me,' he said, holding out a piece of paper and a pen to Delva, You're the newsreader on BTV, aren't you? Could I have your autograph?'

The woman pushed past him and Megan saw a look of confusion on Delva's face. As soon as the café door closed Megan was on her feet. Pushing the door open she gave Delva a brief nod. Delva's face was still creased with anxiety but she had taken the pen and paper and was scribbling something.

'Could you put it "to Nick",' Megan heard the man say as the door thudded shut.

The precinct was full of shoppers but the woman's mane of blonde hair made her easy to spot. Megan caught sight of her running past the chemist's. She was heading for the carpark and Megan ran after her. If she could see what car the woman got into she could follow and find out where she lived. Suddenly Megan stopped. It was too risky. She might lose her. After a moment Megan set off again, walking briskly this time. She had had a better idea. All she had to do was get to the exit barrier. She was pretty sure the woman wouldn't recognise her if she stood discreetly watching the cars leaving the carpark.

Megan stood behind a large bush and peered inside each

car that went past. After six or seven had gone through the barrier she began to panic. What if someone had driven up and whisked her off without going into the carpark? But even as the thought went through her mind she caught a flash of blonde hair at the wheel of a red Ford Fiesta. It was her. As the car slowed to get through the barrier she scribbled down the registration number.

Ten minutes later Megan was sitting opposite Delva in the café with another cappuccino in her hand.

'I couldn't believe it when that bloke came and asked for my autograph,' Delva whispered, glancing over her shoulder towards the servery.

'It's all right, he's gone,' Megan said, 'And actually, I think he did us a favour.'

'Why?'

'Well if you'd tried to follow her yourself she'd have done a disappearing act, wouldn't she? She certainly wouldn't have gone straight to her car.'

'Hmm, I suppose you're right.' Delva rested her elbows on the table, clasping her hands under her chin as she looked at Megan. 'Anyway, what did you make of her?'

'Hard to say, really. What did the photo look like?'

'Well she said it was taken at a party. Tessa Ledbury was on a big sofa with a man each side of her and a couple of other people leaning over the back pulling silly faces. The one she called Raven definitely had his hand on Tessa's knee but I suppose he could have just been fooling around.'

'But she said she had other photos that were more explicit?'

Delva nodded.

'Did she mention whether this affair was supposed to have been going on when Tessa died? I didn't catch what she said when she first came in.'

'She said Tessa ended it about a year ago but she reckoned this Raven character was out for revenge.'

'Well,' Megan said, taking a sip of coffee, 'If Tessa did have an affair the police need to know. It doesn't necessarily mean her lover was the killer, though.'

'So what do you think we should do?'

'Give that car registration number to Steve Foy. I don't particularly want him to know I was in on this, so would you mind doing it?'

'No, of course not.' Delva took the piece of paper Megan pushed across the table.

'The police can check the guy out. I hope for his sake he's got a decent alibi for last Thursday. What did he look like, by the way?'

'Well he was white, about mid-forties, shoulder length grey hair, slim,' Delva shrugged. 'Very intense eyes. Not bad looking, actually.'

'Did you notice a wedding ring?'

'I don't think so.' Delva screwed up her eyes, concentrating. 'No. I think it was his right hand on her knee, anyway. Why, is it significant?'

'Only from the point of view of his wife, if he's got one,' Megan said. 'Like I said last night, I'm not convinced Tessa Ledbury was murdered by an ex-lover or anyone else she was close to, but I have to be sure of my facts. So while the police are tracking down that red Fiesta I'm going to go back to the house to dig around a bit more.'

Delva said nothing, staring at the cloud of steam rising from her mug of hot chocolate. There was a faraway look in her eyes.

'What's the matter?' Megan asked. 'Do you think Des is going to be pissed off about you not getting the story?'

'Oh no, it's not that,' Delva said. 'I just can't help thinking about what this is going to do to Richard Ledbury. Poor sod's been through enough already without finding out his wife was having an affair.'

'He might already know,' Megan said. 'Tessa might have confessed when she broke it off.'

'Yes, I suppose you could be right.' Delva cupped her hands around the hot drink as if she were trying to warm herself. 'But wouldn't he have told the police?'

'Not necessarily. If he forgave her for the affair he might not want to admit the possibility that the murder had anything to do with her ex-lover. He could be in a state of denial about the whole thing and if he is the grief over her death would just compound it.'

'Yes, I see what you mean.' Delva raised the mug to her lips and drank mechanically, her eyes fixed on the tablecloth. 'The way he went on about her when I was interviewing him, it was as if she was some sort of saint. It made me feel quite envious, actually. I was thinking what a fantastic relationship they must have had and wondering how come I never get to meet guys like that.'

'Hmm.' Megan drained her cup. A short time ago she would have empathised wholeheartedly with that sentiment. But now was not the time to tell Delva about Patrick. She pushed her cup and saucer aside. 'It doesn't sit very easily with all this Sunday school teacher stuff, does it?' she said.

'No.' Delva leaned back in her chair. 'Supposing he doesn't know,' she said, thinking aloud, 'If the police track down the lover and find out he's got a cast- iron alibi, would they still tell him, do you think?'

'They'd have to.' Megan shrugged.

'Then it'll be my fault.' Delva's voice was almost a whisper.

'Your fault? Why on earth do you say that?'

'Because if I hadn't agreed to meet that stupid woman none of it would have come out.'

'You know that's not true!' Megan shook her head. 'I was

listening to her, Delva, she's lowlife! If you'd said no she'd have gone to someone else. The police would have got to hear about it sooner or later.'

Delva sighed, pressing her lips into a thin line. 'And it's better for him to be told by some sympathetic police-woman than to see it splashed across the front of one of the tabloids,' Megan went on. 'In fact you've probably done Richard Ledbury a big favour handling it the way you did.' Megan sat back and folded her arms. 'Listen, if you want I'll phone Steve Foy. I'll tell him you phoned me first because you weren't sure what to make of her.'

'No, it's okay, I'll do it,' Delva said. 'There's something I want to ask him anyway.'

Megan looked at her.

'I want to know where Richard's staying so I can send some flowers.'

Megan started to say something but thought better of it. 'Delva,' she said instead, 'Let me know what Steve says – about the woman, I mean.'

'Oh, right, yes.' Delva was in another world. She stood up and reached for her coat. 'I'll phone you later then, okay?'

Megan watched her walk off across the precinct. 'Don't get involved, Delva.' She whispered the words like a prayer.

The net curtains left a gap at the bottom of the window. Easy to watch the passers by. There was a foot. A shapely leg in sheer black tights. Or stockings? Shifting the net inch by inch revealed more. Travelling upwards from the legs, a tight-fitting skirt. Too tight. A bulge where the stomach squeezed over the waistband. A T-shirt that showed the ridges where the bra dug into the skin. Her breasts wobbled as she walked, hair blowing over her face. That familiar feeling. Blood rushing, buzzing in the ears. She was the one.

Chapter 5

'Auntie Megan!' Emily flew along the hallway like a miniature tornado.

'Hello monkey!' Megan limped into the house with Emily clinging to her right leg. 'Where's your baby brother?'

'He's asleep!' Ceri's head appeared round the kitchen door. She was a slightly shorter, paler-skinned version of Megan. Her dark hair was cut in a sleek bob which revealed silver hoop earrings. The nose stud she had once worn was long-abandoned.

'Oh, I thought he might be – good job I didn't ring the bell, then.' Megan replaced Ceri's door key in her bag. Her sister had told her to use it any time she called round but she only really felt comfortable about letting herself in unannounced when she knew Neil wasn't going to be there.

'Would you like a coffee? I've just put the kettle on.' Ceri took off the rubber gloves she was wearing and tossed them into a cupboard under the sink. 'I've just managed to get the house straight. Wednesday is my housework day now. Did I tell you they asked me to do another morning at Pendleton?'

'No. Since when?' Megan perched on a high stool, hoisting Emily onto her lap.

'Last week. One of the lecturers has gone in for an emergency hysterectomy and she won't be coming back until September. I'm doing Mondays, Thursdays and Fridays now.' Ceri poured hot water into two mugs and handed Emily a beaker of juice.

'Is it the same hours?' Megan grabbed a piece of kitchen roll and held it under Emily's chin as she tipped the beaker almost vertically into her mouth.

'Yes, nine 'til eleven. Neil's going to look after the kids when he's on a late shift, otherwise they'll go to Pendleton nursery.'

'Is that the one by the school?' Megan felt a stab of anxiety.

'Yes – I was lucky to get in. Most of the nurseries round here have got waiting lists.' She opened a tin of biscuits and offered Megan one.

'No thanks. I really pigged out in Dublin.'

'Aah yes, Dublin!' Ceri's eyebrows wiggled up and down. 'Emily, why don't you go and put *Cinderella* on the video?'

'I want to play with Auntie Megan.' Emily's mouth turned down and a little frown line appeared above her nose.

'I'll come and play with you in a minute, I promise,' Megan said. 'I've just got to tell Mummy a story first. A story for grown-ups. Then it'll be your turn.'

'So how old is he, then?' Ceri was on her way upstairs in answer to a wail from the baby. Megan followed her.

'Have a guess.'

'Well if he's one of your PhD students, I suppose he could be as young as twenty-two. Your auntie's a wicked woman, isn't she Joe?' Ceri lifted the baby out of his cot and handed him to Megan.

'Bloody hell, Ceri, I'm not a cradle snatcher!' she protested, stroking Joe's blond, downy hair. 'He's only five years younger than me, actually. And he's not *my* PhD student – he changed supervisors before we got together.'

She felt as if she was rehearsing for next week's inter-rogation. 'He spent ten years with the Dutch police before coming to Heartland.'

'Hang on, I'm confused. He took you to see his relatives in Dublin, but he was in the Dutch police?'

'Yes, it *is* confusing. His Mum's Irish and his Dad's Dutch. He lived in Dublin till he was ten, then they moved back to Holland.'

'And he's single? No complications?'

'Only by the skin of his teeth.' Megan shifted Joe onto her hip, rocking him gently. 'He was engaged to a girl in Holland before he came to Heartland, but he broke it off.'

Ceri's eyes widened. 'Wow! Must be serious about you then?'

'Oh, I don't know about that.' Megan laughed off the remark. Past experience had made her very wary of admit-ting her true feelings, even to herself. Ceri leaned towards her sister and sniffed. 'Oh, Joe, you don't half pong! Can you lie him on the change mat while I get a clean nappy, Meg?'

Half an hour later Megan was sitting in Ceri's living room, a *Noddy* book by her side and Emily fast asleep on her lap. 'I'm going to have to go in a minute, Ceri,' she said, 'I've got to go back to Pendleton.'

'To that woman's house? The one who was stabbed?'

Megan nodded. 'I've been there once already today but I want to have another look. I called there before I came to you but the place was empty.' She looked at her watch. 'The police said they'd make sure someone was back there by three o'clock.' Megan lowered Emily's head onto a cushion and slowly eased the rest of her small body onto the sofa.

'I knew her, you know,' Ceri said quietly.

Megan's head whipped round. 'Knew her? You mean she was a friend?'

'No,' Ceri sighed. 'Just knew her by sight, really. She used to go to the same Mother and Toddlers group I took the kids to before I started lecturing. I think I only spoke to her once or twice.'

Megan frowned. 'What was she like?'

'Bit of a loner, really,' Ceri said. 'She only had one of the kids with her. Little boy. Must have been her youngest. She never seemed interested in talking to the rest of us – that's why most of us were there, to get a bit of adult conversation – but she just sat on the floor among the toys and played with him.'

'How long ago was this?'

'Hmm, Ceri pursed her lips. 'It was just after I'd had Joe, so it would have been about eighteen months ago. I remember trying to talk to her about what boys were like as babies compared to girls. I gave up after a couple of minutes because she just gave monosyllabic replies to everything I said.'

'Was there anything else about her? Anything unusual?' Megan stared intently at her sister. 'Her appearance, I mean. What did she look like?'

'Well, she was quite pretty. Quite smartly dressed, for a mum.' Ceri glanced down at her clothes and shrugged. 'Not the usual shapeless tracky bottoms and sweatshirts most of us wear when we're likely to get puked or dribbled on every five minutes!'

Megan's eyebrows lifted. 'So what did she wear?'

'Designer stuff, I suppose,' Ceri said. 'She wore jeans, but they were always very expensive-looking ones. And little jackets with matching shoes. That was one thing I always noticed about her. I've only got a couple of pairs of loafers I wear in the daytime – black and navy to go with everything – but Tessa seemed to have a different pair every week.'

'Hmm,' Megan got up and slung her bag over her shoulder. 'Do you go to Pendleton precinct much? Apart from picking the kids up from nursery, I mean?' 'Sometimes, yes,' Ceri said. 'There's a nice café there – the coffee's much better than the crap they serve in the college.'

'Hmm. You will be careful, won't you, Ceri?'

Ceri frowned. 'Why? You don't think the killer's prowling around there, do you?'

'I don't know.' Megan sighed and stared at the carpet. 'It's possible. The woman who died could well have been stalked by someone who saw her at the precinct. It was the last place she was seen alive.'

Ceri shuddered. 'Poor woman. I can't bear to think of her kids, left without a mother when they're so young.'

'I know.' Megan put out her hand and stroked Emily's shoulder.

'Listen, Meg, don't worry about me – I'm nearly always with someone when I go to the café.' Ceri stooped to gather up the toys scattered on the carpet. 'Quite a few of the students go there after the lecture – there's usually at least half a dozen of us.'

'Well, that's a relief.' Megan bent down and pecked her sister on the cheek. 'You take care, you hear?'

When Megan had gone Ceri plonked back onto her chair, ashamed at having had to lie to her sister. How could she tell Megan about Justin? How could she explain that she, too, had fallen for one of her students? A student who was only twenty-one years old and thirteen years her junior?

Megan thought everything was back to normal between her and Neil. Thought she'd forgiven him for going after one of his much younger work colleagues when she was pregnant with Joe. How could she ever explain to Meg that now she'd got this job she suddenly felt like a real person again?

She picked up Emily's *Barbie* doll and started plaiting its hair. Before, she had been stuck in the house all day changing nappies and felt as if no-one in their right mind could possibly fancy her. But now it was different. She felt a wave of excitement at the thought of seeing him tomorrow. Revenge, she decided, was very sweet.

It was ten past three when Megan pulled up outside the Ledburys' house. Before she had chance to ring the bell the door was opened by a uniformed officer.

'Doctor Rhys?' He sounded even younger than he looked.

'Yes. Is D.S. Todd here?'

'No, it's just me, I'm afraid.' He stood aside as Megan walked in. 'He was here a few minutes back but he's been called out.'

'Oh? Any idea what for?'

'Not really, no. I was on traffic duty when they radioed me to come over. The rest of the team are out doing house-to-house.'

Megan wondered if Dave Todd was off on the trail of the woman in the red Fiesta. She had suspected as much when she called earlier and found no-one around. Perhaps it had gone further than that now. Perhaps Tessa's ex-lover was about to be hauled in for questioning.

'Did they tell you why I was coming?' Megan put her bag down on the kitchen table.

'They said you wanted to do a more detailed inventory of the house.'

Megan nodded. 'Do you mind if I potter around on my own for a bit?'

For a while she wandered from room to room, opening drawers and cupboards. She felt a surge of guilt as she rummaged through clothes that still bore a faint smell of perfume. She wondered what sort of life the contents of her own pockets would conjure up. Would they give her away? She thought of the post-it notes Patrick often left in obscure places for her to find when he wasn't around. Silly, romantic messages that she would stuff in the pockets of her dressing gown or whatever else she happened to be wearing when she found them.

But if Tessa had ever been the recipient of love-letters there was no evidence of them. Megan looked in old handbags and beneath the paper liners of the drawers. She searched bookcases in the living room and bedrooms, shaking out the books in case anything had been tucked inside the pages. But there was nothing.

She paused for a moment in the hall, catching sight of a wooden rack tucked under the staircase. Ceri had been right about Tessa Ledbury's multi-coloured shoe collection. There were seven adult-sized women's pairs. In cream, pink, navy, black, red, brown and turquoise. Most were of a similar style; leather pumps with flattish heels. Conservative, Megan thought. Nothing that could be described as sexy or alluring. She stooped to pick one up, noticing as she did so that all the shoes had a slight bump in the same area of the toe section. The shape of Tessa's toes imprinted on the leather made her far more real than the mutilated figure Megan had seen in crime scene photos. With a shudder, she replaced the shoe and walked away. The last room Megan searched was the conservatory. After flicking through a photograph album she noticed a collection of cookery books tucked into a storage space beneath the wicker coffee table. She began taking them out and shaking them until she came to a cardboard ring-binder at the bottom of the pile. Inside were dozens of clear plastic wallets containing recipes cut out of magazines. They had been put in back-to-back so that recipes appeared on both sides as you turned them over.

As Megan flicked through she noticed something. She stopped and pulled out the contents of one of the wallets. Concealed between the glossy recipes was a piece of white, narrow-ruled paper that looked as if it had been ripped out of a notebook. There was a diagram drawn in biro, with notes scribbled alongside. At the top were the words *Rite of Beltaine* and underneath was a rectangle with the word *Altar* inside. Megan read what had been written next to the rectangle:

> *Athame (pron. ath-a-may) – name of knife placed on the altar (should always be blunt), along with a chalice (of wine or whatever), salt, a wand, hawthorn blossom, a pink or orange candle and a pentagram.*

Megan felt her mouth go dry as she stared at the word on the page in front of her. Then her eyes moved down the page, taking in the circle marked with compass points and the names of the four elements. Turning the paper over she gasped when she saw what was on the other side. Two pentagrams, with arrows indicating which way they had been drawn, sat side by side. One was subtitled *Invoking Pentagram* and the other *Banishing Pentagram*.

Megan shuddered and laid the file down on the table. Forcing open the stiff ring-binder she pulled out a sheaf of plastic pages and began pulling out the contents. The third one she came to contained another sheet of notepaper. This one bore a date. It had been written more than two years ago, on the thirtieth of April:

> *Tonight he gave me the five-fold kiss. At the Rite of Beltaine he chose me from the women of the coven to be his High Priestess, anointing and kissing me on the head, lips, breasts, belly and feet.*

The room was lit with candles and the air sweet with incense and the scent of hawthorn blossom. They were all watching. I felt wonderful. Powerful. I took the athame and drew pentagrams in the air at the four points of the circle. We raised a cone of power and drank metheglin from the chalice.

I was the Beltaine Maiden. The Witch of Spring. I wore a silver robe and a crescent moon in my hair. Some covens perform their rites naked, or skyclad as Raven calls it. We wear robes with nothing underneath. If anything it is more arousing than wearing nothing at all.

Now I am an initiate of Wicca I will need to compile my own Book of Shadows. It will have to be concealed from Richard and the children. I am not sure where yet.

Megan lost track of the time as she pulled out page after page of handwritten accounts of Wiccan spells and rituals. The name Raven cropped up time after time. There was never any other name alongside it. Nothing to convey whether this was a real name or some alias assumed for the purposes of witchcraft.

When she came to the last page Megan threw the empty folder on the table and sank back into one of the cane armchairs. She felt hollow inside. In her hand she was holding evidence that would set any prosecution counsel dancing round the room in glee. How could she have got it so wrong?

She thought about what she had just read, trying to be objective. There was no proof that Tessa was the author. Her name appeared nowhere. But Megan had no real doubt that she had written the notes and it would be a simple matter to compare the handwriting with letters signed by Tessa.

Nevertheless, Megan thought, it seemed bizarre that

such stuff had been penned by a woman who, two years later, was described as a pillar of the local church. She looked again at the last sheet of paper she had uncovered:

> *Raven made love to me in the ruins at Whiteladies Abbey.*
> *We were not supposed to be there. He was due to give a*
> *talk tonight about Candle Magic. We had booked Saint*
> *Paul's church hall and about fifty people turned up to*
> *hear him. But the Born Agains were out in force. They*
> *blocked the doors and refused to let us in. They were*
> *waving banners with phrases like 'Get Thee Behind Me*
> *Satan' and other such rubbish. They have no idea, these*
> *people. They think all magic is Black Magic. They con-*
> *demn us from a position of total ignorance. It is people*
> *like them who were responsible for the Burning Times.*

The Born Agains. Not a very flattering description of the people Tessa had apparently regarded as her friends when she died. So what had happened, Megan wondered? Had the decision to give up her lover been fuelled by a conversion experience? And how would he have reacted to her joining the ranks of the enemy? Whichever way round things had happened, Megan thought, there was plenty of motive for murder.

She was so absorbed that she failed to recognise the tone of her mobile phone, which was ringing inside her bag on the kitchen table. The policeman brought it through to the conservatory, holding the bag out in front of him as if it were a bomb about to explode.

She looked at him uncomprehendingly for a moment before taking it from his outstretched hand.

'Hello, Megan.' Steve Foy's voice was gruff and he sounded excited. 'I think we've got him!'

Chapter 6

'You say she actually mentions him by name? Steve Foy was leafing through Tessa Ledbury's cookery file.

'Yes,' Megan said, 'It's always Raven, though. She never calls him Sean.'

'This is unbelievable, isn't it?' Steve Foy was shaking his head as he pulled out the sheets of notepaper. 'And it was in the conservatory?'

Megan nodded.

'Well the SOCOs are going to get a damn good kick up the arse for missing it. What did you say she called it?'

'A Book of Shadows. It's a sort of work book for a newly initiated witch. But this is more than just a description of rituals and spells. It's a diary of her affair as well.'

'Hmm.' Foy put the file on his desk. 'Well this is really going to nail him. This and the little haul we picked up at his house. Want to come and see?'

He led Megan down two flights of stairs to a windowless room in the basement of the police station. On the left-hand side was a collection of objects in clear plastic bags. Something glinted in the light from the fluorescent strip on the ceiling and Megan lifted it carefully off the table. It was a silver dagger, its handle inlaid with ivory stars and crescent moons.

'So this is the Athame.' Megan turned it over in her hands, examining the edges of the blade. 'Feels pretty blunt, doesn't it?' She handed it to him. 'That's what it said in Tessa's notes: "Athame should always be blunt." Have you had chance to run a comparison with the stab wounds yet?'

'Not yet, no,' Foy was looking at her in surprise. 'How did you know it was pronounced like that? I'd never even heard the word till Kate O'Leary told me.'

'Oh, she'd written it phonetically in brackets,' Megan said. 'It was part of a very detailed diagram of a Wiccan altar and a description of the various objects they have on it.'

'What is this word, *Wicca*?' Foy asked. 'I keep hearing Kate saying it.'

'It's the old word for witchcraft,' Megan said. 'Dates back to Anglo-Saxon times, I think.'

'You seem very knowlegeable on the subject, I must say.' He was looking at her suspiciously. 'I can't believe you've picked all this up in an afternoon at Tessa Ledbury's house.'

Megan glanced at the rest of the paraphernalia on the table before answering. 'When I was a student I had a friend who was involved in a coven. She tried to persuade me to go along. Lent me all her books.'

'But you didn't go?'

'Yes I did, actually. Just the once. There was no dancing naked round bonfires or anything. It was held in someone's living room. They'd decked it out with a lot of candles and incense and we were all given robes to wear. I was quite enjoying it up to the point where we were asked to leave the room so the High Priest could have ritual sex with the High Priestess.' Megan sniffed and picked out a book from the pile on the table, studying the crude drawing of three naked women its cover.

'What did you do?' Steve Foy's eyes were like saucers.

Megan replaced the book and picked up another. 'Not a lot,' she said. 'We sat in the kitchen listening to the moans and groans coming under the door and after about five minutes I decided I'd had enough, so I made my excuses and left, as they say in the gutter press.'

'Well, well.' Foy's expression had changed to something bordering on admiration. 'Why didn't you say anything to Kate this morning? She was giving you chapter and verse on witchcraft like she was the world's leading expert.' He folded his arms and leaned against the table. 'She nearly blew a gasket when I told her I was bringing you in on the interrogation, you know.'

'I can imagine,' Megan said, picking up a disc-shaped brass altar-piece with a pentagram etched into its surface, 'I bet she was jumping up and down when she saw this, wasn't she?'

'Well wouldn't you be? I mean it's a pentagram, for heaven's sake!'

'I'm not blind, Steve.' She looked him straight in the eye. 'And yes, at this point the evidence does look pretty damning. But I don't need to remind you that it's all circumstantial, do I?' She paused but he said nothing. 'All we know for sure,' she went on, 'Is that Sean Raven was screwing Tessa Ledbury until she dumped him about a year ago. That does *not* automatically make him the killer.'

'But come on, Megan, the pentagram . . .'

'Could easily have been used by someone who wanted to implicate Raven,' she interrupted. 'That woman, for instance, the one who told you about him . . . what's her name?'

'Carole-Ann Beddowes.'

Megan nodded, picturing the woman in the red Fiesta. 'Yes, her. She's obviously out for some sort of revenge, isn't she?'

'Tell me about it.' Foy raised his eyebrows and looked at the ceiling. 'I didn't have chance to tell you, did I?'

'What?' Megan turned to him sharply.

'A couple of years back Carole-Ann Beddowes accused Sean Raven of rape. He was acquitted for lack of evidence.'

'Acquitted?'

'Yes.'

'Does he have form for any other sexual offence?'

'Not exactly, no.'

'What do you mean, not exactly?'

'He was convicted of bigamy last year. Must have been around the same time Tessa gave him the elbow. He got eighteen months for that and a fraud charge. Only came out of prison in March. So you see, apart from the bit about Tessa being stalked from the precinct, Raven fits the profile really well. He's the right age, he's been inside and he's got a history of offences against women.'

'Hmm.' The tiny lapis lazuli stud that matched her cobalt blue jacket twitched as her nostrils flared. A bigamy conviction and an unproven rape charge. Not exactly incontrovertible evidence of a violent hatred of women. She looked at Foy. 'Did Carole-Ann Beddowes say he was physically violent when she accused him of raping her?'

'No. She said he spiked her drink.'

'And what about these wives? Did he ever attack them?'

'Well we haven't been able to trace his first wife yet,' Foy said, 'but his current one's in an interview room upstairs. We'll have a go at her once we've decided how to play him. By the way,' he added, holding the door for her, 'the *Crime-watch* people are gagging for us – you okay for Saturday night?'

Megan frowned. 'What do you mean, "gagging"? What have you told them?'

'Well, I had to sex it up a bit, obviously,' Foy shrugged. 'I wanted to make sure we got a decent slot. Probably academic now, of course, with our mate Sean under arrest. But you never know who it'll bring crawling out of the woodwork evidence-wise.' He grinned as he ushered her along the corridor.

Megan blinked. He was enjoying this. Revelling in it. He was going to appear on national television regardless of anything Sean Raven was about to say. What if he mentioned his theory of an occult connection? What would that do to Raven if the case ever came to court? If he was innocent? He'd be tried and convicted by the media before he could open his mouth to deny it.

Her instincts told her to pull out now. Tell Foy she'd have nothing to do with his TV appeal. But what would that achieve? He'd have free rein then. At least she could put across an alternative view. Play down the occult thing.

'Okay,' she nodded. 'What about the reconstruction?

'They're filming it tomorrow morning,' he said. 'Kate's standing in for Tessa.'

'Kate?' Megan thought this an odd choice, given that Kate was dark-haired with a characteristic pale Irish skin, while Tessa had been blonde with a liberal sprinkling of freckles.

'She'll be wearing a wig, of course,' Foy chuckled. 'She's the same age and same height as Tessa, and she really wanted to do it.'

'Really?' Megan muttered. She wondered how many other members of Foy's team were closet TV wannabees.

Delva was asleep when the phone rang. She had gone to bed as soon as she got back from Wolverhampton, hoping that an afternoon nap would help reduce her puffy eyes and get her looking slightly more viewer-friendly for tomorrow's early bulletins.

'Delva it's Des . . .'

'Des?' The sound of the news editor's voice put her into

a blind panic. 'Oh hell! What time is it?' She peered at the clock through bleary eyes, her heart racing as she tried to force her brain into gear.

'Relax, woman, it's still Wednesday – you're not due in for another twelve hours.'

'Oh . . . right . . .' Delva let out a sigh of relief and flopped back on the pillow. But her head was pounding. Bastard, she thought. He's enjoying this. 'What do you want, Des?' she mumbled, trying without much success to keep the irritation out of her voice.

'Just had a tip-off from a mate of mine at Tipton Street nick,' he replied. 'They've lifted someone for the Pendleton murder.'

'You're joking?' Delva sat bolt upright in bed, suddenly remembering the woman in the café.

'His name's Sean Raven,' Des went on, 'They haven't charged him yet but this copper I spoke to reckons it won't be long before they do. And get this.' He paused and Delva heard a crackling at the other end of the phone, followed by something that sounded like teeth biting crisp lettuce. She grimaced at the thought of Des munching away at something as he was talking. When he spoke again his voice was muffled. 'The guy's heavily into black magic,' he said, 'The occult, witchcraft, that kind of thing.'

Delva was not sure she had heard him right. 'Black magic? Did you say black magic?'

'Yeah. Witches' covens, blood sacrifices – the whole nine yards.' His voice was clearer now. 'Bloody brilliant story! Anyway, I want to start doing a background piece right away. I know we won't be able to run anything till he comes to trial but I want you to start putting out a few feelers.'

Delva frowned. She could hear the excitement in his voice and she wondered what was coming next.

'What I'm really after is for someone to infiltrate this coven he was supposed to be running,' Des's voice was getting louder as his enthusiasm took off. 'I want to do a big feature on witchcraft in Wolverhampton. It might even make a documentary.'

'Des, you're not expecting me to con my way into some coven, are you? You don't seriously think I'd get away with . . .'

'No, of course not,' Des interrupted, 'I'm not that stupid. It'd have to be one of the researchers. Someone who's never been on screen, anyway.' Delva heard another strange noise down the line. This time it sounded as if he was blowing his nose. 'No, what I want you to do is use your contacts to get the lowdown on the bloke,' Des said. 'Remember that documentary you did last Christmas? The one about the profiler – Megan whatsername?'

'Yes, what about her,' Delva said guardedly

'Well according to my mate in Wolverhampton she's at Tipton Street now. He said they've brought her in to help them design an interview strategy – something like that, anyway. So I was thinking. You and her hit it off quite well, didn't you?' He paused but Delva remained silent.

'Delva, you still there?'

'Yes.' She knew what he was going to ask and she was wracking her brains to think of a way out of it.

'Thought you'd fallen asleep on me!' His voice was still buzzing with the thrill of the chase. 'Listen, I want you to call her up and pick her brains. She owes us big time. Must have had offers pouring in after that doco went out.'

It would be a waste of breath, Delva knew, to remind Des that Megan had been reluctant to make the documentary in the first place. That she was a respected academic who already had more outside work than she could handle. Des had the instincts of a Rottweiler when it came to a good story, and he didn't care who had to be savaged in order to get it.

'Okay, I'll phone her,' she said resignedly. 'But don't build your hopes up. She's as tight as a cat's arse when it comes to talking about her police work, you know.' Delva felt bad about stooping to his level, describing the woman she had come to think of as a friend in those terms. But it was the only way to get the message across. She hoped that by the time she gave him the news that Megan wasn't going to play ball he might have calmed down a bit.

'Well, we'll see.' There was a devious edge to his voice and Delva got the impression there was something he wasn't telling her. There was no way he could know what the woman in the café had told her. She had decided to lie to him about what happened. Less hassle that way. As far as he knew the woman had failed to show. She glanced at the clock. It was nearly six hours since she had made that phone call to Steve Foy. The man they were holding now had to be the guy Tessa was supposed to have had an affair with.

'Can you get on to it now?' Des's voice cut across her thoughts. 'I'll get someone else to do the early shift. Give us a bell after the programme tonight – let me know what she says, yeah?'

As soon as she replaced the receiver the phone rang again.

'Delva? It's Steve Foy. Thought you might like to know that tip-off was bang on target!'

'What, you mean you've charged someone?' Delva feigned ignorance.

'Not yet, no, but it's looking pretty good. I owe you a drink, okay?'

'Oh, great!' She tried to muster an enthusiasm she didn't feel. 'Is it the bloke in the photo? Off the record, I mean.'

'Yeah. Name's Sean Raven. Right weirdo he is, too. Can't go into detail, obviously, but he certainly fits the bill.'

'Steve,' Delva smiled to herself, astonished at the brilliant solution that had suddenly flashed into her mind. 'Don't s'pose you could let me have the phone number of the woman in the car, could you? It's just for future reference, really – if it comes to court we'll probably want to interview her for a backgrounder.'

'Don't see why not,' he said, 'After all, she doesn't need to know where you got it from, does she? Tell you what, come over for a drink and I'll fill you in on a few more details while we're at it.'

Oh God, here we go, she thought. But she was willing to string him along. Just until she'd got enough out of him to get Des off her back.

The three naked women were standing in front of a huge, golden full moon. All of them had long black hair, swept back to reveal their breasts. The one facing the front had a blazing torch in her left hand. The other two stood back-to-back behind her. One held a vicious-looking whip while the other brandished a silver-bladed dagger that glinted in the moonlight.

Megan pursed her lips. The artist responsible for the cover would certainly not have won any prizes but there was no mistaking what the book was about. Leafing through the pages she found more naked women drawn in various poses alongside each chapter heading. There were sections on Initiation, Sacred Sites, Methods of Divination and Making Magic and these were interspersed with photographs of men and women in long robes and heavy, Celtic-style jewellery.

She smiled wryly as she noted that the men all seemed to have beards and were the wrong side of forty, while the women were much younger and distinctly nubile. It seemed to be a common feature of the library of books on the occult found in Sean Raven's house. She put the book down on the table alongside a biography of Aleister Crowley. One look at the depraved face of the book's subject leering out from the front cover should have been enough to put most people off the occult for life, she thought. But what about Tessa Ledbury? What had drawn her into this shadowy world? Megan remembered what Delva had said about the man with his hand on Tessa's knee in the photograph. *White, about mid-forties, shoulder-length grey hair, slim. Very intense eyes. Not bad-looking, actually.* She wondered how much longer she would have to wait to see Sean Raven for herself.

Steve Foy had asked her wait down in the basement after she had briefed the team on the forthcoming interview. It had been a tense half-hour session, with Kate O'Leary barely concealing her triumph at having apparently been proved right. When Megan had reminded her that there was no forensic evidence to pin on Sean Raven and that the only hope of getting him to admit the crime lay in subtle psychological empathising during interrogation, she had stood up and walked out of the room, muttering something about needing the loo.

'Hi! He's put you in the dungeon, has he?' Dave Todd appeared round the door, two cups in his hand.

'Thanks,' Megan said, 'I'm gasping.'

'I'm not surprised.' He sat down opposite her and took plastic spoons and sachets of sugar from his pocket. 'We're still waiting for Sean Raven's brief to show up. He was supposed to be here half an hour ago.'

Megan raised her cup to her lips and noticed how Dave Todd's glasses had steamed up around the lower edges. He was drinking it black. Must have an asbestos mouth, she thought. Hers was too hot even with milk.

She eyed him over the rim of her cup. The gold-frames suited him. They gave him an interesting, intellectual air. She guessed that they probably made him look older than he really was. If she had had to put an age on him she would have said twenty-six or twenty-seven. But he could be younger.

She tried to imagine his backgound, his progression to detective sergeant. It was something she did whenever she met someone new, a habit so ingrained she couldn't help doing it, even when she didn't need to. She had him down as a graduate who was being pushed through the ranks quickly.

'You don't think Raven's the killer, do you?' Todd's sudden, direct question caught Megan off guard.

'Well, I, er . . . I couldn't really express an opinion until we've done the interview,' she faltered.

'I don't either,' he said simply.

She eyed him curiously. 'Why not?'

'I was the arresting officer when he was up on the rape charge,' he said. 'It was a joke from start to finish. That Carole-Ann Beddowes is an evil bitch.' The venom in his voice was unmistakeable. Megan held his gaze.

'You think she made the whole thing up?'

He nodded. 'She could lie for England, that one. And now she's out for revenge, big style. *Hell hath no fury*, and all that.' He drained his cup and tossed it into the bin. 'If I was the Guv I'd be taking a bit more interest in the cyclist.'

Megan frowned. 'What cyclist?'

'He hasn't told you?' There was a flicker of embarrassment in Todd's eyes. 'One of Tessa's neighbours told us this morning. Said she remembered someone on a bicycle going past the house round the time of the murder. She said whoever it was seemed in a hurry. Nearly knocked her flying as she was coming along the pavement.'

Megan flushed with anger. How could Foy have failed to

tell her something as important as that? 'This neighbour,' she said, trying to control her voice, 'did she give you a description?'

'Not a very good one, no,' Todd said. 'Wasn't even sure if it was a man or a woman. Just said it was a white person in a black tracksuit and a black cycling helmet. Couldn't say what colour hair or eyes because the helmet obscured the face.'

'And the age?' Megan persisted. 'Did she give you any idea of that?'

Todd shook his head. 'She's sixty-nine and she wasn't wearing her glasses

'So what makes you so sure the person on the bike wasn't Raven?'

'He's lost a kneecap.' Todd's gaze was unwavering. 'Car accident a few years back. Can't bend his right leg.'

Delva peered at her A-Z in the twilight. She wasn't sure if this was the right street. She knew she should have left it another day, really. He probably wouldn't even have received the flowers yet.

She checked the address again. Yes. This had to be the right place. She moved the gear stick into first, and was about to start driving slowly along, scanning the house numbers, when she saw him. Richard Ledbury was coming out of the front porch of a pebble-dashed house, brushing aside a trailing frond of wisteria that flopped across his face as he opened the door.

Delva stopped the car and switched off the engine. She could feel her heart pounding and realised how ridiculous that was. He was dressed more casually than when she had last seen him. The T-shirt and jeans made him look younger. His face looked the same, though. A deep frown line between his eyebrows. Not that it made him any less attractive. She felt a powerful urge to run over and take him in her arms.

Strange Blood

Then she saw the woman. Coming out behind him. Dark hair like Megan's. It was the policewoman she had seen yesterday. What was her name? Kate something? Probably come to break the news about Tessa's lover.

Delva watched as they walked along the street away from her. They stopped when they reached a Vauxhall Corsa. Purple or dark blue. She couldn't really tell, it was getting dark. She got in the driver's seat and he went round the other side. Was she taking him to the station? They sat there for a few minutes, talking. Delva wondered if the policewoman was having to use her powers of persuasion again.

When it happened she was so shocked she blinked. They kissed. A quick, furtive movement that she told herself she must have imagined. But no. They did it again. And now he was getting out. Standing there on the pavement gazing after the taillights of the car as it disappeared down the street.

Back in this piss-awful dump. Blew it with that last one. Bitch had company. Should've headed back then, but it seemed such a waste. So many possibilities at the precinct. Click, click, click of heels on concrete. No one with the X-factor, though. Never mind. Bound to be queuing early tomorrow. Ringside seats for the hottest show in town.

Chapter 7

Megan tensed as Foy's arm brushed hers. He was leaning across to rewind the video footage of Raven's interview and his peppermint breath filled her nostrils, making her want to gag.

She was seething inside at the thought of him holding back the information about the cyclist. What was the point of involving her in the case if he withheld crucial details like that? She wasn't sure what game he was playing, but it was obvious he was not to be trusted. She fought back the instinct to walk out; refuse to have anything more to do with the investigation. She *had* to find out about Raven. Weigh him up. She had to satisfy herself that Foy was on the wrong track. And so she would keep silent about the cyclist. For now.

'Would you like something to eat?' Steve Foy glanced at the clock on the wall. 'I can get something sent down from the canteen.'

Megan shook her head. The last thing she had eaten was the ham roll in the café at Pendleton. That was nearly nine hours ago. But she didn't feel hungry. Listening to Sean Raven had robbed her of her appetite.

The expression on Foy's face told her that he was feeling just as frustrated as she was, albeit for a different reason. Nothing had worked. The empathising, the answering of a question with a question, the encouraging nods – all had produced a big fat zero. As they should, of course, if the man was innocent.

She had sat watching the interview through a two-way mirror, directing the questions via an audio link with Foy and O'Leary. She had noted the way he reacted, his facial expressions, the way he moved his hands and altered his posture. Now she and Foy were going over it again on the tape.

It wasn't hard to imagine what had drawn Tessa Ledbury to him. He had an angular face with well-defined cheekbones and an aquiline nose. But the most arresting feature was his mesmering, indigo blue eyes. At times during the interview Megan had felt as if he could see her through the mirror. He seemed to be looking right at her. But that was impossible, she told herself.

She flicked a switch, freezing his face on the screen. Although attractive, it was drawn-looking. Megan could guess what must be going through his mind. He had been out of prison for just seven weeks. And now this. Yes, he had had an affair with Tessa Ledbury. No, he had not seen her since he came out of jail. No, he could not care less whether she had become a Christian. And no, he did not kill her. He was at home on the morning she died. Working on a magazine he published on his PC. Yes, it was a contact magazine for swingers. So what?

Foy clicked the off button and Raven's image disappeared from the screen.

'What about his wife?' Megan asked, 'Are you planning to interview her tonight?'

'Yes', he replied with a heavy sigh, 'You up for it? Need to phone home?' He gave her a sly look. 'Don't want young Patrick waiting up, eh?'

Megan felt her cheeks burning. Was he fishing or did he know? She could just imagine him sniggering to his colleagues, telling them she was knocking off one of her students. She pretended she hadn't heard, scribbling observations about Raven on the pad in front of her.

'I'll get some coffee brought down,' Foy said at last. 'His wife's name's Mariel, by the way. Like Muriel but with an 'a'. Looks like a real witch too – long black hair and big on body piercing.'

Megan nodded, her face angled slightly so that her pierced nostril was directly in his line of vision. It gave her a perverse sense of satisfaction to see him shift uncomfortably and look away.

Mariel Raven looked like a pin-up from a bondage magazine. She stood up in a flurry of chains, studs and biker leathers, her blue-black hair swinging round her face like a pirate flag in a gale. She was thirty-nine, but looked at least five years younger.

Megan watched through the mirror as Kate O'Leary walked into the room and took a seat next to Steve Foy. Kate was rather like a toned-down version of the woman she was about to interview. Same long dark hair, but hers was marshalled into a thick French plait. She had the same pale skin and brown, almond-shaped eyes as Mariel Raven, but the only jewellery she wore was a pair of tiny garnet studs in her earlobes. Catherine Zeta Jones meets Cher, Megan thought with a wry smile.

As the interview progressed Megan began to understand why Sean Raven had broken the law to make Mariel his wife. She was supremely confident. The sort of woman Megan could imagine inadequate men paying to dominate them. Totally unfazed by anything Steve or Kate threw at her, she gave as good as she got.

'Yes, I suppose you could describe me as a swinger,' she said, leaning back in her seat and folding her arms so that the chains on her jacket rattled. 'I love Sean but I've never restricted myself to a single sexual partner – male or female. He knows that. I don't expect him to be monogamous. As long as we're honest with each other, that's all that matters.'

'Ask if he was honest with her about his affair with Tessa.' Megan spoke into the microphone that connected her with the two police officers.

Steve Foy put the question. Megan watched Mariel Raven's face closely as she replied. The lips pushed into an inverted 'U' and the eyebrows, one pierced with a silver ring, shot towards her hairline. When they came, her words were laced with biting sarcasm.

'She was just another little glitter-witch. We get them all the time. Bored housewives with a 'vacant' sign slung across their fannies.'

Megan couldn't see the faces of the police officers but she heard Steve Foy cough slightly before he spoke again.

'What do you mean by 'glitter witch'?'

'It's what serious Wiccans call people who are just playing at it. All they're really interested in is the trappings – it's like kids dressing up.'

'But didn't Tessa go through the initiation ceremony?' Kate cut in. 'Surely that involved some level of commitment?'

Mariel smiled wryly. 'Well she was on what you might call a fast-track entry,' she said. 'Sean was desperate to fuck her and he knew she wouldn't do it unless he told her it was part of the deal of becoming a witch. She was quite prim and proper when she first started coming, but he soon cured her of that.'

'How long were they . . . lovers?' Kate hesitated slightly before enunciating this last word as if she found it somehow inappropriate.

'About a year, off and on, I suppose.'

'You suppose?' Steve Foy said, 'You mean you're not certain?'

'Well he didn't tell me every single time they did it, if that's what you mean,' she retorted, 'I mean, it would have got a bit boring, really, wouldn't it? I used to like to hear about it at first. It's always interesting when one of us is screwing someone new. But she was so full of shit.'

'What does she mean?' Megan whispered.

'What do you mean?' Kate O'Leary's head tilted forward slightly, as if inviting a confidence.

'Oh, she turned into a real prick-teaser. Spent most of the time telling him how guilty she felt about her husband and her kids. That's what I meant about her being a glitter witch. She liked to pretend she was a free spirit but what she really wanted was monogamy. She couldn't cope with the idea of sex without commitment.' She paused, her fingers stroking a silver pentacle pendant that rested on the smooth white cleavage above her black lycra vest. 'I'm sure she would have ditched her old man if she'd thought there was a chance of something permanent with Sean.'

'But that wasn't on the cards?' Kate was still using her sympathetic voice.

'Not a chance!' She almost spat the words out, her hand flying from the pendant and thudding on the table. There was a pause as the officers exchanged glances.

'Ask her why she married him,' Megan said.

'Mrs. Raven,' Foy picked up, 'can I ask you why you agreed to marry Sean? You see, I don't understand what the attraction would be for someone like yourself. Of marriage, I mean.'

'It was for my son's, sake, not mine.' There was another clink of metal as she shifted in the chair.

'Your son?'

'Yes. He was seven when I met Sean and he was having problems at school. Sean offered to marry me and adopt him. He thought it would help, you know, give him a bit of stability.'

'But he failed to tell you that he was already married?'

Megan could hear a noise like a snake hissing. 'Yes, Detective Superintendent, he failed to tell me he was still married. I don't know why you're asking – you already know all the gory details, don't you?'

'And yet you married him a second time while he was in prison.' Foy carried on as if he had not heard the last part of what she said. ' Now why would that be? Not for your son's sake, surely? I mean, he must be what, eighteen, nineteen now?'

'He's twenty-one,' she said through gritted teeth. 'And like I said before, I happen to love Sean. I can't expect someone like you to understand the way we live but I think that's our business, don't you?'

'As long as it doesn't involve breaking the law, yes,' Foy said. Megan could imagine his expression as he said it. The pale, bushy eyebrows would rise, the nostrils would curl slightly and he would rub the index finger of the hand he was leaning on up and down on his chin. He reminded her of a fox. But Mariel was no silly chicken cowering in a corner of the henhouse.

Megan watched and listened as Foy tried to break the woman down with the shock tactics she had suggested. At one point he thrust one of the crime scene photographs at her, staring pointedly at the pendant around Mariel's neck. There was a flicker of revulsion as she took in the sight of Tessa Ledbury's mutilated face, but no other sign of emotion.

'Okay,' she said, nodding her head slowly, 'Now I can see what this is all about. But it's a set-up. It has to be. Can't you see that?' Her eyes flashed angrily as she tossed the photograph back across the desk. 'There are plenty of people who rubbed their hands in glee when Sean got sent down. You should have seen some of the letters I got!'

'You mean Sean has enemies?' Kate O'Leary's words were more of a statement than a question.

'You know he has!' There was a sound like fingernails on a blackboard as Mariel leaned forward, the studded leather bracelet on her wrist scraping the table. Megan winced.

'No, we don't actually.' Steve Foy was being bloody-minded now. 'Surely you don't mean those nice people at Saint Paul's church?'

'If you're trying to wind me up you can forget it!' Mariel gave him a withering look. 'They're pathetic. Misguided, blinkered but ultimately pathetic. Certainly wouldn't have the balls for anything like that.'

'Even if they discovered that one of their new converts had been dabbling in witchcraft?'

'Don't ask me!' she replied indignantly. Foy shrugged. There was a long pause.

'Ask her if she owns a bicycle.' Megan's voice was deadpan. She watched Foy shift in his seat and felt a surge of adrenalin.

Kate O'Leary looked at Foy. Neither spoke. Foy glanced at the clock on the wall. 'Interview terminated at twenty-two thirteen,' he growled.

Delva couldn't understand why Megan hadn't called back. She had left two messages on her mobile and one on her answerphone at home. She wondered whether to try her office but decided there would be no point. The university's switchboard would have closed down for the night by now.

Her head felt as if it was going to explode. The image of Richard Ledbury and that policewoman sizzled as if it had been branded on her brain. Questions flew like sparks. What the hell were they playing at? Was it *Richard* who had killed Tessa because he was in love with Kate? But how *could* he have killed her if he was at work all day? Had someone done it for him? Had the *policewoman* done it?

Delva was desperate to tell Megan what she had seen.

She was within a couple of streets of her own house when she suddenly steered the car sharp right. Megan's house was only five minutes away. There was just a chance she had arrived home and forgotten to check the answering machine.

There were no lights on but Delva rang the bell anyway. When nothing happened she stepped back onto the pavement, looking up at the bedroom windows to see if the curtains were drawn. Delva walked over to a streetlamp and peered at her watch. Twenty past ten. Surely she wouldn't be in bed?

She rang the doorbell again, pressing her face to the glass like an impatient child. After a couple of minutes she got back into her car, slamming the door and striking the steering wheel with the heel of her hand. She sat for a while in the darkness before snatching up her mobile phone and punching out Steve Foy's number.

Steve Foy sat down next to Megan in the video room. She was waiting for him to speak. Apologise or come out with some excuse. But he said nothing.

'Why didn't you ask her about the bicycle?' She fixed him with a hard stare.

'Sorry?' His forehead creased in puzzlement like someone waking up in a strange bed.

'Before you ended the interview I asked you to ask Mariel Raven if she owned a bike.' She cocked her head, waiting for a reply.

'Oh,' he shrugged. 'Didn't hear that. Must've been the audio link. Plays up sometimes.'

Megan leaned back in her chair, arms folded. Did he really expect her to swallow that? 'Why didn't you tell me about the cyclist seen outside Tessa's house?' she persisted. 'I only found out by accident.'

'Sorry!' He slapped his forehead with the heel of his hand.' Must have slipped my mind with all the kerfuffle over Raven.' He gave her a lopsided smile. 'I'm a bit knackered, that's the problem. Haven't had much sleep since all this kicked off.'

Before Megan could reply Kate O'Leary walked in to the room followed by Dave Todd.

'What did you make of her, Kate?' Foy said. Obviously glad of the interruption, Megan thought.

'Well, she certainly had a motive, Guv.' Kate pushed a stray lock of hair back into the French plait. Over the course of the day Megan had watched the plait slowly loosen from a severe, schoolmarmish creation to something wispy and quite vampish.

'Yes, I suppose there's no reason why the pair of them couldn't have done it,' Foy nodded. 'What do you think Megan?'

Megan's eyes narrowed. She was still not sure he was being straight with her. 'Well,' she said slowly, 'I have to admit she's the sort of person who could act her way out of anything if she chose to.' She reached across the table for the coffee. 'But I wouldn't like to jump to any conclusions until I've had a word with the woman who shopped Sean Raven.'

Foy nodded. 'Carole-Ann Beddowes. You taken that statement off her yet, Dave?'

'Yes, Guv.'

'Where is she now?'

'Still in the interview room. Hollis was fetching her something from the canteen.'

'Does she know about the tip-off?' Megan asked.

'No,' Foy replied, getting to his feet, 'When Delva Lobelo gave us the car registration and mentioned the name Raven we put two and two together. Didn't actually need to talk to the woman before we lifted him. We hauled her in a couple of hours ago. Told her we're questioning everyone with a known connection.' He stepped back, holding the door open for Megan. 'Dave,' he said, 'can you take Doctor Rhys to the interview room? I want to have another go at our mate Sean. You coming, Kate?'

As she followed Dave Todd along the corridor to Interview Room Number 3 Megan caught sight of Mariel Raven through an open doorway. She was leaning back in a chair, the spike heels of her black leather boots resting on the formica table and a steaming polystyrene cup in her hand. She glanced up at the sound of footsteps, clocking Megan. Her lip curled in a look of pure hatred. Megan looked quickly away. Had Mariel Raven recognised her from the TV documentary she'd appeared in last year? Guessed she was in on the case? Far more likely, Megan told herself, that the woman gave such looks to anyone and everyone in the building; anybody remotely connected with the criminal justice system that had put her husband behind bars and now seemed hellbent on doing it again.

There was was a strong smell of steak and kidney pie as Megan pushed open the door of the room Carole-Ann Beddowes was in. An empty plate had been pushed to the edge of the table and the woman Megan had last seen at the wheel of the the red Fiesta was flicking ash onto it from her cigarette.

She looked less intimidating than she had appeared at the café, but the harsh fluorescent lighting did her face few favours. A year younger than Mariel Raven, she looked old enough to be her mother. The blonde hair had a straw-like quality, the legacy of years of bleaching and perming . And her skin reminded Megan of the tights everyone had worn at school in the 'seventies, the orangey-brown shade called *American Tan* that had borne no resemblance to the colour of her own legs and had looked even more ridiculous on her pale-skinned friends.

There was no flicker of recognition as Megan introduced herself. Obviously the woman had been so focussed on Delva this morning she hadn't taken much else in.

'I know you've already given a statement to the police,' Megan began, 'And I'm not here to ask you about Sean Raven.' She sensed Dave Todd shifting slightly in his chair a few inches from her own. He wasn't going to approve of what she was about to do but the time had come to fight dirty. 'What I want to know,' she said, 'is more about Tessa Ledbury. I'd like you to tell me what she was really like.'

'Don't know why you're asking me. I didn't know her that well.' There was a faint sizzle as the woman's cigarette ash dropped into a blob of gravy.

'Really? That's not what I've heard.' Megan leaned forward slightly, her elbows on the table. 'Sean Raven's wife's just been telling me that you and Tessa were bosom buddies.' She held her breath, looking her straight in the eye, willing her to take the bait.

'That cow! Well if you believe her you'll believe anyone!'

Megan allowed her eyebrows to rise slightly in feigned surprise. 'Oh, so it's not true, then?' She paused for a moment, choosing her next words like an archer selecting an arrow. 'Only she told us you'd got some very explicit photographs of Sean and Tessa together. Said Tessa had probably given them to you because you get off on that sort of thing . . .'

'Frigging bitch!' Carole-Ann Beddowes was out of the chair, making for the door, 'Where is she?' she screamed, 'I'll fucking kill her!'

'Sit down, please, Mrs. Beddowes.' Dave Todd took her arm and managed to get her to sit down, shooting an anxious look at Megan before moving his own chair closer to the table.

'You know her bastard husband bloody raped me, don't you?'

'I know that he was charged with raping you but was acquitted for lack of evidence,' Megan replied in an even voice. 'I'm not here to discuss the rights and wrongs of that. But that's another thing Mariel Raven said.' She paused again, watching the expression on the woman's face. 'She said the reason you accused Sean of raping you was because you were jealous. Of Tessa.'

'Bullshit!' Carole-Ann Beddowes mouth was the only part of her face not covered in a thick layer of makeup. Her lipstick had rubbed off with the meal and now Megan could see that her lips, pressed into a tight ball, had turned white with rage. 'If anyone's jealous it's her! Do you want to know how I got hold of those photos?' Her head quivered as she spoke. 'Sean gave them to me. Said Mariel was so angry when she found them in the house he'd had to promise to get rid of them. But he didn't want to, so he asked me to keep them for him.'

'And was this little favour granted before or after you accused him of raping you?' Megan asked in a deadpan voice. The woman didn't bother replying.

Foy listened to her account of what Carole-Ann Beddowes had said, rubbing his chin and saying nothing.

'I'm really not convinced, Steve,' she said. 'I mean, if you're wrong about Raven – if Tessa's died at the hands of a stranger – he could be out there stalking another victim while you're stuck here trying to get blood out of a stone.'

Foy's eyes narrowed. 'Oh, I think we'll let our friend sweat it out a bit longer.' He gestured to a set of clothes and a blonde wig lying on a table at the side of the room. 'Let's wait and see what the reconstruction throws up before we make any hasty decisions, eh?'

Megan sighed in exasperation. 'Well, I hope you'll have that precinct crawling with plain clothes people tomorrow. Because if you're wrong and I'm right . . .'

'I know, I know!' Foy held up his hands, palms out. 'Don't worry – I've got it covered.'

She shook her head as she walked across the room to inspect the outfit Kate O'Leary would be wearing in a few hours' time. A pair of cream Armani jeans, a patterned blouse and a pair of cream leather pumps lay beside the wig. 'You found out what shoes she was wearing, then?'

'No, we didn't. None of the people who saw her could remember, so we figured it would probably be the ones that blended in with the trousers.'

Megan looked at the blouse. It too was mainly cream, with a pattern of small swirls of black, red and brown. Hard to say what shoes Tessa would have selected to go with that, but yes, Foy was probably right to go with the cream ones. Still, it irritated her, not knowing. In her experience it was often the smallest details that yielded the biggest insights. She wanted to know more about this woman and if Foy was determined to stick with his theory she was just going to have to dig it out for herself.

It was nearly midnight when she left the police station. She'd left her car in the street because the carpark had been full when she arrived. She didn't notice what had been done to the windscreen until she was about to drive off. Turning the key in the ignition, she looked up to see a pattern of thick lines obscuring her view.

'What the bloody hell . . .' she said aloud, scrambling out and peering at it in the weak orange light of the street-lamps. It was a pentagram. Someone had scrawled a crude imitation of the same five-pointed star she had seen on Tessa Ledbury's head. Reaching out a finger she touched one of the points. It felt greasy and as she pulled her finger away a smear was left behind. The tip of her finger was stained dark red. She sniffed it. Lipstick. Someone had lip-sticked a pentagram on her car. Her hand dropped to her side and she realised she was trembling. The memory of Mariel Raven's face flashed before her eyes. The look of pure hate she had given her. Had she done this? Who else could it possibly be?

Patrick van Zeller slumped back onto the hard bed, stunned by what he'd just heard. He lay there staring at the ceiling, studying the cracks and the dirty gobs of blue tack left behind by some former occupant of this miserable cell of a room.

The mobile phone was still in his hand. He should have changed the number. She would never have been able to get hold of him then. She'd have tried the flat in Birming-ham and found the phone disconnected. Then she would have phoned Heartland and been told that he was no longer registered as a post-graduate student. Would they have told her he'd transferred to Liverpool?

He sighed. It was stupid, trying to think of ways he might have avoided it. She would have tracked him down sooner or later. He went to dial a number but paused, his finger hovering over the buttons. He couldn't tell Megan over the phone. She would go absolutely apeshit. No. He was going to have to break this to her face to face.

Chapter 8

Megan was awake at 5.30 the next morning. Unnerved by what had been done to her car, she had been tempted to spend the night at Ceri's rather than go home to an empty house. But it had been too late to disturb her sister. A large slug of whisky in a mug of hot milk had helped her get to sleep, but after a series of nightmares she had woken up bathed in sweat, her heart thumping.

Stumbling out of bed she peered through the curtains at the street below. In the grey morning light she could see her car. There was still a faint red smudge in the bottom corner of the windscreen on the driver's side. She must have missed it in her frantic effort to obliterate the lip-sticked pentagram.

She shuddered at the memory. The duty officer at the station told her Mariel Raven had been released half an hour before. And so had Carol-Ann Beddowes. Either one of them could have done it. The Heartland University parking permit stuck inside her windscreen would have been a dead giveaway to anyone with half a brain.

By seven o'clock she was ready to leave the house, having breakfasted and showered and applied twice the usual amount of make-up to conceal the dark rings under her eyes. She set off for Wolverhampton, knowing she was going to get to Pendleton precinct a good hour before the police. Never mind. It would be useful to hang around and watch before the media circus began. Reconstructions were like funerals. If the killer was the type she believed him to be, she was sure he'd be unable to stay away.

It was just before eight when she pulled into the carpark. There were quite a few people about. Mainly delivery men unloading at the back of the shops. She sat in the car watching for a few minutes. She noticed a bleary-eyed couple emerge from a doorway and realised there must be flats above the shops. Five minutes later a girl emerged from another doorway. She looked no more than eighteen and was dressed in a baggy sweater and jeans, carrying what looked like an art portfolio case under her arm. A student, Megan thought. These flats would be very handy for students, being a few minutes' walk from the college. She looked up at the windows of the flats, thinking how easy it would be for the occupants to watch people coming and going in the precinct below. There were so many possibilities. What she needed was a caffeine injection to kick-start her brain.

On her way to the café she spotted Delva. She was standing in front of the chemist's, sorting out equipment with a cameraman. She bounded across the precinct in response to Megan's wave.

'Megan! I was trying to get hold of you all last night!'

'Were you? I was at the police station in Wolverhampton until gone midnight.'

'The bastards! I phoned them about half ten and they said you weren't there.'

'Well I was holed up in an interview room most of the time so they wouldn't have been able to get me anyway. I had to switch the mobile off. What's happened?'

'Something pretty mind-blowing, actually.' Delva glanced around. 'Can we talk in the café?'

The man behind the counter brought their coffees over, beaming at Delva as he set them down. 'Keeping you busy?'

He cocked his head at the police car nosing slowly into the precinct's main square. Delva nodded and smiled pleasantly. A practised smile, Megan thought. She must get fed up of being recognised everywhere she went.

'You don't think there are any plain clothes people in here, do you?' Delva whispered when he'd gone.

Megan glanced over her shoulder and gave a quick shake of her head.

'Only I wouldn't want any of them hearing this.'

Megan listened in silence as Delva told her what she'd seen.

'So you see,' Delva said, 'I was totally confused. I mean, when I interviewed Richard I was convinced he was a thoroughly decent bloke who was completely devastated by his wife's death. But when I saw them kissing I suddenly had this horrible feeling that Kate O'Leary could be the killer. That she and Richard somehow cooked it up between them.'

'Yes, I see.' Megan thought for a moment, more troubled about Delva's revelation than she cared to admit. There was a sinister flicker of a possibility in what Delva was suggesting. Kate was an expert in the occult. A policewoman familiar with murder. It would be frighteningly easy for a person with that kind of knowlege to fake something like this. And if the motivation was there . . .

'I can't believe they would have been stupid enough to be seen kissing in public if there was anything sinister going on, can you?' Megan said. 'Was it an actual snog, would you say, or more of a peck on the cheek?'

'Oh, definitely not a snog,' Delva said, 'It was hard to tell, really, from where I was sitting, but it looked like a quick kiss on the lips.'

'And did it look as if he was the one making the running?' Megan asked. Did he move towards her or was it the other way round?'

'Hmm.' Delva thought for a moment. 'It happened so quickly it's hard to tell. They both seemed to move at the same time, I think.'

'Well, I know it *sounds* absolutely damning,' Megan admitted, 'but bereaved people do some very strange things. Look at it from his point of view. Suddenly he's alone with three kids to look after. He could be the sort of man who's never been on his own before – you know, the type who goes straight from living with his mum to living with his wife.'

Delva thought about this for a moment. 'But he's gone back to live with his mother – why does he need Kate O'Leary?'

'Well, we don't know how well he gets on with his parents. And Kate's a very attractive woman, isn't she?'

'And presumably she's been with him nearly every day since the murder.' Delva nodded. 'I remember the day I interviewed him. He was sitting in the back of the car, refusing to budge and she spent ages trying to talk him round.' She sniffed. 'Still, it's not very professional, is it?'

'Oh, I agree,' Megan replied, 'But it happens. And Richard Ledbury's not exactly repulsive, is he?'

The look on Delva's face gave her away.

'Oh, Delva,' Megan sighed. 'You're well out of it, believe me. Talk about emotional baggage . . .'

'I know. You're right. It was stupid of me to send those flowers. I've always tried to avoid getting emotionally involved with people I interview, but this time, I don't know, I . . .' She shook her head and shuddered, as if trying to cast off the events of the past few days. 'Anyway,' she said, leaning forward. 'What about this Sean Raven? Do you think he did it? The news editor's got this mad idea about infiltrating his coven.'

'Hmm. I'd tell him to hang fire,' Megan said. 'Unless he's

interested in running a feature on witchcraft for its own sake.'

'You don't believe Raven's the killer?'

Megan bit her lip. 'This is off the record, but you could find it out for yourself with a bit of digging. That woman you met yesterday – Carole-Ann Beddowes – she accused Sean Raven of rape. He was arrested but it never came to court.'

Delva gave a low whistle. 'I think she was jealous when he took up with Tessa,' Megan went on. 'Threatened to send those pictures she was offering you to Richard. I've no proof of that, you understand, but to me it's patently obvious she hates Sean Raven's guts and is trying to drop him in it a second time.'

'Wow!' Delva rubbed her chin with the back of her hand. 'How did Steve Foy react to all this?'

'Didn't take a blind bit of notice,' Megan said. 'He's applying for an extension so they can carry on with the interrogation.' She sniffed and folded her arms. 'I don't really know why he called me in in the first place. He's got his own little theory about the murder and he's sticking to it. I think when he came on the sex crimes course a few weeks back he got a bit carried away with the idea of profiling. It's almost as if he's getting off on trying to prove me wrong in front of his colleagues. And he's obsessed with the media. Seems more interested in getting his face on the box than catching Tessa's killer.'

'Sounds about right from what I've seen of him.. Hey, talk of the devil!' She jerked her head at the window. Steve Foy was getting out of an unmarked car which had pulled up in the main square. 'I'd better get back out there.' She glanced at her watch. 'They're due to start in half an hour.'

Megan nodded. 'I'm going to stay here for a while. I want to see who comes nosing around Foy and his mates.'

Megan left the café five minutes before Kate O'Leary began her progression from the school to the precinct. Knots of people had gathered along the route to watch in sombre silence. Mostly women, Megan noticed. Many of them were clutching babies and toddlers. They were probably mothers from the school, no doubt thanking their lucky stars it wasn't *their* last moments of life being acted out by a policewoman.

Megan stared at Kate O'Leary as she walked from the doctor's surgery to the chemist's. The blonde wig made her almost unrecognisable.

She thought about what Delva had seen. Kate was not an easy woman to deal with, but she mustn't let that cloud her judgement. If there had been an affair going on between Richard Ledbury and the policewoman before Tessa's death, was it *really* likely the pair had planned the murder? Even if Kate was capable of such a thing, Megan reasoned, the pentagram signature would have been pure folly. Foy knew all about Kate's familiarity with the occult. It simply didn't make sense for her to have done something so obvious.

Megan moved between the onlookers, following in Kate's wake. What she was looking for was a man with a bicycle. She scanned the shop doorways and the metal bollards at the entrance to the square. Not even a chained-up bike in sight, let alone someone pushing one.

When the reconstruction was over Megan waited outside the café until Foy had finished talking to the waiting reporters. His body language spoke volumes. Before the cameras started to roll he checked himself in a small hand mirror taken from his jacket pocket, running his fingers through the gelled spikes of hair before turning on a suitably stern expression.

'Well?' she asked, when the show was finally over. 'Anything happened?'

Foy shrugged. 'No-one suspicious hanging around, if

that's what you mean,' he said. 'Just got to see if the telly can work a bit of magic, now, eh?'

He seemed very confident all of a sudden. Not the dejected, frustrated man she had seen last night. Megan wondered what he wasn't telling her. She got the feeling he had something up his sleeve.

'I'd like to interview the couple from the church,' she said. 'Okay with you?'

His eyes narrowed. 'Any particular reason? They've both got provable alibis.' 'I know.' She held his gaze. 'But from what I can make out they were Tessa's only real friends. I want to know more about her life as it was last week, not the life she was living eighteen months ago. I think that's important, don't you?'

It was impossible now. No chance of getting out. So frustrating, with the crowds out there. But the first one was still cooking. Nothing on the news about her. Must be pretty high by now, weather being so warm. There'd be flies. Maggots as well, probably. Doing their worst. What a shot that would make. Camera panning round the room. Silence except for the buzz of the insects. Zoom in to what looks like a bundle of rags on the bed. Close-up of the head. Cut to titles . . .

Chapter 9

The silver chalice glinted in the rays of sunshine that slanted in through the kitchen window. There was a blackened rag beside it and the air was thick with the smell of polish. Across the kitchen the ironing board was still out, a white altar cloth draped across it and the iron propped up on the heatproof end. Jenny Spelman had left it that way when she went to answer the door. She had told Megan that she and her husband were preparing for a communion service at an old people's home.

'You see, when Tessa came to the church that evening she was on the verge of a breakdown.' Bob Spelman was speaking. Seated at the kitchen table he was looking straight into Megan's eyes in a disarming way. He was a slight man with a ruddy face and thinning brown hair. Not attractive in the conventional sense. But there was something very arresting about him. Megan couldn't quite put her finger on it.

'She'd sat through the service,' Jenny Spelman, sitting close to her husband, took up the story, 'but as she left, one of the people whose job it is to make newcomers welcome went up to speak to her. Gwen, I think it was.' She turned, her eyebrows raised in a question mark and he nodded. 'Anyway,' she went on, 'Gwen only got as far as asking if she was from Pendleton and Tessa burst into tears.' The woman paused, casting her eyes down as if she was embarrassed to be betraying a confidence.

Megan studied her for a moment. Her long, naturally curly brown hair was greying slightly at the temples, but it was pulled back from her face with two slides. No attempt at concealment. And not a scrap of make-up. Her blue-grey eyes were imprisoned by thick-lensed glasses.

'When exactly was this?' Megan asked.

'It was just over a year ago. I remember it was Easter Sunday. Bob and I were on duty that night, weren't we?' She looked at him again. 'We have a prayer team every Sunday night. If anyone needs to be prayed for they can come up after the service and whoever's on duty will stay and pray with them.'

'And Tessa came up, did she?' Megan asked.

'Not exactly, no,' Bob Spelman replied. 'It was Gwen who brought her to us. After she started crying, I mean.'

'And did she tell you why she was so upset?'

'Not the whole story, not then.' He reached for the bottle of polish, screwing the cap back on. 'She said she was having problems with her husband, that was all.'

'Did she tell you about the affair?'

'Not that night, no. It wasn't until she started coming to our house group that she really opened up about . . .' He paused, exchanging glances with Jenny. 'Well, about things in her past,' he went on. 'I'm sorry,' he said, 'But this is something we both find very hard to talk about. You see we only found out yesterday . . .'

'I know,' Megan said, 'and I do appreciate you talking to me.' She caught a sudden flicker of movement. Jenny Spelman had pulled a handkerchief from the sleeve of her sweater and was dabbing her eyes.

'I'm sorry to have to ask you this,' Megan went on, 'but it could be important. Did Tessa ever hint that her husband had been unfaithful too?'

Bob Spelman shook his head. 'No. When she came to us

she was weighed down by guilt. She said it was all her fault and she wanted to try to save her marriage. I think it was touch and go when she confessed she'd had the affair, but we prayed that Richard would forgive her.'

'And do you think he did?'

'Oh yes. They were very happy, you know, these last few months. That's what makes it so tragic.' Bob Spelman sniffed loudly and for a moment Megan thought he was going to cry too. Instead he reached for the rag he had been polishing the chalice with, rubbing a corner of the cloth between his finger and thumb until it formed a stiff point.

'Did she ever suggest that she was being persecuted in some way? That someone was out to get her?' Megan asked.

'In the beginning, yes,' the man replied, looking at her with a trace of surprise. 'That's why we urged her to make a clean breast of it with her husband. Someone was threatening to tell him about the affair.'

'Did she say who, exactly?'

He shook his head.

'And you didn't suggest going to the police? After all, what you're describing sounds like blackmail to me.'

'No, Doctor Rhys.' Bob Spelman sighed. 'It wasn't blackmail exactly. And we thought prayer and honesty were a better solution than getting the police involved. I don't really think that course of action would have helped anybody.'

'I suppose you know that the man the police are holding over Tessa's murder is her ex-lover?' Megan's voice came out sounding harsher than she had intended. She heard something like a muffled sob and half expected Jenny Spelman to start crying again. But the woman had composed herself and was staring down at the handkerchief in her hand.

Bob Spelman looked shocked. 'It's Sean Raven, is it? I didn't know that.' He sighed. 'I've encountered him quite a few times – nothing to do with Tessa – but on occasions when he's tried to use the church hall for occult meetings.' He paused, screwing the rag into a ball and clenching his hand over it. 'From what I've seen of him he's not the sort of man to get jealous over a woman. He's surrounded by them. They stand there hanging on his every word. Tessa described him as a sex addict, and as far as I can see he's the last person who would commit a crime of passion.'

Megan looked at the man with a certain admiration. It would have been easy for him to condemn Sean Raven. After all, Raven represented everything he despised. But instead he was defending him.

'What makes you think this was a crime of passion?' she asked.

He frowned, a single line appearing between his dark eyebrows. 'If Tessa was killed by her ex-lover, what other sort of crime could it be?'

'Well, you mentioned the occult, Mr. Spelman.'

The frown deepened. 'Are you suggesting Tessa's death was some sort of black magic ritual?'

'Is that something you've ever encountered?'

He closed his eyes, screwing up the lids as if he was concentrating hard. Then he opened them again, taking a deep breath. 'No, Doctor Rhys. I've heard all kinds of stories about the appalling things witches are supposed to involve themselves in, but I have no first hand experience of anything of that kind.' He glanced at the rag in his hand. 'I spoke to Sean Raven about his beliefs when I visited him in prison. It's basically a nature religion. Obviously I don't agree with it, but there was nothing he described to me that could be construed as deliberately evil or malicious.'

Megan's eyes narrowed. 'You visited him prison? Why?'

'We have an outreach group at St Paul's,' he explained. 'We hold services at Whiteladies Prison once a month and some of us do visiting as well.'

Megan's heart began to pump faster. Whiteladies was an open prison in Shropshire. About, what, ten miles from Pendleton? What if Tessa Ledbury had been involved in this? If Pendleton was the nearest community there was every chance that inmates of an *open* prison would be allowed a certain amount of access. 'Was Tessa part of the outreach group?' she asked. Bob Spelman shook his head. 'It was something we advised her against. We thought it best that she avoid Sean Raven completely. Make a clean break.'

Megan felt frustrated. For a moment she'd thought she was on to something. But she'd got it wrong. And anyway, she reasoned, what would a violent sex offender be doing in an open prison?

'Actually,' Jenny Spelman piped up, 'she made the decision to stop seeing all the people that were connected with her old life, didn't she Bob? She said she didn't want to expose herself to any temptation.' Her face crumpled and a tear dripped from the rim of her glasses. 'She was so lovely,' the woman gasped. 'We all loved her – I just can't believe she's gone!'

Bob Spelman put an arm around his wife's shoulders and stroked her hair. There was an uncomfortable silence as Megan tried to judge whether she should attempt to carry on. 'I'm sorry, Dr Rhys,' he said at last. 'Is there anything else you wanted to ask?'

His tone was kindly rather than dismissive, so she decided to try another tack. 'Tessa telephoned you a few minutes before she died,' she said. 'Have you any idea why that might have been?'

'I think it was about the church flowers,' Jenny Spelman whispered. 'You told the police that, didn't you, Bob?'

He nodded. 'Yes.' He smiled grimly. 'Once I'd managed to convince them I really did spend all of Thursday morning giving driving lessons, that is. I told them Tessa probably phoned to find out whether she was meant to be doing the flowers for church. Jenny was down for it on the rota but she'd been ill, hadn't you?'

The woman nodded, lifting her glasses to wipe her eyes. 'Yes. I missed the Bible study on Tuesday and Tessa had told Bob she'd do the flowers if I wasn't better.'

'Do you think there's any chance she went to St. Paul's on the morning she died?' Megan asked. 'If she thought she might be doing the flowers would she have called in there first?'

'She couldn't have,' Bob Spelman said simply, 'The church isn't open until noon on Thursdays and she's not one of the keyholders.'

'So the church is kept locked most of the time, is it?' Megan frowned. 'People can't just wander in and pray if they want to?'

'Yes. It's a shame, but it's one of those sad facts of modern life. There's been lot of burglary in Pendleton over the past few years and unfortunately St. Paul's is a prime target. That's why we've started keeping things like this in our own homes. He stroked the neck of the chalice with his finger and thumb. 'But I can guess what you're thinking, Doctor Rhys,' he said slowly. 'Religious maniacs? Nutters? I'm not sure what the correct psychological term would be. And yes, we do get people like that at Saint Paul's occasionally. It's unavoidable. The church is there to help people with problems and we don't turn anybody away.'

He paused, looking searchingly into her eyes. 'But if you believe someone like that is responsible for what happened to Tessa,' he said, 'I can only say she couldn't possibly have been followed home from the church that morning.' He paused, his fingers moving away from the chalice. Taking his wife's hand he squeezed it gently. 'We'll be praying for you,' he said softly.

Megan cast a nervous glance at her car as she left the Spelmans' house. She was in the heart of the Pendleton estate. Five minutes' drive from Tessa Ledbury's house and just a few streets away from the address on Sean Raven's police file. The more she thought about it, the more certain she became that Mariel Raven was responsible for the lipstick pentagram. Apart from the police, she was the only one who knew what had been done to Tessa's body. But why do it? The question had been hammering away in Megan's head since the previous night. Was it a reckless, opportunistic thing or something much more sinister?

The car was just as she had left it and she jumped in, pulling the A-Z from the glove compartment and scanning the index for the name of the Ravens' street. It was even closer to the Spelmans' house than she had realised. After a couple of right turns she was cruising past the houses, looking for number 171. She didn't have to look for long. As she rounded a bend she caught sight of a gaggle of people on the pavement. Photographers and journalists camped out on the Ravens' doorstep. Megan put her foot on the accelerator and sped past. Nothing to be gained by wading into that lot, she thought. Had something happened? Had Sean been released?

She switched channels on the car radio, trying to catch a news bulletin. But by the time she got home all she had managed to learn was the latest cricket score and the best way to keep slugs off plants without using pesticide. The press pack didn't necessarily signify anything new, she reflected. Could have been hanging around ever since Sean Raven was arrested.

Draping her coat on the banister she went straight to her study. Nothing on e-mail from Steve Foy. Just two messages from Patrick. One was about an academic reference he had been unable to track down in the library at Liverpool and the other simply said, 'See you tomorrow.'

Megan stared at the screen, frowning. He had e-mailed her yesterday to say his mobile phone had broken. There was no phone in his room at the hall of residence, so unless he went to a payphone, e-mails were the only means of communication.

But his messages were usually longer and a lot more romantic. He'd always been into leaving little notes around the house for her to find and now he was away she had expected him to be, if anything, even more communicative via the computer. She had a nagging feeling something was wrong, but without being able to speak to him properly it was impossible to suss out what it was.

Megan tried to put it out of her mind. They could have a long chat when he got back tomorrow night. She went downstairs and switched on the television, leaving the door of the living room open as she went to the kitchen to make a coffee. Just as the kettle boiled she heard the familiar opening sting of the local lunchtime news and she wandered back through to catch the headlines. A shot of forensics people in white overalls going up a path bordered by red and white police tape alerted her before the presenter had even opened his mouth: *'Fears of a serial killer on the loose as the body of a second woman is found in Wolverhampton . . .'*

Megan sank onto the sofa, staring at the newsreader but taking in nothing as he announced job losses at a local car plant and news of a Birmingham woman giving birth to sextuplets. Then pictures of a Victorian house very similar to her sister's came up on the screen and her brain ground back into gear as he picked up the lead story. '*The discovery of a woman's body at a house in Wolverhampton has sparked fears that a serial killer has struck again. Twenty-five-year-old Joanna Hamilton was found dead after police broke into her home this morning . . .*'

Pictures of scenes-of-crime officers flashed back onto the screen and the van transporting the body was shown driving away from the house. Megan's mind was in a whirl. If the body was found this morning, she reasoned, the woman was probably killed last night. When Sean Raven was still in custody . . .

'*Police have refused to confirm reports that the victim was stabbed to death. They say there will be no official confirmation of the cause until a post-mortem examination has been carried out. But they are not ruling out the possibilty that the death is linked to the murder of mother-of-three Tessa Ledbury, who was stabbed to death at her home in the Wolverhampton suburb of Pendleton a week ago . . .*'

The shrill sound of Megan's mobile phone cut across the newsreader's voice and she ran into the hall to retrieve it from her bag.

'Megan? It's Steve Foy . . .' He sounded breathless, excited.

'I've just heard it on the news,' she cut in, stealing his thunder. 'When did it happen?'

'Oh, our friend Sean's not off the hook yet. Not by a long chalk.' He sounded like a snake about to strike. 'We're waiting for official confirmation from the pathologist, of course, but the word is the poor woman's been lying in that house for more than a week.' He paused, waiting for the impact of his words to sink in. 'I thought you might like to be in on the post-mortem,' he said in the sweet voice she had heard him use when he was being deeply sarcastic. 'Looks like it could be another case of overkill.'

Chapter 10

Megan's fingers left trails of perspiration on the steering wheel as she battled to reverse into a space in the mortuary car park. She was still wearing the navy wool trouser suit she'd put on that morning and now she wished she'd changed into something cooler. As she straightened the car up she caught sight of a familiar-looking figure in the rear-view mirror. It was Dave Todd. He was coming down the steps, hunched over, supporting someone much shorter than himself. As Megan watched, Kate O'Leary caught them up. They reached a black Ford Mondeo and Dave opened one of the rear doors. Now Megan could see that the person he was with was a young woman. Her face looked very red and she was holding a handkerchief a few inches from her mouth the way someone would if they were afraid they were going to vomit.

Kate got in beside the woman and Dave jumped into the driver's seat, pulling out in a single manoeuvre and picking up speed as he headed for the exit at the other end of the car park.

Steve Foy was waiting for Megan in a small, sparsely furnished room. A pair of heavy, dusky pink curtains screened the window and there was a faded artificial geranium in a pot on the sill. There was a partition in one wall and through it she could see a long metal trolley covered in a white sheet. The sheet was wrinkled, as if something heavy had been lying on it. Now Megan knew why the woman she had just seen looked so awful. This was the viewing room. The place relatives were bought to identify a body.

'Who was that?' Megan jerked her head towards the car park.

'Young lady by the name of Vicky Tomlins,' Foy replied. He let out a sigh and shook his head. 'Poor cow. Not a pleasant sight for anyone, but when it's your best friend . . .'

Megan sighed and shook her head.

'It was her raised the alarm,' he went on, 'They were supposed to meet for lunch yesterday but Joanna didn't show. Vicky said she phoned her a couple of times and kept getting the answering machine. In the end she went round to the house.' He felt in his jacket pocket and pulled out a packet of mints, offering one to Megan. She shook her head. 'Anyway,' he went on, the mint making a bulge in his cheek, 'there's an alleyway down the side of the house and when she peered through the back gate she noticed one of the rubbish bins had been knocked over. An animal had dragged out a chicken carcass and made a right mess. That what made her suspicious.'

'Why?' Megan frowned.

'She said Joanna was obsessively tidy. The sort who'd spot something like that straightaway and clear it up before she did anything else.'

'But how did she know she hadn't just gone away somewhere?'

'Because she hadn't put the bins out the front. Vicky said she would never have gone off without doing that.'

'Hmm.' Megan thought for a moment. 'And there are no relatives? No-one else who missed her, I mean?'

'Well there's an ex-husband but he's in Australia. They didn't have any kids. And according to Vicky there's no boyfriend either.'

'And she didn't work?'

'Oh yes, she was a freelance illustrator. She worked from home.'

'So nobody missed her, apart from this Vicky?'

Foy shook his head. 'Frightening isn't it?'

'Well, yes,' Megan said, 'Didn't the neighbours notice anything?'

'They're not really the type who would,' Foy said. 'On one side there's an old lady who's bedridden and the other side there's a houseful of students. I don't think they even knew her name. She'd only moved in a few months ago, evidently.'

'Where exactly did she live? It looked like an old house. Too old for Pendleton, anyway.'

'It isn't in Pendleton,' Foy said. 'It's in Stockhall. About three miles away, towards Wolverhampton town centre.'

'Yes, I know where it is.' Megan felt a cold sensation in her stomach. 'My sister lives there. What street is it?'

When Foy said the name, Megan wracked her brains, running a mental map of the area around Ceri's house through her brain. No, it wasn't a street she could place. But that didn't make her feel any less anxious. She would have to look it up in the A-Z when she got back to the car.

The door opened and a bespectacled man in a white lab coat appeared. 'Doctor Laine says he's ready for you now if you'd like to come through,' he said.

The smell hit Megan before she had even entered the room. It had drifted through the gaps under the doors and along the corridor like some invisible, malevolent spirit, assaulting her senses so that her hand shot involuntarily to her mouth.

'Sorry about the stink,' the pathologist shrugged as they stepped gingerly over the threshold. 'We've got the extractor fan going flat out but it's not making much of an impact, I'm afraid.'

Slowly, Megan looked up, trying to prepare herself for the appalling sight she knew was going to meet her eyes. She had attended maybe a dozen post-mortems since she'd started working with the police, but never one in which putrefaction was this far advanced.

It was the feet and legs she looked at first. This was deliberate. She would focus on those and work herself up slowly to viewing the rest of the body. The head she would try to avoid seeing until she absolutely had to. Without the head she could distance herself. Pretend that the pale green limbs with their dark marbling of veins were not real but some prosthetic creation borrowed from the set of a horror film.

'As you can see,' the pathologist was saying, 'The putrefaction at the site of the wounds is considerably more advanced than for the rest of the body.'

Megan's eyes travelled up the legs to the trunk. The stomach was so swollen that an untrained observer might have mistakenly believed the victim to be pregnant. But she had anticipated this. Anything over a week, she knew, meant that the stomach gases would have expanded alarmingly, giving this characteristic bloated appearance.

'This is consistent with trauma to the body,' the pathologist went on. 'The destruction of haemoglobin by bacteria means blood at the site of the wound or abrasion gives a blackened appearance to the surrounding skin.'

Megan allowed herself to move slightly so that she could see the victim's chest. The pale green skin of the neck gave way to a blackened mess of torn flesh.

'Have you been able to estimate the number of stab wounds?' Steve Foy bent closer to the body, apparently unmoved by its appearance.

'It's difficult to say until we begin the dissection,' the pathologist said, 'Because the extent of putrefaction tends to blur the boundaries between points of entry. We'll get a better idea when we examine the heart and lungs although I'd say the majority of the wounds were superficial.'

'Can you give a ballpark figure though?' Foy pressed him. 'I mean, is it less than say, fifty? More than twenty?'

'At a conservative estimate, I'd say no less than a couple of dozen.' The pathologist motioned to his assistant who produced an outline diagram of a human body. The chest area was peppered with red biro marks. 'This is a representation of the surface appearance of the upper trunk,' he said.

'Hmm.' Foy studied the diagram and passed it to Megan. 'What do you think?'

'It's very similar to the distribution of wounds on Tessa Ledbury's body, isn't it?' she replied. 'What about clothing? Was she wearing anything when they found her?'

'Yes' Foy said. 'This one was fully dressed. She was stabbed through her clothes, like Tessa, but they weren't removed afterwards.'

'What about the weapon?' She turned to the pathologist. 'Has the flesh decayed too much to be able to tell what kind of knife was used?'

'I'm afraid so,' he said. 'Again, we might get a better idea when we dissect the body but you have to take into account that the swelling of the internal organs will have altered the dimensions of any laceration to the tissue.'

'And what about the head?' Foy took a step towards the top of the steel trolley. 'It's a real mess, isn't it?' He addressed the question to the pathologist but his eyes were on Megan. She couldn't put the moment off any longer. She had to make herself look.

The face was hardly recognisable as human. The features were so grotesquely altered that it was impossible to imagine what the woman had looked like in life. The mouth and cheeks were swollen and discoloured and the skin around the eyes so dark and puffy that it looked as if she had been punched.

'Don't be misled by the appearance of the face,' the pathologist said, as if reading her thoughts. 'The only area of trauma is on the forehead – the rest is consistent with this stage of decay.'

Megan allowed her gaze to inch up the woman's face. Those eyes would come back to haunt her, she knew. Tonight, maybe. Or tomorrow, when she was lying in Patrick's arms.

'How on earth did her friend manage to identify her?' she asked.

Foy pointed to the corpse's right shoulder. 'Tattoo in the shape of a Chinese character on her back,' he said. 'Means "happiness", evidently.'

Megan shuddered. She glanced at the woman's forehead, concentrating on that area of blackened flesh, about three inches square, which held the key to this killing.

'You saw Tessa Ledbury,' Foy said to the pathologist. 'Could this be a similar type of injury, do you think?'

'It's impossible to say,' he replied, shifting his position so that the scalpel in his hand hovered over the woman's forehead. 'There's no way we can tell from the state of the skin. The only possible clue would lie in the bone immediately underneath.' He waved the scalpel in a circular movement, as if stirring a cup of tea. 'There's a slim chance that the killer left an impression of his handiwork on the skull, although I have to say that was not the case with Tessa Ledbury. The mark on her forehead was a straightforward flesh wound.'

'So you're saying that unless the killer used more force in cutting the pentagram on this victim, there'd be no damage to the bone?' Foy frowned.

'That's about the size of it, yes,' the pathologist nodded.

'What about the hair?' Megan was staring at the long, matted, dark brown locks which stuck to the flesh at the temples. 'Tessa Ledbury's hair was held back from her face with a pair of tights . . .'

'Sorry I didn't tell you,' Foy said quickly. 'There was a hairband. A gold-coloured, beaded sort of thing. It's been removed. Vicky Tomlins said it was one Joanna often wore.'

'So you think she was wearing it when she was attacked?'

'It's hard to say. He could have found it and used it instead of tights.'

'What about a gag?' Megan glanced at the swollen mouth with its unnaturally dark lips. 'Tessa's killer left a dishcloth sticking out of her mouth.'

'We haven't opened the oral cavity yet,' the pathologist said. 'You could stay and watch the dissection if you want, but I warn you, it'll be a long and very messy business. There were maggots on the body when it was found and I expect we'll find more when we open her up.'

'No, it's okay.' For the first time, Foy's face betrayed the fact that he was finding this every bit as distasteful as Megan. 'You'll phone me if you find anything.' This was said in lieu of any goodbye as he made for the door, pulling off the surgical cap concealing his carroty hair. It looked even more startling than usual against the pallor of his skin and for a split second Megan had a vision of him lying in place of the woman on the mortuary trolley. It was terrifying, she reflected, to think that a living, breathing human being could be reduced to nothing more than a stinking parcel of bones in the space of just a few days.

She left the place feeling, as she always did after such encounters, a mixture of emotions. On the one hand she felt a powerful urge to run away. To refuse to have anything more to do with the depravity whose end result she had

just witnessed. She knew that the memory of Joanna
Hamilton's wretched body would be with her for the rest
of her life, squeezing unbidden into her mind's eye to
curdle the moments of joy.

She was in the car now, following Foy's Audi to the car
park exit. She didn't have to follow him. She could drive to
her sister's instead, play with Emily and Joe; do the things
normal people do. She hesitated at a junction as Foy turned
left. And then a voice welled up in her head, drowning out
the rest. *If you chicken out now, someone else is going to die. Get
whoever did this off the streets.*

Ceri was sitting in the café at Pendleton. It was far more
crowded than usual, but they had managed to get a table to
themselves. She glanced around. Thank God there were no
other students in here. Under cover of the chequered tablecloth Justin was rubbing his knee against her thigh.

'Are you sure you want this?' The way he looked at her
made her feel completely reckless.

'You know I do.'

'When, then?'

'Soon,' she smiled, easing her foot from its shoe and
rubbing her bare toes against his crotch. 'He's going away.'
She held his gaze, her private fantasy taking over, blotting
out the sights and sounds of the café: The house empty.
Justin naked in her bed. The feel of him on her skin as he
took her in his arms. She closed her eyes.

As Megan followed Foy back to the police station she ran
through the facts. The number and pattern of the wounds
were the same for both women. Each had also had something incised on to their foreheads, and in both cases the
hair had been drawn away from the face. But without hard
evidence of the mess on Joanna Hamilton's face being a

pentagram, there were still enough differences to question whether the two women were victims of the same killer.

Tessa was thirty-six and blonde while Joanna was twenty-five and brunette. Tessa's body was naked while Joanna had been found with her clothes on. Questions crowded Megan's mind. She needed to talk to Vicky Tomlins. Find out if there were any connections between the two women, however slight. What she most wanted to know was if Joanna Hamilton ever went to the precinct at Pendleton.

Foy was waiting for her outside the entrance to Tipton Street police station. As they went in, a couple of drunks were shouting at the duty officer on the desk. Foy didn't bat an eyelid.

'Dave and Kate back?' was all he said, raising his voice slightly above the din.

'Incident room, Guv,' the officer called back without looking up. One of the drunks had begun ripping a 'wanted' poster off the wall and the other was staggering towards Megan, looking as if he was about to throw up. Suddenly, three uniformed officers materialised from behind a door. Foy ushered her quickly away, shouts of abuse following them down the corridor.

'Guv?' Dave Todd looked up expectantly as they entered the room.

'Where's Kate?' Foy sat down heavily at a table strewn with evidence bags.

'Out the back, collecting stuff from the SOCOs,' he said. 'Any joy?'

Foy shook his head. 'Body was a total abortion. Zero forensic evidence because of the state of decay.' He shrugged. 'If there was any ejaculant this time we'll never know. How about you?'

'Well, we haven't found anything that connects her with Tessa Ledbury,' he replied, 'But I think we're getting somewhere with the time of death. That Vicky woman said they always met for lunch on Wednesdays.'

'Yeah, she already told me they were supposed to meet yesterday.' Foy sounded impatient. 'How does it help us with the time of death?'

'Well, the reason they didn't meet last Wednesday was because Joanna was due to fly to Paris. She was leaving the day after their last meeting, which was two weeks ago.' Todd brushed away a fly that had settled on his arm. 'Vicky said Joanna was planning to spend a week in Paris to get inspiration from the art galleries for her latest book commission,' he went on. 'But she never caught the plane from Birmingham International on the Thursday afternoon. That means she must have died sometime between 2.30pm on the Wednesday and about 11am on the Thursday.'

'I see,' Foy nodded. 'Which means she's been dead a fortnight.'

'Looks like it, Guv, yes.'

'There could be a pattern, there, couldn't there?' The men looked up, startled at the sound of Megan's voice, as if they had forgotten she was there. 'Tessa dies on a Thursday morning; Joanna dies sometime between Wednesday afternoon and Thursday morning. Where was it they met for lunch?' She had suddenly remembered the café in Pendleton and her mind was racing ahead like an express train.

'Beatties,' Todd said, derailing her theory with a single word. 'That's where they always met. You know – the department store in Wolverhampton town centre?'

Megan nodded. 'Do we know where she went after she'd had lunch? I mean, did she tell Vicky she was going shopping or anything?'

'She told her she was going straight home to pack for the holiday.'

'What if she needed something last-minute for the trip?'

Megan asked. 'Pendleton's the nearest supermarket to Stockhall.'

'She could have gone to the local shops,' Foy said slowly. 'They're only two minutes walk from the house.'

'Yes, but they all shut at half past five,' Megan countered. 'The supermarket at Pendleton stays open until at least eight o'clock most nights, doesn't it?'

'Well I suppose she could have done that,' Foy grunted. 'But I don't think it's very likely because she didn't own a car.'

'She could have got there some other way, though, couldn't she?' Megan persisted. 'On a bus. Or a bicycle.' She looked pointedly at him. She still hadn't forgiven him for witholding that witness statement from her.

'Okay, okay!' Foy glanced at the ceiling. 'Have you checked her handbag yet, Dave?'

'Yes Guv. No receipts for anything after the day she met Vicky Tomlins for lunch.'

'But were any of those receipts from shops in Pendleton?' Foy sounded exasperated.

'I, er, think so, yes.' He flicked through his notebook. 'I was looking at them more from the point of view of establishing the time of death.' His face had flushed and Megan felt a twinge of sympathy. 'I'll have to check,' he said.

'Tell the SOCOs to get onto it, will you Dave?' Foy barked. 'Get them to check barcodes with the supermarket. Oh, and don't forget those rubbish bags outside.' He sounded serious enough but Megan had a feeling all this was window-dressing. He had given himself away in that phone call he'd made to her when the body was found. Sean Raven was still his prime suspect.

There was an uncomfortable silence after Dave Todd left the room. Megan wondered what Foy was thinking.

'What I find hard to believe,' she said, 'is that Vicky Tomlins was Joanna Hamilton's only friend. It's odd, don't you think? Both murder victims having such a limited social circle.'

He frowned. 'Well, in Joanna's case it might not have been that limited. She hadn't long moved from Australia, but we're checking out local groups she might have joined, that sort of thing.'

'By which you mean Sean Raven's coven, I assume?' Megan looked at him. 'And?'

'And nothing.' He sounded sheepish. 'Carole-Ann Beddows said she'd never clapped eyes on her. So did a couple of others we've tracked down.'

'And the man himself?' Megan's eyebrows arched. 'Come on Steve, don't tell me he wasn't back in the interview room the minute Joanna's body was found?'

'Guv!'

Before Foy could say anything, Kate O'Leary appeared, almost staggering into the room. She was carrying an enormous pile of books, each one encased in a plastic evidence bag.

'Just look at these, Guv,' she said, leaning over the table so that they slid gently out of her arms.

Foy picked one up, reading the cover through the plastic. 'The Thoth Tarot,' he announced, 'An introduction to the Occult-Inspired Designs of Aleister Crowley.' His eyes narrowed as he stared at the book before tossing it aside and grabbing another. 'Queen of the Night,' he read. 'Exploring the Astrological Moon.' Megan could hear the excitement in his voice as he reached for another, this time a thick hardback with a brightly illustrated jacket. 'Parker's Astrology: The Definitive Guide To Using Astrology In Every Aspect Of Your Life.' He gave a low whistle. 'Thank you, God,' he breathed, pushing the books towards Megan and grabbing another handful.

'They were just sitting there in a bookcase in the bed-room,' Kate said. She sounded out of breath. 'Can't believe I didn't notice them myself.'

'Is there anything on witchcraft?' Megan sifted through the books Foy had not yet seized.

'Not actual witchcraft, no,' Kate said. 'But there's loads on Tarot and Astrology. She was obviously one of the wacky brigade.'

'I think that's going a bit far, don't you?' Megan said, pulling a book about crystal healing from the pile. 'I'd say this was pretty mainstream stuff. Or are you suggesting that everyone who reads their horoscope and burns scented candles is a closet occultist?'

'Oh come on!' Kate gave her a withering look. 'Aleister Crowley? Don't you know the kind of perverted filth he was involved in?'

'Of course I do,' Megan replied, reaching for the book Foy had picked out first. 'But the woman was an illustrator and this has the word 'Designs' in the title. For all we know she bought it for the pictures, not the content.'

She looked at Foy but his eyes were full of righteous zeal. He breathed in deeply and sat back, folding his arms. When he opened his mouth Megan caught a whiff of peppermint. 'Come on,' he said, his nostrils flaring. 'Let's get the bastard up here!'

Mariel Raven drew the thick green velvet curtains in her living room. She could see no reporters or photographers outside, but she wasn't taking any chances. It had been hard, running their gauntlet every time she left the house. But at lunchtime they'd streaked off like sharks scenting blood. She'd seen the news later and breathed a sigh of relief. What she couldn't understand was why those bastards were still holding Sean.

She heard the sound of her son's bicycle on the gravel path. He would have to eat quickly and get himself ready. The others would be here soon. She took candles, wine, a silver goblet and a knife from the kitchen cupboard. 'Justin!' she called. 'In here!'

An hour later, Mariel, her son and eleven others stood in a circle in the living room. The candlelight flickered on translucent white robes, beneath which each one was naked.

'I call on the spirits of the air,' Mariel cried out, sweeping the point of the knife above one of the candles. Working her way round the circle, she invoked spirits of the earth, fire and water, cutting the air in a succession of intricate patterns.

'Now choose your high priestess,' she whispered to her son. Justin stood in the centre of the circle. Tall and slim-hipped, he had his mother's jet black hair and high cheek-bones. Mariel watched his eyes as they travelled over the bodies of the six young women she'd selected. By candle-light they were all beautiful. He was gazing at the large, pendulous breasts of the girl nearest to the altar. In a sudden movement he crouched at her feet, the folds of the robe hiding his swelling penis.

He sank to his knees and bent his head. His mother wondered what was going through his mind. He knew how to perform the five-fold kiss. He had watched Sean do it many times. Mariel saw the girl's legs quiver as his lips moved up her body. She was enjoying this as much as he was. And soon they would be left alone.

Twenty minutes later Mariel and the others filed back in from the kitchen. The girl was lying on the floor by the altar. Taking up the knife, Mariel plunged it into the goblet of red wine. 'The Great Rite is finished,' she hissed. 'Raise the cone!' The others sank to the floor. Mariel took Justin's hand and held it high above the circle. She could smell the girl on his body.

'We raise a cone of power for our brother, Sean,' she chanted, 'We call on the spirits of earth, air, fire and water! By the power of the Goddess! Free him!'

'Free him!' the others echoed.

Mariel breathed deeply and slowly, soothed by the scent of the jasmine oil burning on the altar. The spell would work. She *knew* it would work.

When she opened her eyes she saw that Justin's robe was smeared with blood.

Chapter 11

Dave Todd picked up the phone and punched out a number. 'Al, it's Dave. Can you get Raven up from the cells?' He caught Megan's eye as he replaced the receiver. His expression was one of resignation and she got the impression he was as unhappy as she was about the direction the investigation was taking.

Steve Foy was rifling through plastic evidence bags piled on a table in the far corner of the room. He picked one out and waved it under Megan's nose. She peered at the dark brown scrap of fabric inside and then at the label. It was Tessa Ledbury's bloodstained bra.

'Might come in handy!' Foy sniffed and cocked his head at the door. 'You coming?'

'You don't really need me for this, do you Steve?' Megan tried to keep her voice steady, but her anger and frustration were mounting.

He looked surprised. 'Well, I suppose it's not *vital*. But I thought you'd want . . .'

'I think my time might be better spent at the crime scene,' she cut in. 'There's a lot more I want to know. Okay by you?' She looked him in the eyes, daring him to challenge her.

'Okay,' he shrugged. 'Whatever turns you on.'

'Shall I take Dr Rhys, Guv?' Dave Todd piped up.

Megan wondered why he was so eager to escape. Perhaps he was thinking along the same lines as she was.

'Might as well,' Foy grunted. 'Don't forget to check out those receipts, now.' There was an edge of sarcasm in his voice. *Bastard*, Megan thought. The man had total self-belief. It was an unpleasant trait in any human being, but in a policeman it was positively dangerous.

'We're picking up Vicky Tomlins on the way,' Dave Todd said as they got into the black Mondeo. We need her to tell us if anything's been nicked from the house.'

'Good,' Megan replied. 'I want to talk to her as well, if that's okay.'

'Get in the back when we stop at her house, then,' Dave said. 'You can talk on the way to Joanna's. There won't be anywhere private once we get there 'cos the SOCOs'll be all over the shop.'

Megan gave him a sideways glance. 'Were you there when the body was found?'

He nodded. 'Not a pretty sight. I've come across all kinds since I started this job, but that was definitely one of the worst.'

'I didn't get a proper look at the crime scene photographs,' Megan said. 'She was clothed, though, wasn't she? What was she wearing?'

'A red vest top and red trousers.' A line appeared above the bridge of Todd's glasses as he frowned in concentration. 'Black bra and knickers. A gold beaded hair band. Nothing on her feet.'

'Oh?' Megan said. 'No shoes?'

'No socks or tights either. She must have been barefoot when he broke in.'

'Like Tessa Ledbury, then?'

'Yes.' Todd shot her sideways glance. 'Does that tell you something?'

Megan pursed her lips. 'Not sure. It could be down to the warm weather, of course. But it could also tell us something about the killer's *modus operandi*.'

'Do you think he took their shoes? Like a trophy or something?'

'It's possible.' She looked at him. 'Presumably Richard Ledbury was asked about that? Whether any of his wife's things were missing?'

'Yes, he was. I was there when Kate was going through it with him.'

Megan's eyebrows flicked up at the mention of the policewoman's name. 'The thing is,' she said, thinking aloud, 'Would a man necessarily know if a pair of his wife's shoes were missing?'

The bloodstained bra shot across the table, coming to rest against Sean Raven's left hand. At first he couldn't work out what it was. It looked like a dirty brown rag.

'Recognise it?' Foy barked.

Raven looked up, confused.

'Go on! Pick it up!'

Gingerly he lifted the fabric with his finger and thumb. 'Jesus!' He dropped it as if it had burnt his fingers, his other hand shooting to his mouth as he retched. 'Oh Jesus!'

'Not a very appropriate expletive for a Black Magician, is it?' Foy sneered. 'Was Joanna another of your sacrifices to Satan?'

'I . . . I don't know what you're talking about.' Sean Raven's voice was a hoarse whisper. 'I've never seen that . . . that *thing* before in my life.'

'Don't give me that bollocks!' Foy was shouting now. 'You took it off Tessa's body after you'd killed her, didn't you? Was that before or after you left your sicko sign on her head?'

Sean Raven stared at the coffee-stained table, not moving.

'Let me guess,' Foy went on, 'You got bored of dancing naked round bonfires. You wanted to see how far you could go. How far you could push the poor slappers who fell for your witchcraft bullshit. You murdered Tessa and Joanna, didn't you?' For a moment there was no sound but the ticking of the clock on the wall. 'Didn't you?' he roared.

Raven jumped as Foy's fist came down on the table. 'You can't do this,' he croaked, cradling his head in his hands. 'Where's my brief?'

Vicky Tomlins looked much younger than her twenty-five years. Her short, wispy blonde hair framed a chubby face with red-rimmed eyes. Talking to her was like waiting for an icicle to drop from a roof. The way she held her head, the constant clenching and unclenching of her hands, spoke of a soul in torment. After a few minutes Megan became convinced she was holding something back. She wondered if Dave Todd's presence in the driver's seat was the problem.

'Would you mind pulling in at this garage?' Megan leaned forward, catching his eye in the rear view mirror. 'I've got a thumping head. Could do with some paracetamol or something.'

'No problem.' He nodded and she knew he'd taken the hint. 'I'll pop in and get it,' he said, swinging the car off the road. 'Could do with some petrol, anyway.'

As his door slammed shut Megan glanced after him. Without looking at Vicky she said: 'It's odd, you know. The police say they can't trace anyone who was close to Joanna. Apart from her ex in Australia, I mean.' She paused, still avoiding Vicky's eyes. 'I'd have thought she'd have had other people in her life.'

'You know, that's what makes me feel so terrible.' The voice was a whisper.

Megan said nothing, but turned to look at the girl, trying to keep her face as expressionless as possible.

'She asked me to move in with her,' Vicky went on. 'And if I hadn't turned her down, she'd still be alive now!'

Megan sat in silence as Vicky dug in her pocket for a handkerchief and dabbed at her eyes.

'I'm sorry,' she sniffed, 'it's just that I . . . I . . .' The rest of the sentence dissolved in a stream of tears.

'It's alright, ' Megan said gently. 'Take your time. You say she asked you to move in with her?'

'Yes.' Another sniff and a deep breath. 'You see Joanna was . . . well . . .' She paused, looking down at the screwed up hanky in her hand. She took another deep breath, as if mustering her courage and looked straight at Megan. 'She was gay.'

'Oh, I see,' Megan replied evenly, trying not to let the surprise register on her face.

'I know it sounds strange, with her having been married and everything.' Vicky blinked at Megan, obviously taken aback by the lack of reaction to what she had just divulged. 'But that was why her marriage broke up,' she went on. 'She had a fling with a girl in Australia but it didn't work out. She was really cut up about it and that's why she decided to move back here.'

'How long ago was it that she asked you to move in?' Megan asked, avoiding the obvious question about Vicky's own sexual orientation.

'The last time I saw her,' Vicky said, her eyes filling with fresh tears. 'Up until then I didn't know. I didn't know anything.' She blew her nose loudly. 'She'd never explained exactly why her marriage had failed. I had no idea she was a . . .' She faltered, struggling with the word. 'You know, a *lesbian*.'

'So what happened? When she told you, I mean?'

'It all came out in a rush. We were sitting there in the middle of Beatties restaurant and she started telling me all this stuff about the girl in Australia. She started crying and told me how lonely she'd been since she moved here. She knew I wanted to move out of my parents' house and in the next breath she was asking if I'd go and live with her.'

'What did you say?'

'Well, I was so shocked I didn't know what to say at first. She started backtracking very quickly, saying she didn't mean anything by it. She said she just wanted us to live together as friends.'

'As friends?' Megan echoed.

'Well that's what she said.' Vicky bit her lip. 'But by that time I was so confused I didn't know what to say or do.' She looked away. 'It's a while since I've been in a relationship, but I've been quite happy to be single for the past year or so. Joanna knew that. I couldn't work out if she thought *I* might be interested in a gay relationship and whether that was the real reason she was asking me to move in.' She sighed. 'To be honest, the whole thing really freaked me out.'

'So what did you do?'

'I said I'd have to think about it. But that was just an excuse, really. I wanted to get up and run from the table, I felt so embarrassed. We arranged to meet again after her trip to Paris but my brain was in a whirl. I didn't even know if I was going to turn up myself.'

'But you did.'

'Yes. I thought about it a lot over the next few days. I decided I'd tell her I couldn't move in because it might spoil our friendship. And that was the truth, you know? I really liked Joanna. We've known each other since primary school . . .' She tailed off, blinking in a vain attempt to stop her eyes overflowing again. 'If it hadn't been for her telling me she was gay I probably would have gone ahead with it. But I couldn't get it out of my mind that sooner or later she might make a pass at me. And I couldn't have coped with that.' She sniffed and then blew her nose again. 'When she didn't turn up yesterday I thought it was because I'd offended her by not saying yes straight away. I wanted to put things right between us. When I couldn't get through on her mobile I thought it was because she was still angry. That's why I ended up going round to the house.'

The steady trickle of tears now gave way to a rush of sobbing. 'I . . . I don't think I can do it again,' Vicky stammered. 'I . . . can't face going to that house!'

Megan saw Dave coming out of the forecourt shop. She put a hand on the girl's shoulder. 'I'm so sorry you're being put through this,' she whispered. 'But we have to know everything we can about Joanna. Anything you can tell us, no matter how embarrassing or insignificant it might seem, might help us find out who killed her.' Megan paused, hoping she hadn't blown things for the SOCOs. 'Will you do that? For her sake?'

Patrick sat on the hard, narrow bed he'd lain awake in for most of the previous night. He was rehearsing what to say to Megan. This time tomorrow he would be doing it for real.

He thought of Megan's bed, conjuring the smell of her skin; the way her hair brushed against his shoulder when she lay beside him. He wished he was there with her now.

But then it dawned on him that he would probably never lie in that bed again. How could he possibly expect her to understand? What good would it do to explain that he had not meant it to happen? That he had been the unwitting victim of emotional blackmail?

He knew how weak that was going to sound. *Oh, you poor, pathetic creature.* He could hear her now, taunting him. *Are you trying to make out you just couldn't help yourself? Whatever happened to self-control?*

How would he answer that? There was no defence. And it was too late to halt the damage now. He felt the same sensation he had experienced as a child on his first ride on a rollercoaster. He was there at the apex of the arc, staring down. Suddenly sick to the stomach but completely power-less to avoid the nightmare about to engulf him.

The light was beginning to fade when the black Mondeo reached Stockhall. They drove past the top of Ceri's road and took the next right. Megan shuddered to think of her sister living so close to the scene of such a grisly murder.

Vicky Tomlins had composed herself enough to start talking about Joanna again. 'She was so pretty,' she said wistfully. 'Always had fantastic clothes. Really different, you know? Stuff she'd picked up in the Far East when she was travelling. And she was so slim.' She glanced at her stomach. 'Not like me. She was a vegan. Never ate any of the rubbish I like.'

Megan turned her head sharply. 'A vegan?'

'Yes. Eating out was a nightmare. That's why we went to Beatties – not many places do vegan stuff.'

Megan's mind was racing. 'Do you know where she did her food shopping?'

Vicky Tomlins gave her puzzled frown. 'Not round here,' she said. 'Why do you ask?'

'It might be important if she went shopping the day she died.' Megan could see Dave Todd's expression in the rear view mirror. He was thinking the same thing she was. 'Where did she go? Anywhere in particular?'

'The supermarket at Pendleton,' the girl said. 'She was always moaning about the shops in Stockhall not having the kind of things she needed. Pendleton was the nearest place that did.'

It felt good, listening to the news. Hearing people talk about it in hushed voices. Little did they know the next episode was already a wrap. Each time the performance was a little more polished; the scene a little more artistically set. What a pity the TV cameras weren't allowed inside the bedrooms. It was a waste, really. They were missing the money shot. The key action.

Against the dark blue square of sky the stars were beginning to come out. It was going to be fine again tomorrow. Would they find her then? Or would days go by, shoppers passing beneath the window, never guessing what lay rotting behind the Venetian blinds?

Chapter 12

Vicky Tomlins was sitting in Joanna Hamilton's white-painted living room clutching a mug of black coffee. Nothing would persuade her to enter her friend's bedroom and Megan could understand why. Going up there herself had been bad enough. The mattress, bedding and rugs had been taken away but the smell of rotting flesh hung in the air. The window sill and dressing table were littered with dead flies.

Megan had looked through the clothes in Joanna Hamilton's wardrobe. The shoes and boots were arranged in two neat rows in the bottom of it. They were of a variety of colours but the styles were very different from the collection at Tessa Ledbury's house. With the exception of a pair of moccasin slippers, all were high-heeled. A pair of red suede shoes caught Megan's eye. The toes tapered to a narrow point and the heels were stilettos. Dave Todd had said Joanna was wearing a red outfit when she was found. Could she have been wearing these shoes as well? There were no gaps in the rows. Nothing to suggest a pair was missing.

Megan had brought the red suede shoes downstairs. She hadn't yet shown them to Vicky. 'Do you remember what Joanna was wearing the last time you saw her?' she asked.

Vicky glanced at the framed watercolours on the wall in front of her, blinking, as if trying to summon the image of her friend. 'A dress, I think,' she said. 'A blue dress with a sort of batik pattern.'

'Hmm,' Megan pressed her lips together. 'When she was found she was wearing a red sleeveless top and trousers. You're sure that's not what she had on?'

Vicky nodded. 'She did sometimes wear red, but she wasn't wearing it that day.'

'And when she wore a red outfit, would she have worn matching shoes?'

'Definitely,' Vicky said. 'She always liked her clothes and shoes to match.'

'I found this pair in her wardrobe.' Megan held up the shoes in the evidence bag she had taken from the SOCOs. 'I couldn't see any other red ones. Would she have had a second pair, do you think?'

'I don't think so.' Vicky frowned. 'She didn't have a lot of cash to splash around. She liked nice things and she went for quality rather than quantity.'

So much for the trophy theory, then, Megan thought. That left two possibilities. Either Joanna had taken off her shoes and replaced them in the wardrobe before being attacked or her killer had put them back there. The second scenario seemed pretty unlikely. Still, Megan thought, the fact that both Joanna and Tessa were found barefoot was a connection. Both had also shopped at Pendleton. What else might there be?

'You said Joanna did her shopping at Pendleton super-market,' Megan went on. 'How would she have got there?'

'On the bus,' Vicky replied.

'She didn't have a bicycle or anything?'

The girl shook her head.

'So apart from shopping, would she have gone to the precinct for any other reason? To the hairdresser's, doctor's anything like that?'

'She wasn't registered with a doctor,' Vicky replied. 'It was something she'd been meaning to do but hadn't got round to.'

'And the hairdresser?'

'She never went to a hairdresser. She had long, straight hair and if the ends needed trimming she'd do it herself.'

'What about the church? Was she a religious person?'

Vicky shook her head. 'She was a spiritual person, but I wouldn't call her religious. She told me she'd taken evening classes in astrology when she was out in Australia. She was really into stuff like that.'

Megan bit her lip. 'What about the occult? Was she into that kind of thing?'

Vicky frowned. 'Why do you ask?'

'Oh, it's just some books the police said they found here. They got it into their heads she might belong to a witches' coven or something.' Megan held her breath.

'Not to my knowledge. She was, like, totally anti any form of organised religion, whatever the beliefs.' Vicky swallowed hard, tears welling in her eyes. 'She was a free spirit.'

Megan was aware the girl was close to breaking down again. 'There's just one more thing I need to ask.' Her voice was barely more than a whisper. 'You said Joanna took evening classes when she was in Australia. Might she have signed up for something at Pendleton college?'

Vicky shook her head. 'She wasn't taking any classes, no. But she'd talked about trying to get work there. The freelance stuff was a bit patchy, I think.'

'Oh?' Megan's stomach churned. 'Do you know if she'd been offered anything?'

'She'd done odd days, I think.' Vicky sniffed. 'She was hoping for something a bit more permanent come September.'

'Could she have gone there that afternoon you last saw her, do you think?'

'She didn't say so.' Vicky pulled a tissue from her sleeve and dabbed at her face. 'I . . . I'm sorry. I don't know.'

Dave Todd's head appeared round the door. 'Dr Rhys? Have you got a minute?'

Delva was waiting for the lift when a familiar voice hailed her. Her heart sank. Sharing a lift with Des was all she needed. She had managed to avoid him all day by lying low in one of the editing suites and now she just wanted to get home.

'How's it going?' He was panting from the effort of walking the few yards from his desk to the lift. And one of his shirt buttons was undone, revealing a pallid patch of his overstretched stomach.

'Oh, er, fine!' Delva said in a brittle voice, 'I've nearly finished editing the interview with Carole-Ann Beddowes.' She pressed herself against the wall of the lift to get as far away from him as possible. 'But it's all a bit up in the air now, isn't it?'

'How do you mean?' He moved forward slightly and Delva stiffened. Des had a horrible habit of rubbing his beer belly against female members of staff when he found himself alone in the lift with them. If anyone complained he would accuse them of being pre-menstrual or meno-pausal, depending on their age. And as he only ever did it in the lift, there were never any witnesses.

'Well the police haven't confirmed that the murders are linked, have they?' Delva said. The lift doors opened and she shot out. 'So this witchcraft thing could turn out to be a complete red herring,' she called over her shoulder.

'Oh, I don't think so.' Des stepped out after her and smiled, revealing wet teeth which glinted in the fluorescent lights. He reminded Delva of a crocodile.

'Word is,' he said, tapping the side of his nose, 'there's going to a presser at Tipton Street nick. I'm sending the OB van. Might get it live on the late bully with a bit of luck.'

Delva stared at him. A press conference? Did that mean Sean Raven had been charged?

Megan followed Dave Todd into Joanna Hamilton's kitchen.

'I found this in the pocket of one of her jackets.' He produced a crumpled scrap of paper. 'It's a receipt from the supermarket at Pendleton. She was there at five-fifteen on the Wednesday evening.'

Megan took the receipt from his outstretched hand. It showed that Joanna had purchased a carton of soya milk, hair conditioner, three packets of mixed nuts and a travel adaptor plug.

'Sounds as if she was stocking up for the trip, then?'

Todd nodded.

'I wonder why she went to the trouble of catching a bus to Pendleton?' Megan said, waving the receipt. 'She could have got all these things in Wolverhampton town centre when she went to meet Vicky.'

'I know,' he shrugged. 'Doesn't make sense, does it?'

'Which jacket did you find this in?'

Todd pointed to a black leather one hanging on a hook on the back of the kitchen door.

'Were there any cases or holdalls lying around the house when you first got here?' Megan asked. 'Anything to suggest she'd started packing?'

'No.' Todd rubbed the five o'clock shadow on his chin. 'It's looking more and more likely she was killed on the Wednesday night, isn't it?'

Megan nodded slowly. 'Vicky told me that when she last saw Joanna she was wearing different clothes to the ones you found her in,' Megan said. 'So she must have come home and got changed for some reason before going out again.' She cocked her head on one side, remembering the red suede shoes. An odd choice of footwear for a trip to the supermarket, she thought. 'Unless she changed *after* she got back from the supermarket.' She looked at Todd. 'Why would she do that?'

'Can't think. Unless she was going out again?'

Megan frowned. 'I suppose there's a chance she was just trying on outfits for the holiday – you know, deciding what to pack?'

'I suppose that might have been what happened.' Todd's face told her that this was a totally alien concept. She wondered if he was married or living with someone. Possibly not, she thought.

Half an hour later he was driving her back to the police station. 'If it *is* the same killer,' he asked, 'Why would he have left Joanna's clothes on but taken Tessa's off?'

'Do you remember that first briefing, when I said I thought whoever murdered Tessa had killed before?'

He nodded. 'You said the amount of time he'd spent with the body *post mortem* suggested a level of experience.'

'Yes. Now I'm wondering if killing Joanna is where he got that experience. Taking the clothes off could be a progression – in terms of what he gets out of it, I mean. But if Joanna was his first-ever victim he might not have had the confidence to hang around.'

Dave frowned. 'Does that change your theory then? About him having form for sex offences?'

'It means it's not as clear-cut as it looked,' she admitted. 'I still think it's someone who's done time, though – someone whose DNA is on file.'

'Because of the forensic awareness?'

'Yes. I mean, I know Joanna's body was too badly decayed for any semen to show up, but the SOCOs have found nothing in the rest of the house, have they? Not a single print, or hair or anything?'

Todd shook his head.

'So has Foy run those checks I asked for?'

'Yes. We've got the lowdown on every convicted sex offender released from jail in the past six months.'

'And?'

'There are six living within a twenty-mile radius of Pendleton. All their alibis check out.'

'Hmm.' Megan cast him a sideways glance. 'Twenty miles isn't much. I'd have cast the net a bit wider than that.'

'But what if it's the cyclist? The one Tessa's neighbour saw?'

Before Megan could reply Todd's mobile rang out. He grabbed the earpiece dangling over his shoulder and inserted it in his left ear.

'Nothing after four thirty-five?' He spoke into the tiny microphone pinned to his lapel. 'You'll check that number out, then? Okay. Cheers.' He turned to Megan, yanking the earpiece out. 'Joanna's mobile,' he said. The last call she received was at four thirty-five on the Wednesday afternoon. It was from another mobile. They're checking it out now.'

'And she didn't make any calls herself that afternoon?'

He shook his head. 'Nothing all day. And there was no land-line in the house.'

'So no e-mails, either,' Megan said, thinking aloud. 'Vicky Tomlins said Joanna had been doing some supply work at Pendleton College. Wonder if she popped in there before she went to the supermarket? It makes more sense than her going all that way for a few last-minute bits and bobs she could have bought in town.'

'Why would she go there when she was just about to go off on holiday?'

She pursed her lips. 'Vicky said she was trying to land a permanent contract at the college. What if she got a call from them that afternoon asking her to attend some sort of interview? That would explain the clothes – the red outfit and the black leather jacket – the sort of clothes that would make a real impression.'

'But we'd have known straight away if the call to her mobile was from the college. It would've come up on the computer.'

'That doesn't necessarily rule it out though, does it? Could be one of the staff using a mobile for some reason?'

Megan knew it was a long shot. The supermarket receipt was the only concrete evidence of Joanna's link with Pendleton. But as the car pulled into Tipton Street she made up her mind to go to the college in the morning. It was a gut feeling that probably had more to do with her fears for Ceri than anything else, but it was something she felt compelled to do.

'What the hell's going on?'

The tone of Todd's voice startled her. Glancing up she was dazzled by headlights. As she blinked she saw that a huge white van was parked in front of the police station. The BTV logo was emblazoned above the windscreen.

'It's the Outside Broadcast van.' Todd grimaced as he pulled off the road. 'Wonder what the Guv's got up his sleeve this time?'

They could hear the scrum inside the police station before they got through the doors. The foyer was milling with photographers, cameramen and reporters. Todd shouldered his way past them and led Megan to the conference room where microphones were being set up on a long glass-topped table.

'What's kicking off?' Todd asked one of the uniformed officers on the door.

The man grinned. 'Guv's about to throw Raven to the wolves.'

Ten minutes later Megan stood at the back of the packed

room watching Steve Foy's performance, wondering what the hell he was up to.

'The occult is a difficult strata of society to get into,' he said, leaning towards the microphone. 'We don't have much intelligence on it – unlike terrorism or organised crime. It's a very secretive area.'

'What's made you aware of the fact that both victims had links with the occult?' The question came from a reporter with the BTV logo on his hand-held microphone.

'I'm afraid I can't divulge that information for operational reasons,' Foy replied.

'But Tessa Ledbury was a Sunday school teacher,' a woman standing a few feet from Megan piped up.

'Yes,' Foy nodded, 'but we now know that before she became involved in the church she was a member of an occult group – a coven of witches – and we believe that connection may have played a part in her murder.' There was a murmuring from the floor as the journalists digested this tasty morsel.

'We understand that the man you're questioning has links with the occult.' The BTV reporter again. 'Is he one of the witches?'

Megan slipped out of the room. She had heard enough. Foy had obviously been unable to wait for his star slot on *Crimewatch*. He'd got nowhere with Raven so he was getting the press to do his dirty work for him; pinning his hopes on someone coming forward to say they'd seen Joanna Hamilton at a coven. Perhaps he'd got it into his head that Raven was operating a whole chain of covens with different women at each one. The tabloids were going to have a field day.

When she got home it was on the late-night news. *Occult link in horror stabbings.* It was the kind of headline that would make anyone sit up and take notice. Foy was a real operator, there was no doubt about that. She hoped he could sleep at night, because she was damn sure Raven wouldn't.

Lying in the miserable little bed the memories came flooding back. The two of them dancing round the Christmas tree in taffetta dresses and lace petticoats. Turning on the TV in time for the film. Watching Dorothy swept up by the twister. The house landing on the witch. Looking up at the sound of the key in the lock. Dad's face framed in the doorway. Catching them. The shame of the clothes being ripped off. Mum screaming behind the sofa. Dorothy tripping down the Yellow Brick Road while Dad beat shit out of them both.

Chapter 13

Patrick was heading back to Birmingham with a feeling of dread. He'd seen the news about the second body and had e-mailed Megan about it but she hadn't replied. Perhaps she'd been up all night. He wondered what sort of mood she'd be in when he got back. Probably not great, he reflected. She would give him a hug, flop onto the sofa and suggest whiskies in the bath and then bed. She might even be too tired to make love. *Make love?* What was he thinking of? Sex was going to be right out of the question when he'd delivered his little bombshell.

Perhaps it would be better to wait until Saturday morning. Tell her after she'd had a good night's sleep. He tried to persuade himself that would be the best course of action, realising even as he mulled it over that it would be himself he was putting first, not her. Because if he left it until tomorrow they would almost certainly make love. If not tonight then first thing in the morning. And that was what he wanted. More than anything. Because it would probably be the last time.

Megan was in her office before any of the rest of the staff had arrived. There was a pile of post lying unopened on her desk and a stack of exam papers waiting to be marked. But her eyes kept wandering back to the newspaper she had bought. 'BLACK MAGIC KILLER'. The headline screamed at her in letters that filled most of the front page.

A report of last night's press conference was illustrated with a photo of Steve Foy in front of a bank of microphones. And then inside was the double page spread that had made Megan gasp when she'd first seen it. The words of the article were carefully chosen but the innuendo was clear. There was a head-and-shoulders shot of Sean Raven alongside photos of Tessa Ledbury and Joanna Hamilton.

But dominating the page was a bigger picture of a man in a black robe holding his arms aloft. The face was Sean Raven's and the only clue that this photo was nothing but computer trickery lay in the caption beneath, which read: 'Sean Raven as he would look at a witches' coven.'

Further inside the paper was a photo of Mariel Raven with her hand up to her face. In the background was the house Megan had driven past yesterday. Mariel was obviously trying to escape from the media feeding frenzy Foy had unleashed with last night's press conference. Megan thought about the lipsticked pentagram on her car windscreen. If the woman was responsible for that she was certainly getting her comeuppance now.

She wondered how much longer Foy would hold Raven without charging him. In theory, with the extension he'd got from the magistrate, he could be kept at Tipton Street for a total of ninety-six hours. She worked it out in her head. He'd have to be released by Sunday afternoon, then. Unless Foy got the information he was hoping for. She picked up the phone and tapped out the number Dave Todd had given her.

'Dave, it's Dr Rhys. Any news on that mobile phone number?'

'No, not yet.' His voice sounded different. Distracted. She got the feeling she'd caught him in the middle of something important.

'Any developments with Raven?' She should have phoned

Foy to ask this but after last night she didn't feel she could be civil to the man.

'Not that I'm aware of, no.' She heard a noise in the background that sounded like a door slamming. 'Plenty of nutters calling in, but that's par for the course, as you know. Oh, one thing . . .' There was another pause and a crackle on the line. 'Pathologist found a dishcloth in Joanna Hamilton's mouth – same colour and type as the one found in Tessa Ledbury's.'

'Oh, that's much clearer evidence of a link, then, isn't it?' The news strengthened her resolve. 'I'm going to Pendleton later,' she said. 'Thought I'd do a bit of digging.' There was silence at the other end of the line. 'Just to let you know,' she added.

'Fine by me.' She could hear someone else's voice in the background. It sounded like a woman. Megan wondered where he was. 'Give me a call if you need anything, yeah?'

As she replaced the receiver Megan pondered exactly what he had meant. Did he think she was going to need some sort of back-up? What she had in mind was something fairly low-key. Snooping, Patrick would call it. She sighed as she reached for her jacket. Patrick would be home soon. It would be good to be able to talk to him about this. Get his angle on all that had happened in the past three days. Before she reached the door the phone rang.

'Megan, it's Delva – have you got a minute?'

'Er, yes, if it's a quickie.' Megan could hear the hubbub of the newsroom in the background.

'I won't keep you – just wanted to know your thoughts on this other woman they found yesterday. My boss is leaning on me to chase up this black magic angle. That stuff Steve Foy came out with – is it for real?'

'You mean what he said about both victims having links with the occult?'

'Yes.' There was a pause. 'I mean, I know there's only so much you can say.'

'Okay,' Megan frowned. In the months since they'd made the documentary together she had come to regard Delva as a friend. She had to keep reminding herself that as a journalist, she would have divided loyalties. 'Don't tell Des or anyone else this, but they've found some books in Joanna Hamilton's house. Nothing particularly way out – astrology, tarot, that sort of thing.'

'And that's the occult connection?' Delva grunted.

'My feelings exactly,' Megan said, 'but Foy's chosen to run with it – hence the press conference.'

'What are you going to do now?'

'Let's just say I'm following other lines of enquiry. I'll let you know if anything comes of it.'

'Thanks, Megan. You take care, you hear?'

Megan smiled as she put the phone down. Delva seemed a lot more positive than when she'd last seen her. It sounded as if she was far too busy to dwell on that business with Richard Ledbury.

On her way out of the building Megan bumped into Christopher Jessop. He was struggling through the plate-glass doors with a pile of box files stacked in his arms.

'Morning Megan,' he said, with a smile that didn't reach his large green eyes. 'Off again?' The sarcasm in his voice was unmistakeable and she didn't grace him with a reply, merely nodding as she passed by. She wondered if he knew about her meeting with the Vice-Chancellor next week. Taking a breath, she thrust her shoulders back and strode purposefully towards the car. Whatever happened, she was not going to let the likes of *him* get to her.

At Pendleton College, Megan found a parking space beneath a large horse chestnut tree whose pale young leaves brushed the rear windscreen as she reversed. It was a good spot from which to observe the comings and goings from the grim-looking building in front of her. The college had been built in the 'sixties. Its walls were grey and the design uninspiring. The trees lining the path from the main entrance were the only softening feature.

To the right of the entrance groups of students sat on the grass with cans, cups and cigarettes in their hands. They were a mixture of ages, Megan noticed. From kids barely past adolescence to men and women who might have been their grandparents. The gravel path forked at the point where they were sitting, one branch leading to the carpark and the other veering left across a field that bordered the precinct. She wondered if Joanna had walked along that path in her high-heeled red shoes. Unlikely, she thought, looking at the dust kicked up by a couple of girls as they trudged past.

She needed to know if there was any substance to this gut instinct about a link with the college. She would go to the reception and see if there was a visitors' book. A quick flick through the pages would tell her if Joanna had been there on the day she was last seen. Megan went to open the car door but stopped short. Was that Ceri walking along the path? She watched as a woman with the same dark hair as her sister's took the fork leading to the precinct. Large sunglasses obscured her face. Did Ceri have a pair like that? As she peered through the windscreen something else caught her eye. A helmeted figure pushing a mountain bike appeared from behind a tree. He was staring after the woman in the sunglasses. As Megan watched he glanced at the entrance to the college, then back over his shoulder, as if checking that no-one was looking. Then he jumped onto the bike and started pedalling slowly along the path, gradually gaining ground on the woman. In a moment both had disappeared from sight round the corner of the building.

Megan sat stock still, her heart thumping in her chest. *What if that was him? What if that woman was Ceri?* What should she do? Run after them? No, that wasn't the answer. If he *was* the killer he'd see her running and do a disappearing act. She turned the key in the ignition. She must drive to the precinct and find the place where the path came out. Once they were in the shopping centre she could track his movements without him noticing her.

Her heart missed a beat when she got there. Ceri's yellow Peugeot was parked right by the exit barrier. There were no spaces anywhere near it and she swerved through the rows of cars, frantically searching for a space. She found one at the far end and shot into it, catching her offside wing mirror in her haste. She scrambled out of the car, squeezing past the bent-back mirror and ran towards the precinct's main square.

Shading her eyes from the sun she scanned the rows of shops. Where did the path come out? She ran past the chemist's and the newsagent's and round a corner, pausing when she got to the lake. There was a path round the edge of it but she couldn't see where it led because the land rose up in a series of hillocks on the other side. There was an elderly woman sitting on a bench a few feet away.

'Excuse me,' Megan panted, 'Can you tell me how to get to Pendleton College from here?'

The woman pointed back towards the precinct. 'You need to go back through there and turn right by the church, love.'

Megan gasped her thanks and ran back towards the main square. As she passed the newsagent's she caught sight of the woman in the sunglasses. She was walking past the supermarket in the direction of the carpark. A few yards behind her the cyclist stood with his back to Megan, looking in the window of the electrical shop. In the strong sunlight she could see that his helmet was black – just like the one Tessa Ledbury's neighbour had described to the police.

Megan quickened her pace as the woman disappeared from view. She saw the cyclist mount his bike and pedal off in the same direction. Megan ran as fast as she could, but when she reached the carpark there was no sign of the woman or the cyclist. As she stood gasping for breath she caught sight of a yellow car driving through the exit barrier. *Ceri*'s car. It *was* her, then. So where was the cyclist? There was no chance of catching Ceri up so Megan ran towards her own car. If he was following Ceri he might have gone on ahead to the junction to see which way she went at the lights.

By the time she reached the junction Ceri's car had gone and the lights were on red. 'Damn!' Megan thumped the dashboard with the heel of her hand. At least she knew which way Ceri would be going. If she put her foot down she could catch her up before she got home. *Home*? Megan frowned. Why was she going home? Why hadn't she gone to Pendleton nursery to collect the children? It was only a stone's throw from the carpark, but she wouldn't have had chance to fetch them in the short time it had taken to follow her out of the precinct. Neil must be looking after them, she reasoned. She fervently hoped that he was; that Ceri was not going back to an empty house.

Reaching into her bag she punched out Dave Todd's number on her mobile. She was certain he would think she was over-reacting, but she didn't care.

'Dave? I need your help.' In a few brief sentences she told him what she'd seen.

'I'm in Stockhall now,' he said. 'What's the address?' From the tone of his voice he was taking it seriously. 'Okay, I'll be there in five.' And that was it. No questions asked. *Thank God for that*, Megan thought.

As the lights changed she sped past fields of green barley on the road that led to Stockhall. A few seconds later she was forced to slow right down as a tractor pulled out of a farm gate up ahead. She craned her neck, trying to overtake, but it was impossible. By the time she reached the turn-off to Ceri's road perspiration was sticking her clothes to her skin.

She pulled up sharply outside the house. The car was in the drive. There was no sign of the bike. In her rear view mirror she caught sight of Dave Todd at the wheel of the black Mondeo. There were four other people in the car. Then she spotted a squad car coming along the road towards her. Bloody hell, she thought, he's pulled out all the stops.

As she jumped out of the car something shiny caught her eye. Her insides froze. It was the rim of a bicycle wheel. Almost hidden by her sister's green wheelie bin. 'Oh my God!' She stood on the pavement, rooted to the spot.

A split-second later Dave Todd was by her side. 'No-one else in the house has a bike?' She could hear the urgency in his voice.

She shook her head. 'I've got a key to the front door.' Her hand trembled as she groped in her bag.

'Right. No point pussyfooting around.' Todd motioned to the officers in the two cars. 'Go up to the front door with Penny,' he said to Megan. 'Don't call out or anything. Just stay on the step, okay?'

Megan's legs were like jelly as she walked up to the house. She glanced at the upstairs windows. What if her sister was lying dead in the bedroom? She tried to shut out the images that came crowding into her head. Her arm was shaking so much as she lifted the key to the lock that she had to steady it by grasping her wrist with her other hand. The woman police officer pushed the door open slowly.

The hallway was deserted. Megan could see the children's anoraks hanging on pegs by the kitchen door. In the split second before Dave Todd and the others rushed up the path Megan heard someone coughing. A man's cough. And it had come from upstairs.

Chapter 14

Megan pressed her back against the wall as Dave and five other officers hurtled past. The thunder of footsteps on the stairs was followed by shouts and the sound of furniture and bodies crashing onto the floor. Amid the chaos Megan thought she heard a scream.

'Oh my God!' she cried out. 'Ceri!'

Before the policewoman could stop her Megan raced up the stairs. She froze in the doorway of her sister's bedroom. Ceri was on the bed, naked but for a pair of red stiletto shoes. Her wrists and ankles had been lashed to the brass rails with what looked like her own black stockings. Megan could not see her face. It was turned to one side, away from the doorway.

Megan felt as if her whole body was paralysed. She wanted to run to Ceri but she couldn't move. Beyond the bed, on the floor beside the window, the detectives were holding a man face down on the floor. He was naked except for a pair of white boxer shorts and as he struggled his black ponytail swished against the wooden floorboards. One of the officers grabbed it and he was still.

For a split second nobody moved. The room and the people in it were like freeze-frame images from a film. Suddenly a scream filled Megan's ears. Ceri's body began to writhe on the bed.

'Justin!' Ceri screamed, her back arching as she struggled against her bonds.

'Let him go! Bastards!'

Mariel Raven was lying low at the house of a friend who lived ten miles from her Pendleton home. She had driven off at high speed last night, pursued by reporters from the tabloid press, and had only managed to shake them off by driving into a multi-storey carpark in Wolverhampton town centre. Abandoning her car she had hidden in the ladies' toilets while phoning her friend, who had picked her up in a dimly-lit back alley a few streets away.

She was glad Justin had friends he could stay with. She wouldn't have wanted him going back to the house. She wondered how long it would be before the vultures gave up. Her hand shook as she picked up the newspaper lying on the coffee table. It was open at the photograph of her husband's head grafted onto a figure in a black cloak. *Sean Raven as he would look at a witches' coven.* What bollocks! How *dare* they do that to him! Seizing the paper in both hands she screwed it into a ball and stamped on it with her spike heels.

'My name's Justin Preece. I'm a Media Studies student at Pendleton College.' The boy looked barely out of his teens. He was on his feet now, his wrists handcuffed. 'She'll tell you! Tell them Ceri! You invited me here, didn't you?'

Megan cringed as she watched her sister struggle into jeans and a sweater. Ceri wouldn't even look at her.

'Is he telling the truth, Mrs Richardson?'

Dave Todd's use of Ceri's surname just rubbed it in. 'Yes! Of course he's telling the truth!' Her eyes had narrowed to kohl-rimmed slits and her nostrils flared. 'Would you mind telling me what the hell's going on?'

'We're investigating the murders of Tessa Ledbury and Joanna Hamilton, Mrs Richardson,' Todd said, voice matter-of-fact. He turned his attention back to the boy. 'Your address?'

'One-seven-one Linden Close, Pendleton, Wolverhampton WV30 1QR.' He recited it robotically, staring at the ceiling. Megan blinked. Linden Close? That was the name of Sean and Mariel Raven's road. She saw Dave Todd exchange glances with the officer making notes.

'Mr Preece,' Todd said, emphasizing the title with a hint of sarcasm, 'are you related to a Mr Sean Raven?'

Justin's lip curled. 'You know damn well I am,' he snarled. 'What is this? Some bloody vendetta? First my stepfather, now me! Why don't you go and lift my mother while you're at it?'

Megan stared from the boy to Ceri. The look of confusion on her sister's face told her that the name Sean Raven meant nothing to Ceri. Unless she had seen the morning papers there was no reason why it should.

'Where were you between nine-fifty and eleven o'clock on the morning of Thursday the twenty-fourth of May?' Todd was standing in front of Justin now. Megan couldn't see the expression on the boy's face.

'He was with me!' Ceri's voice was shaking. 'He was in my lecture at Pendleton College! Satisfied?'

Todd glanced at her then turned back to the boy. 'Can you account for your whereabouts between the hours of 2.30pm on Wednesday May the sixteenth and 11am on Thursday the seventeenth?'

There was a moment's silence. Megan saw that her sister's head was shaking in disbelief. 'He was at college, weren't you Justin?' There was a note of hysteria in her voice now. 'He's always in my lectures on Thursday mornings! He'd have been in another class on the Wednesday afternoon!'

Todd nodded an acknowledgement without turning his head. 'And the Wednesday night?' he said to Justin. 'Where were you that evening?'

'I was at home with my mother and stepfather.' The tone was defiant. 'But I'm sure you're not going to believe me when you haven't believed a single word *they've* told you!'

'Justin Preece,' Todd said, 'I'm arresting you on suspicion of murder.' He recited the standard clause about the boy's right to remain silent before ushering him out of the room.

'No! Justin!' Ceri reached out to grab him but was held back by the WPC and another officer. Megan could have wept at the sight of her. She looked completely bereft, as if the bottom had fallen out of her world.

'Please,' Megan said, 'let me talk to her.'

Ceri turned her face away.

'We'll have to take a statement first,' the WPC said. 'But we can do it here if you'd prefer, Mrs Richardson?' Ceri nodded dumbly. 'You'll be free to talk to your sister as soon as we've finished, Dr Rhys.'

Megan walked out of the bedroom in a daze. She went outside to see the squad car pulling away, Justin Preece in the back between two police officers.

Dave Todd was standing on the pavement with his back to her, talking into his mobile.

'She's his lecturer, yes,' Todd was saying. No doubt he'd been telling Steve Foy all the gory details. She felt numb. Could Justin really be the killer? Had he and Sean Raven carried out the murders together? Or had she just subjected her sister to a terrifying, degrading experience for nothing?

Ceri had *invited* Justin into her house. She was having an *affair* with him. That in itself was devastating enough for her family, but it didn't mean he was capable of murder. She thought about Tessa Ledbury. Tessa had once had an affair with Sean Raven. What if it had started up again? What if she'd been involved in some sort of bizarre three-some with the stepfather and the stepson? But what about

Joanna Hamilton? Yes, she had a connection with the college and could possibly have met Justin there. But she was a lesbian. She had been trying to persuade Vicky Tomlins to move in with her. No, Megan thought, it just didn't add up.

'Yes, Guv,' she heard Todd saying, 'I'll ask Dr Rhys if she'll come.' He shoved the mobile in his pocket and swung round. Behind the gold-rimmed glasses his eyes were full of concern. 'This must terrible for you,' he said. 'I'm so sorry.'

Megan nodded. She didn't trust herself to speak.

'I don't know how you feel about coming to the station, but the Guv would like you there if you feel up to it.'

She swallowed hard. 'I could come later.' Her voice was hoarse with emotion. 'I'd like some time with my sister first.'

'Of course,' Todd said. 'Take as much time as you need. Would you like one of the officers to stay with you?'

She shook her head. 'I'd just like to be alone with her, if you don't mind.'

Half an hour later the other officers had gone. Megan sat on a chair in the living room, her sister on the sofa. The room was unusually tidy. No toys lying on the rug or clothes draped over the radiators. Ceri must have wanted the place spick and span for entertaining her boyfriend. Megan wondered how old he was. She couldn't believe her sister had risked her marriage, her home, *everything* for a fling with one of her own students. She opened her mouth to speak but checked herself. Who was *she* to stand in judgement?

'I know how you must be feeling,' she began. It sounded lame. As far as Ceri was concerned she had been violated. Violated and humiliated. She probably felt that being murdered would not have been much worse than the experience the police had put her through.

'I don't know how you can say that.' Ceri's voice was full of bitterness. 'And I don't want to talk about it – to you or anyone else!' She rose to her feet. 'I need to get the children.'

'Where are they?'

'At the nursery, of course!' The corners of her mouth turned down. 'Did you think I'd abandoned them somewhere? Terrible mother as well as a tart?'

'No, of course I didn't,' Megan said. 'I thought that Neil . . .'

'He's at a conference in Brussels,' Ceri cut in. She paused in the doorway. 'If you want to know why I didn't tell you it's because I knew you wouldn't approve!'

God, is that what she thinks of me? Megan looked away, tears blurring her vision. There was a silence. She waited for the door to slam. Instead she heard a strange, muffled, sighing sound. Running into the hallway she saw Ceri slumped against the coat rack, her shoulders heaving with sobs.

'Oh Ceri! Please don't cry!' Megan hugged her sister to her. 'I never meant for you to get mixed up in all this, but when I saw him following you . . . '

'I . . . know!' Ceri stuttered through her tears. 'I . . . do understand.'

Megan led her back into the living room and sat down on the sofa beside her. 'Shall I get you a cup of tea? Or could you do with a brandy?'

Ceri shook her head. 'The way I feel, I'd just end up drinking the whole bottle.' She reached for a tissue and blew her nose.

'I'll make some tea, then,' Megan said. 'What time are you supposed to be picking the kids up?'

'Well, not until half past three, really,' Ceri sniffed. She followed Megan into the kitchen. By the time the kettle boiled she had begun telling the story of her affair with Justin. She described how miserable things were between her and Neil. How much more attractive she had begun to feel in the new clothes she had bought for work. The admiring glances from some of her students and her irresistible attraction to Justin. 'I knew it was mad,' she said. 'But I couldn't stop myself. It was like a drug, Meg. I couldn't stop thinking about him.'

'How old is he?' Megan tried to keep her voice neutral.

'Twenty-one.' Ceri tapped the side of her head. 'But he's much older than that in here.' She looking pleadingly at Megan. 'You don't believe he's a murderer, do you?'

'I don't know, Ceri.' Megan sighed. 'I don't know what to think.' She looked at her sister, dreading asking the question that had been on her mind since the moment she'd seen Ceri on the bed. 'There's something I need to know,' she began. 'Please don't hate me for asking you, but those shoes – the ones you had on when, you know . . .' she tailed off, gauging her sister's reaction.

'Oh God!' Ceri buried her face in her hands. 'I can't bear the thought of all those people seeing me like that!' She rocked back and forth in her seat and Megan reached out to touch her shoulder. 'He wanted me to dress up for him.' Ceri's voice was muffled by her hands. 'It was all part of the excitement. I bought stockings and suspenders and those tarty shoes and he . . .' She broke off, wiping away the tears that were now streaming down her face.

'He what, Ceri?' Megan held her breath. She was thinking about the red suede shoes in Joanna Hamilton's wardrobe. The ones she might have been wearing when she was murdered. 'Did he ask you to wear red shoes?'

Ceri stared at her, her eyes puffy with crying. 'Why? Is that what the other women were wearing? Tessa Ledbury and that Joanna woman?'

Megan bit her lip. She mustn't allow Ceri the opportunity to cover for Justin Preece if he was guilty. It was obvious her sister was besotted with him; that she would defend him to hell and back. 'They weren't wearing any shoes,' she said, 'but the police have a theory the killer might go for women who wear red.' This was a lie, but it took attention off the shoes. She felt bad, doing this to her sister, but she had to get to the truth.

'He wanted me to wear black, actually.' Ceri cupped her hands over her nose and mouth, as if to keep the next sentence from Megan. Megan waited. Eventually the hands dropped and Ceri began to speak, her eyes fixed on the floor. 'He said he'd fantasised about me giving my lectures in a black mini skirt. He said he'd imagined what it would be like if I was wearing stockings and suspenders; getting a glimpse of them when I reached up to write something on the board.' Ceri closed her eyes and pressed her lips together until they turned white.

'And the shoes?' Megan's voice was barely more than a whisper. It was like walking on eggshells.

'They were my idea.' Ceri took a deep breath and tipped her head back. 'I got them off e-Bay,' she said to the ceiling.

Patrick pushed open the door and picked up the letters that lay on the mat. He had half-expected Megan to be at home, but the place had a neglected look that suggested she'd been far too busy to spend much time there. There were dirty dishes in the sink and the pedal bin in the kitchen looked as if it could do with emptying. As he carried the rubbish through the hall the phone rang. He hesitated a moment before going to answer it. He was almost certain it would be Megan, ringing to see if he was back. It rang five times before the answering machine cut in. He stood there listening to the recording of her voice, his stomach tying itself in knots. He knew he should pick it up. But if it was Megan he knew he would be unable to speak without giving himself away.

The machine beeped. There was no message.

Megan was worried about leaving her sister. They had driven off at the same time, Megan heading for Tipton Street and Ceri for the nursery. Megan had suggested she take the children over to her house for the night. She would have to let Patrick know. She glanced at her watch. He probably wouldn't be back yet. She must remember to phone later.

As she negotiated the Friday afternoon traffic in Wolverhampton town centre Megan wondered what on earth her sister was going to do. Neil wasn't due back until next Wednesday. That meant plenty of thinking time. But Megan couldn't see how Ceri was going to avoid coming clean about Justin. Even if she decided to try to make a go of it with Neil, there was a good chance he'd find out what had happened. If Justin Preece was charged with anything Ceri would probably end up in court as a witness. And even if he wasn't, the college would be bound to find out that Ceri had been caught *in flagrante* with one of her students. She would almost certainly lose her job. How would she explain *that* to Neil?

Megan shuddered. She couldn't help thinking of the children. Their little world was about to come crashing down around their ears and she desperately wanted to protect them. But there was nothing she could do. It was all down to Ceri.

At Tipton Street Dave Todd came to meet her in the foyer. 'Guv's got Sean Raven in Number One,' he said, ushering her along the corridor to the suite with the two-way mirror. 'I thought you'd like to sit in.'

In silence she seated herself at the table placed up against the mirrored window. Foy and Kate O'Leary were in the next room, sitting opposite a haggard-looking Sean Raven. She glanced at the clock on the wall. He had been in custody for more than forty-eight hours, during which time he probably hadn't slept. No wonder he was looking so rough.

'We've got your stepson in the cells downstairs. Young Justin.' Foy had his back to Megan but she could hear the sarcasm in his voice. 'He's been telling us all about your nasty little habits.' There was a pause. 'About the sick things that turn you on!'

Megan glanced at Dave Todd, her eyebrows raised. He gave a quick shake of his head. Rising to her feet, she walked out of the room. Todd followed.

'I'm sorry, Dave, I'm going. I can't listen to any more of this.' Foy had gone too far, trying to play the man and the boy off against each other with blatant lies. It was one thing fighting dirty with the likes of Carole-Ann Beddowes, but when it was someone facing a murder charge . . .

'Keep me posted, will you?' she said. 'And tell your boss I won't be available for *Crimewatch* tomorrow night.'

Megan battled her way through the worsening traffic, tapping out her home number when she came to a standstill in one of the inevitable jams. All she got was the answerphone. Perhaps Patrick's taxi from the station was stuck in traffic too. She hoped he hadn't missed his train. As she pressed the 'off' button her mobile rang out. It was Ceri, saying that she was going to have to stay at her own house because Emily had been invited to a party. Megan suggested they came over later but Ceri said the children would be too tired. She would come tomorrow instead.

As the traffic began to move Megan flexed her shoulders, rubbing the back of her neck with her hand. She felt worn out. Her mind was in a turmoil, running through endless scenarios. She needed to talk it all through with Patrick. Perhaps in the morning she would have a clearer idea of what to do. Her stomach rumbled and she realised she'd had nothing to eat since the slice of toast she'd grabbed for breakfast. And there was no food in the house. She groaned. Never mind. She would stop off for a takeaway and a bottle of wine.

The pages of the newspaper fluttered in the breeze from the open window. Black Magic Killer. In letters four inches high. And on pages three, six and seven, a storyline and a cast of characters to fool a gullible world. The photograph of the witch was laughable. Is that what those idiot journalists thought a witch looked like? How ridiculous they would look when the next one was found. Then they would realise they were dealing with a far higher intelligence.

'Oh, am I glad to see you! I thought maybe you'd missed the train.' Megan flung her arms round Patrick. He had been coming to the front door, hearing her scrabbling with her key in the lock.

'I've missed you,' he whispered.

'Me too. I've had the most god-awful day.' She had a bulky white plastic carrier hooked over her elbow and as he drew her to him it jabbed his skin.

'Ow,' he said, flinching.

'Oh sorry. It's the takeaway. I didn't have chance to do any shopping so I called for a Chinese on the way home.'

Patrick looked into her eyes and saw that they were filled with tears. 'Meg! What's the matter?'

'I . . . I'm sorry,' she stammered, 'It's just that . . . it's Ceri . . . something terrible happened . . .'

'What? Oh my God! She's not . . .'

'No, no . . . she's not hurt or anything,' Megan sniffed.

'What then?'

'It's a long and very depressing story,' she said, pulling a tissue from her pocket and dabbing her face. 'And I'm going to need a large glass of wine.' She glanced at the carrier bag in her hand and held it out. 'This is probably stone cold. Will you stick it in the microwave while I open the wine?' Her voice trailed off as she headed for the kitchen.

Patrick stood in the hall like a lost child. Seeing her had changed everything. Before she arrived he had worked out exactly what he was going to say. But how on earth could he tell her now?

He followed her to the kitchen. On automatic pilot he pulled bowls from the cupboard and doled out the contents of the aluminium cartons. Perhaps he could go to Holland without saying anything. Pretend he was going back to Liverpool. He could easily do that without her finding out. And then he could sort things out. Decide what to do. Perhaps he would never need to tell her . . .

'Patrick, what's wrong?' Megan was standing in front of him, a glass in her hand.

'Oh, nothing.' He forced a smile.

She smiled back, stroking his jaw with her finger. 'I'll take this through to the living room,' she said, picking up the wine bottle and the other glass. 'Will you bring the food?'

He nodded, perching on the edge of the table as he waited for the microwave. The takeaway had been wrapped in yesterday's newspaper. He glanced at the pages. There was a photograph of Joanna Hamilton, her face smeared with sweet and sour sauce where one of the cartons had leaked. How he wished he could turn back the clock.

When he carried the tray through Megan was halfway through her glass of wine. He topped her up and watched her picking disinterestedly at her food as she talked about her frustration with the murder investigation and the trauma of the police raid on her sister's house.

'I don't know what Ceri's going to do,' she said, pushing a chunk of pineapple around the plate with her fork. 'I keep thinking about the children. What's it going to do to them if she and Neil split up?'

Patrick stared at the food on his lap, unable to look at her.

'Patrick?' She pushed her plate aside. 'What's up?' She took his hand and looked into his eyes. 'You've been really quiet all evening. Something's happened, hasn't it? Please, tell me what's wrong.'

He took a deep breath, still avoiding her eyes. 'I wasn't going to tell you,' he mumbled. 'I didn't want to spoil things . . .'

'Tell me what?'

He looked up slowly, blinking away the tears that pricked the corners of his eyes. 'If I tell you,' he said, 'There's something I want you to remember.

She stared at him, shaking her head in confusion.

'I love you Megan.' He pulled her to him, clinging on like a drowning man.

'And I love you!' Her words were muffled by his chest.

'It's Kristine,' he whispered into her hair.

Megan recoiled at the sound of the name of Patrick's ex-fiancée. The woman he had been planning to marry. *Would* have married had he not come to study at Heartland. 'Kristine?' She frowned. 'What about Kristine?'

'Megan, she's pregnant.'

For a moment she stared uncomprehendingly at him. 'You mean she's met someone else?'

His eyes dropped to the carpet.

'But that's good, isn't it?' Megan began. 'That makes everything . . .'

'That makes everything totally fucked up.' He snatched her words and threw them back in her face. 'She's six months pregnant, Megan. She says the baby's mine.'

Chapter 15

Megan stared at Patrick, unable to believe what he had just said.

'What do you mean? How can it possibly be *your* baby?' Her mind had already done the calculation. Six months. December. Christmas. He had gone back to Holland at Christmas. To *finish* with Kristine.

'You did it with her at Christmas, didn't you?' Megan leapt off the sofa. You callous bastard! Screwing her and then dumping her . . .'

'Meg, it wasn't like that!' Patrick tried to grasp her arm as she ran for the door. She broke free and he heard her footsteps on the stairs. He ran after her but she darted into the bathroom. He heard the clunk of the bolt as she locked herself in. 'I know you're not going to believe this,' he pleaded through the door, 'but I never intended it to happen. It was you I wanted. You know that! I only went back to explain why I was breaking off the engagement.' He sighed, leaning heavily against the door. 'When I got to the flat she was in such a state. Threatening to kill herself. She asked me to stay the night and I was afraid that if I left her she might do something stupid. I'd had a lot to drink and, well, next thing I knew she was lying on top of me . . .' He broke off, realising that nothing he could say was going to make it sound any more acceptable.

'So you screwed her to cheer her up? My God, what a hero!' Megan's voice was muffled but the venom in it was unmistakeable.

'She did it deliberately, Megan! Can't you see that?' He rattled the door. 'Let me in for God's sake!'

He heard the sound of taps being turned on.

'Why do you think she waited this long to tell me?' He paused but there was no sound other than the splash of water tumbling into the bath. 'She knows it's too late to do anything about it. Don't you see? She's using the baby to try and get me back.'

'Well she's bloody well succeeded as far as I'm concerned!' Megan's voice was so loud it made Patrick jump. She must be standing right behind the door.

'Oh, come on Meg!' He rattled the lock again. 'We're never going to get anywhere like this!'

'Get anywhere? You honestly think you're going to talk your way out of this one?'

'Listen, try and see it from my point of view, will you?' There was a note of anger in his voice now. 'For God's sake, we hadn't even started seeing each other properly last Christmas, had we? I didn't even know if you'd be interested in me when I got back from Holland.'

'Oh, I see! Hedging your bets, were you?'

The roar of water from the taps suddenly stopped. He heard the pad of her footsteps on the wooden floor and a splash as she climbed into the bath. No chance of her letting him in now. He slumped onto the carpet, hugging his knees. He had been a fool to think she could be persuaded to talk rationally about something so painful. Of all the things he could possibly have done to hurt her . . .

The sound of her laughing broke the silence. It was a hollow kind of laughter and the bath water gave it an eerie echo.

'It's ironic.' She sounded as if she was talking to herself rather than to him. 'The man who won't even mention the word *baby* is about to become an almost instant father.'

'Oh come on, Megan, that's not fair!' He was on his feet with his cheek pressed against the door frame. 'If I've never talked about kids it's because the idea of having them's never really occurred to me before. I was happy the way things were with you and me!' He slammed the heel of his hand against the wood. 'I know this is a mess but won't you at least give me a chance to try and sort it out?'

'Just go, will you, Patrick!' She spat out his name like something poisonous.

'So that's it, is it?' He tried to shout but his voice was hoarse with emotion. 'You're just going to throw everything down the pan?'

'Just go!'

Her words were still ringing in his ears when he slunk off down the stairs.

Megan stared at the clock, trying to work out whether it was morning or afternoon. The sun was streaming through a crack in the living room curtains. She blinked. Why was she on the sofa? As she lowered her legs over the edge one foot landed in the congealed remains of a plate of Sweet and Sour King Prawns and the other sent an empty whisky bottle skidding across the floor. That was when she remembered.

'Shit! Shit! Shit!' Her first instinct was to jump back onto the sofa and bury her head under the cushions. Shut it all out. But the sole of her foot was a sticky mess. Smearing it over the furniture was not going to make this crappy day any better.

Instead she hopped up the stairs to the bathroom, her head pounding with every movement. Hooking her foot over the washbasin she turned on the tap, cursing again as the cold water splashed her skin.

'My God you look awful!' The bathroom mirror was not

flattering at the best of times, but today her reflection made her wince. She stared at the puffy skin and smudged mascara, playing back Patrick's words in her head. Her eyes filled and she looked away, feeling the tears run down her face to land with a plop in the washbasin. She let out the water and collapsed onto the bathroom floor, a wave of nausea suddenly sweeping over her. Crawling over to the toilet she crouched like a wounded animal, hating herself for having got into such a state.

She was still there when the phone rang ten minutes later. Patrick, she thought. Don't answer it. After a few rings the answering machine clicked in. Seized by a sudden urge to hear his voice she limped onto the landing, clutching the banister rail for support.

'Hi, Megan.' It was a woman's voice. 'There's a piece in the morning papers I wanted to ask you about: something a bit odd. It's Delva, by the way – sorry, forgot to say. I'm at home if you want to call me back. Bye.'

Megan made for the stairs and then stopped. She couldn't phone Delva. Not yet anyway. She couldn't trust herself to speak without cracking up. She might be a wreck but there was one thing she was sure of. She would tell no-one about what had happened with Patrick. Not Delva. Not even Ceri. It was too painful. Too humiliating. If either of them asked she would simply say he had gone back to Holland to sort out some family business. Later she would say he had had to stay on. It would be easy enough to cook up a reason. No-one would be surprised when she told them the relationship had fizzled out.

By the time she was dressed she had started rationalising what had happened. It was for the best, she thought. Sooner or later Patrick would have realised that he wanted children. Better for them to split up now than five years down the line. Suddenly her mind filled with an image of him cradling a new-born baby in his arms. Her legs crumpled and she sank to the floor, burying her head in her knees. Tears seeped into the fabric of her skirt and when she finally picked herself up there were two damp patches where her eyes had been.

Megan walked mechanically over to the wardrobe and pulled out a change of clothes. She would get through this. If she had survived the break-up of a five-year-old marriage she could surely get over something that had lasted a mere five months. She took a deep breath and made her way downstairs to the kitchen. Grabbing a black bin liner from the cupboard she walked purposefully into the living room. Pausing only to yank open the curtains, she gathered up everything in her path; the plates of Chinese food, the cutlery, the empty bottles of booze and the wine glasses. Marching into the back yard she tossed the bag into the wheelie bin, where it landed with a satisfying crash. Then she went inside, made herself a large mug of black coffee and phoned Delva.

'Hi Meg, thanks for calling back,' Delva said. 'It's something I spotted in one of the tabloids.'

'I can't hear you very well,' Megan said, 'Did you say tabloids?'

'Yes – sorry,' Delva raised her voice a little. 'It's this cordless phone. I'm in the garden, actually. Trying to tart it up a bit, but I could do with the *Groundforce* team, I think.'

'Oh you should see mine,' Megan said, 'Lawn's like a jungle.' She was glad the line was bad. Delva wouldn't be able to detect the shakiness in her voice. 'What's the story?' she asked.

'Hang on a minute,' Delva said, 'I'll read it out to you.' There was a crackle as she went inside. When she spoke again her voice was much clearer. 'The headline is "Red Faces As Police Raid Kinky Sex Couple". It's a diary piece on the inside pages.' Megan's stomach churned and she fought down the urge to throw up as Delva read on. '"Police hunting Wolverhampton's Black Magic Killer burst in on what they thought was the murderer attacking his third victim, only to find a couple having kinky sex. It's thought that officers raiding the house had been tipped off by a woman involved in the investigation who feared the killer had targeted her sister. But it turned out that the sister had sneaked off from her job at a local college for a lunchtime bondage session with her student boyfriend. A source close to the hunt for the killer said: 'She was tied to the bed and all she was wearing was a pair of red stilettos and a smile. The look on her face was priceless. Imagine being in the throes of passion when half a dozen coppers burst through the door. Her sister was pretty red-faced too.' A West Midlands police spokesman refused to confirm whether or not the raid had taken place."'

Megan stared at the wall in front of her, her head thumping.

'Megan? You still there?' Delva said.

'Sorry, I, er,' Megan mumbled. 'Which paper was it in?' She wondered if Delva could hear the panic in her voice.

'*The Sun*,' Delva replied. 'What do you make of it? I was wondering if the woman they're talking about could be Kate O'Leary's sister? Or maybe the police got the tip-off from that Carole-Ann Beddowes?'

'No,' Megan said with a heavy heart, 'it wasn't either of them.'

'You weren't there, were you?' Delva's voice was tentative. Then the penny dropped. 'Oh, my God! It was you, wasn't it? Oh, Megan, I'm so sorry – you must think I did this deliberately, but honestly, I had . . .'

'It's okay,' Megan cut in. 'There's no way anyone could have known from that piece that it was me.' She breathed in sharply. 'I just wish I knew which bastard tipped off the newspaper.'

'Listen, Megan, I don't want to pry – I only phoned because I wondered who the bloke was. The piece gives the impression the police have ruled him out and I wondered if *The Sun* had got that right.'

'No, they haven't,' Megan sighed. 'As far as I know the police are still holding him.' She paused. Delva knew so much anyway there seemed little point keeping the truth from her. No doubt Foy would make sure Justin's name was leaked to the press before the day was out. 'His name's Justin Preece,' she said. 'And he's Sean Raven's stepson.'

There was a gasp from the other end of the line. 'And he's been . . .?' Delva's voice tailed off. Obviously she was too embarrassed to finish the sentence.

'Yes, he's been seeing my sister.' Megan couldn't bring herself to use the word *The Sun* would have chosen.

'Megan, can I give you a word of advice?' Delva's tone was serious. There was no hint of sarcasm. 'Watch who you open the door to today and leave the answerphone on – if any hack susses who this story's about they'll be doorstepping you and your sister.'

Megan closed her eyes, wondering how much worse this day could possibly become. 'What about you, Delva?' If ever there was a time when her friend was going to have divided loyalties, Megan thought, this was surely it.

'Don't worry, it's not the sort of thing that makes teatime viewing.' Delva's voice sounded strained now. Megan wondered if she was trying not to laugh. She imagined it was the kind of story that would give most reporters a good giggle.

She stood in the hall for several minutes after her conversation with Delva had ended, wondering what to do. The desire to run away was almost overwhelming. She and

Ceri and the children could drive to the house their Welsh grandmother had left them; the tiny fisherman's cottage that overlooked Cardigan Bay. They would be safe there; from reporters; lovers; two-faced detectives . . . The sound of the phone cut her short.

'Meg, it's me.' It was Ceri. She sounded much calmer than when Megan had last spoken to her. 'I know we were meant to be coming over today but I've had a lot of time to mull things over, and I really think it'd be best if the kids and I stayed here. I've got to face people sooner or later, and running away's not going to help.'

Megan bit her lip. 'Oh, Ceri, you're being really brave, but there's something I've got to tell you.' There was no sound from the other end as she related what Delva had told her. 'So it probably isn't a very good idea for you to be at home.'

'I'm not going to let it get to me, Meg.' Ceri's voice was quiet but determined. 'People are going to find out sooner or later. Best to just brazen it out, eh?'

'What about Neil? Have you decided what you're going to tell him?'

There was a long sigh from the other end. 'It's over, Meg. If I'm honest I've known it for a long time. It's nothing to do with Justin – he just brought things to a head.' There was a pause. 'Do you know what's happened to him, by the way?' The sudden shakiness in her voice betrayed the fragility of her emotions. 'I keep trying his mobile but it's switched off.'

'Do you want me to find out?'

'Yes, please, Meg.' Ceri's voice had become a hoarse whisper. 'I can't bear to think of him lying in some police cell.'

Megan's face was set as she punched out Dave Todd's number. Asking about Justin Preece would give her an excuse to find out if he was the one who'd sold that story to *The Sun*. In her heart of hearts she didn't want to believe it. He had seemed so likeable; so keen to help her in spite of his boss. She grunted. She'd managed to balls-up pretty much everything else – why should her judgement of *him* be any different?

The mobile number rang out several times before he picked up.

'Dave Todd.' He sounded out of breath. She wondered if she'd disturbed him on a morning off.

'It's Dr Rhys.' Two days ago she had told him to call her Megan. Now she felt inclined to be formal. 'Any news on Justin Preece?'

'Still holding him,' Todd said. 'I was at the station about an hour ago. No prospect of charging him with anything at the moment, I shouldn't think.'

'Oh? Why do you say that?'

'Well, like you said with Sean Raven, it's all circumstantial, isn't it? I mean, at least with Raven there's a definite link with Tessa Ledbury. I think the Guv's going to be on very shaky ground if he tries to hold Justin beyond tomorrow morning.'

'So you think he'll let him go?' Megan wondered what the papers would make of that. 'What about Raven?'

'I wouldn't be surprised if he lets them both out tomorrow. If they're released without charge, the papers'll be free to sling even more dirt – perhaps that's his plan.'

'Hmm.' The moment had come to say what was on her mind. 'Talking of the papers, have you seen today's *Sun*?'

There was no sound from Todd's end of the line. 'Are you there, Dave?' She heard him cough.

'Yes, I have seen it. I hope you don't think it came from me?'

This threw her. She hesitated a moment, then said: 'I

don't know who it came from, but I think I've a right to know, don't you?'

'Well, if I was you I bloody well would!' She heard him tutting under his breath. 'I don't know who it was. It could have been anyone at Tipton Street – a relative of an officer, even. I'm afraid that kind of thing gets round pretty fast.' He sounded genuinely angry, Megan thought. She wished she could see his face. It was so easy to lie over the phone.

'I was going to phone you anyway,' he said, the tone of his voice changing. 'I've got some news about that call to Joanna Hamilton's mobile.'

'Oh?' Was he trying to distract her?

'It came from Bob Spelman – d'you remember? The driving instructor from the church?'

'Spelman?'

'I know,' Todd said. 'Bit of a coincidence – that's what I thought. But we've been round there. He said she'd been enquiring about driving lessons. Said he was phoning to give her an appointment.'

'So why didn't he come forward before'

'He said he only knew her as Jo. She hadn't given her surname. Said he would have taken all the details at the first lesson. He saw it on the news but he didn't make the connection.'

Ceri was upstairs, crouching on the bathroom floor. She lifted a corner of the rectangle of patterned muslin hanging across the window. She was right. It *was* a photographer. The phone had alerted her. It had rung ten minutes ago but she had taken Megan's advice and left the answering machine on. There had been no message, but for a split second she had heard office sounds in the background. A newspaper office, she guessed. She crawled out of the bathroom on her stomach, getting to her feet only after she had closed the door behind her. Walking along the landing she called to Emily, who was playing in her room. Then she scooped Joe, still asleep, from his cot and made her way downstairs.

There was a gate in the wall of the back garden that led to an overgrown footpath. It ran the length of the houses and came out by the shops. 'Come on,' she said to Emily, 'we're going for a little walk.' Placing Joe gently down in his buggy, she eased her way down the back steps to the cobbled patio. They would go to the park. It was a hot day and there would be lots of people. No-one would recognise her in her in her baseball cap and sunglasses.

Megan had pulled her phone out of its socket. Anyone who needed to get hold of her could call her on her mobile. She fished the small silver phone from her jacket pocket and picked out the digits of the Spelmans' home number. It was engaged. She would have to try later. The more she thought about it, the more odd it seemed that Bob Spelman was the last person to have telephoned both Tessa and Joanna. She wondered if the police had checked his alibi for the evening Joanna died. Driving instructors must do a lot of evening work, she reflected. How would he account for the gaps between clients? Times when he was driving from one appointment to the next? And surely there must be the odd session when a client failed to show?

These questions buzzed round her head as she searched for her bag. Where had she left it last night? There wasn't even a crust of bread in the house and she needed to go to the shops. Not that she was hungry – Patrick had seen to that. She found her bag in the hall, where she had dropped it when she'd come in last night with the Chinese take-away. Her insides flipped over at the memory of Patrick coming to greet her. 'Oh God,' she wailed. 'How long before I stop thinking about him?'

She swallowed hard and headed to the door but stopped before turning the latch. What if there were reporters outside? She darted into the living room and peered through the thin lilac sari fabric that served as a net curtain. She could see no-one. Good.

Her car was parked right outside the house and she scrambled in. Still no sign of anyone. She went to the big *Sainsbury's* half an hour's drive away. When she'd done her shopping she decided to linger in the café for a while. The thought of going home depressed her. When Patrick left it had suddenly seemed so empty. She bought a copy of the local evening paper and tucked it under her arm as she went to get a black coffee. There were plenty of empty tables and she chose one in a corner by the window that overlooked the carpark. She poured two sachets of brown sugar into her cup and while she stirred it she watched the people going to and from their cars. It struck her how easy it would be to single out a lone woman and follow her home. Even on a pushbike it would be possible, she reflected, given the congestion on the roads.

She took a sip of coffee and scanned the front page of the newspaper. 'Occult Killings – Second Man Held,' the headline read. She scanned it quickly to see if Justin Preece had been named. It appeared not, but the column ended mid-sentence. 'Turn to Page 3', it said. She opened the paper and did a double take. Her own face was staring up at her.

Dave Todd sat in the canteen at Tipton Street police station. Through the window he could see Sean Raven and Justin Preece on their way to a waiting squad car. Beyond the compound a gaggle of reporters and photographers were waiting. He wondered where the two men would go; certainly not home, he thought. Suddenly a newspaper came skidding across the table, almost knocking his cup out of its saucer.

'Looks like your friend's turned into a Page Three Girl!'

He looked up to see Detective Constable Craig Hollis standing at the other side of the table, arms folded and a silly grin on his face. Todd opened the newspaper and stared at the photograph on page three.

'The sister of a top criminal profiler has been revealed as the woman involved in a sex romp that sparked a police raid in Wolverhampton,' the text read. 'Ceri Richardson, the sister of Heartland University academic Dr Megan Rhys, was named as the woman found tied up by police who raided the house in the Stockhall area of the city yesterday. Married mother-of-two Ceri Richardson, 34, of 23 Church Terrace, Stockhall, is a part-time lecturer at Pendleton College.' Dave Todd read on, his eyebrows arching when he got to the quote about Ceri wearing nothing but red stilettos and a smile. The last line of the article read: 'Neither Dr Rhys nor her sister were available for comment.' *I bet they bloody well weren't*, he thought.

Megan grabbed her mobile and punched out Ceri's number. It rang five times before the answering machine cut in. Then she tried her sister's mobile, but it was switched off. She phoned the house a second time. 'Ceri, it's Meg,' she said, as the machine bleeped. 'There's a piece in tonight's paper. It gives our names and your address. I really don't think it's a good idea for you to be staying there. Ring me back, will you?'

Megan hurried back to the car and loaded her shopping into the boot. She thought about driving over to her sister's. But would Ceri be back by the time Megan got there? Had she perhaps gone to a friend's house? It would make more sense to go home and wait for her to call.

Megan drove up and down her street twice before pulling in a few houses up from her own. She glanced up and down the pavement before going to her front door, wary of any lurking reporters. Perhaps she was being paranoid. Perhaps, now the story was out, they would lose interest.

After unpacking the shopping she tried to distract herself by preparing a salad of mozzarella cheese, tomatoes and basil. She still didn't have the slightest appetite, but she must eat something. Phrases from the newspaper article rattled around inside her head. How was Ceri ever going to live it down?

It was nearly dark outside when her sister phoned. She had seen the article in the local paper and and had decided not to return home until the evening. She told Megan about the photographer she had seen outside the house earlier, but seemed almost unbelievably calm about it all.

'I thought you'd be beside yourself when you saw the paper,' Megan said.

'Oh, I was,' Ceri said. 'But what could I do? I had the kids with me. I couldn't break down in front of them, could I?'

'What are you going to do? Will you come over?'

'No, but thanks for asking. I'm going to take the kids to Wales first thing in the morning. I'll stay at the cottage for a couple of days; give things a chance to die down.' Megan heard her give a heavy sigh. 'I'll have to come back Tuesday night because Neil's due back from Brussels on Wednesday.'

'Have you decided what you're going to say to him?' Megan held her breath.

'We'll have to work out what's going to happen with the house,' Ceri said, her voice wobbling. 'Get an estate agent round to value it.'

'The house? You're going to sell up?'

'I think so, Meg.' There was a pause, then the sound of Ceri blowing her nose. 'What I said before, about brazening it out – it's not going to work is it? Imagine what it'd be like for the children when they're a bit older; other kids in the playground teasing them about their mum. People round here have got long memories.'

'And what about . . .?' Megan could hardly bring herself to say the name.

'Justin?' Ceri cut in. 'I don't know, Meg. I still don't believe he's done anything wrong.'

'Will you see him? When you get back I mean?'

'If those bastards ever let him out, then yes, I probably will.'

The television had been on in the background while Megan was talking to Ceri. She had put it on to see *Crime-watch*, wanting to know how much further Steve Foy was going to go in his bid to nail Sean Raven. As she said goodbye to her sister his face suddenly filled the screen.

Foy looked every inch the assured senior officer. He oozed confidence and his delivery was word-perfect. 'Tessa Ledbury was involved in a local witches' coven before she converted to Christianity,' he said. 'She was last seen at the shopping centre near her home in Pendleton.' His face disappeared, to be replaced by a shot of Kate O'Leary in the blonde wig, walking towards the chemist's at Pendleton precinct.

Megan picked at the limp salad that lay untouched on the coffee table. She wondered why Steve Foy was being so blinkered. *But what if he's right?* The voice nagging inside her head was Patrick's. What if both murders *were* linked to the occult? She shook her head. Patrick's bombshell had knocked her confidence. She reminded herself that the only reason for the occult theory was the pentagram on Tessa Ledbury's head; no-one knew if the wounds on Joanna's head were a pentagram, and even if they were, it didn't *prove* the killer was involved in the occult. There were other lines of enquiry that needed to be followed up. She must try to get hold of Bob Spelman. Find out more about his call to Joanna Hamilton.

She also wanted to know more about this link between St Paul's and the open prison at Whiteladies. If they held services there, perhaps they held them at other prisons in the area too. What about Featherstone? That was near Wolverhampton and it held Category 'A' offenders. What if someone from St Paul's had befriended a sex offender who, on his release, had started hanging around Pendleton for the want of anywhere else to go?

But when she tried ringing the Spelmans there was still no reply. She looked at her watch and groaned. It was nearly ten o'clock – too late to keep trying for much longer. Then an idea struck her. She could catch them if she went to Pendleton church in the morning.

Foy's voice made her glance back at the television. 'I'd like to appeal to anyone who might know of any dabbling in black magic by the two victims to come forward,' he said, looking gravely into the camera. 'Any information we receive will be treated in the strictest confidence.'

'In confidence? Bollocks!' Megan threw her slipper at the screen.

It was only a portable TV, but watching the reconstruction was as good as any Hollywood blockbuster. They'd managed to dig out a new photograph of Joanna Hamilton as well, tanned and happy-looking on some Australian beach. A wide shot of the studio next, with all the coppers manning the phones. Still no idea about the third woman, then. It was so tempting to call in. Easy enough to do, thanks to the stolen mobile. Concealing it in the lining of the cycle helmet, along with the craft knife, had been a stroke of genius. No chance of anyone stumbling across it there. And finding a weapon to kill them with had been a piece of piss.

A vegetable knife from their own kitchen drawer had done the
trick on all three occasions. The craft knife was for the artwork.
Oh. Number coming up now. Better write it down.

A policewoman picked up the phone. Foy was standing
nearby, eager to stay in shot.

'Hello, my name's Dorothy and I've got something
important to tell you.' The policewoman frowned. It didn't
sound like a woman. Difficult to say. The line wasn't very
good.

'Can you speak up?' the WPC said. 'I can't hear you very
well.'

'My name's Dorothy and I'm wearing the witch's ruby
slippers. There's a number three, you know,' the voice said.

The policewoman blinked. 'I beg your pardon?' The line
went dead.

'Anything?' Foy asked, bending over her.

'Just another nutter, Guv,' she replied.

Chapter 16

Megan had had a bad night. She had lain awake until dawn began to lighten the curtains, turning things over and over in her head until it ached. Eventually she had drifted into sleep, only to dream about Patrick. When she came to she'd reached out for him before she'd woken up enough to realise he wasn't there.

She groaned and stumbled into the bathroom. She must get herself dressed and drive over to Pendleton. She showered quickly, then dabbed concealer under her eyes in a vain bid to hide the dark circles. She stared at her reflection and took a deep breath. In the past her job had always provided a refuge from any troubles in her personal life. Whatever else happened, she was not going to let this affect her work.

It was odd driving through the centre of Birmingham on a Sunday morning. It was something Megan didn't do very often. The streets were so quiet, so empty of cars. *What if he's out there now, killing again?* The thought sprang into her head out of nowhere. 'But I don't think he would be,' she said aloud. Sundays were days when women were most unlikely to be at home alone. Normal women. Not women like Delva and herself. Or Joanna Hamilton.

As she turned onto the Birmingham New Road the news came on the radio. Sean Raven and Justin Preece had been released. She whistled under her breath. Foy must be getting desperate, then.

At Pendleton precinct the newsagent and the super-market were the only shops open. Megan stopped outside the paper shop, running her eyes over the stands. The headline in the *News of the World* caught her eye. *MURDER SUSPECT'S SEX ROMP WITH VICTIM*. She pulled the paper from the rack. There were head-and-shoulders shots of Sean Raven and Tessa Ledbury on the front page. The article itself was only a few paragraphs long, but there was a line in bold type at the end saying the full story and pictures could be found on the centre pages. Were these the photos Carole-Ann Beddowes had tried to sell to Delva, Megan wondered?

She was about to open the paper when she heard a loud cough from inside the shop. A young girl was staring pointedly at her from behind the counter. Megan took the paper inside and dug out her purse.

'My mum knows him,' the girl said, cocking her head at the picture of Sean Raven as she scanned the paper through the till.

'Oh, really,' Megan replied, looking at her with a little more interest.

'Tessa used to come in here too,' the girl went on. 'Used to bring her kids into get sweets after school.'

Megan took her paper and her change, acknowledging this snippet of information with a slight tilt of her head. The girl was obviously showing off, but Megan had the feeling that any direct questions would make her clam up. So she fumbled with her purse, trying to prolong the encounter in case she came out with anything else. She didn't have to wait long.

'Richard Ledbury was in here earlier as well, you know.'

'Oh, was he?' Megan put on an expression of polite concern.

'Couldn't believe it when I saw him.' The girl shrugged.

'He didn't come in, just hung about outside the shop while this woman he was with came and bought the paper.' She flicked her tongue over her teeth and Megan caught a flash of chewing gum. 'You'd think he'd be the last person to want to see it wouldn't you?'

'Yes, you would.' Megan paused for a moment longer but the girl turned away and started filling the shelves behind her with cartons of cigarettes.

What woman? Megan pondered the girl's words as she walked out of the shop. Could it be Kate O'Leary? She glanced at her watch. It was another ten minutes before the service was due to end. There was a low wall running along the path and she sat down to read the paper.

The photographs were every bit as sordid as she had imagined. Sean Raven must have taken them with a time-release mechanism attached to his camera. The pictures had been doctored with black blobs over the points where the naked bodies made contact. In the main shot Sean Raven's face leered into the camera. He was lying on top of Tessa. She was looking away but her profile was unmistake-able. Megan thought about what the girl in the newsagent's had said. Why would Richard Ledbury want to torture himself with this? Had it been the woman's idea, whoever she was? Bite the bullet and get it over with?

Megan got up and walked across to the path that led to the church. She stopped short. There was a photographer standing behind a bush a few yards in front of her. His telephoto lens was pointing at the entrance to the church. She slipped behind a large concrete litter bin, wondering what to do. He must be after Richard Ledbury. Trying to get a reaction to the story in the *News of the World*. Richard must have bought that paper on his way to the service. She would have to think of some way of catching Bob Spelman without passing the vulture lurking behind the bush.

She scanned the shrubbery bordering the church's salmon-coloured walls and caught a flash of movement. Three figures were moving slowly away from the back of the building, their bodies hunched over. The one bringing up the rear kept glancing backwards. As they drew nearer the first one grabbed the second one's hand and the pair of them broke into a run. Megan caught her breath. It was Kate O'Leary and Richard Ledbury. She stared after them as they disappeared round the side of the supermarket. She glanced at the photographer, whose posture hadn't altered. Obviously he hadn't spotted them. The third figure had come to a standstill a few yards from Megan. It was Bob Spelman. He shaded his eyes against the sun, as if double-checking that the others had got away safely, then he turned on his heel and walked back the way he had come. Megan ran after him.

'Mr Spelman!' She didn't want to shout for fear of alerting the photographer.

She caught up with him and he wheeled round.

'Oh! Dr Rhys!' He looked rattled.

'I'm sorry, I didn't mean to startle you,' she panted. 'I need to talk you. I tried phoning yesterday but there was no reply.'

'We were out all day,' he replied, his features settling into the serene expression she remembered from last time. 'Would you like to come into the vestry?' He showed her through a narrow door that gave onto a small room.

She could hear the muffled sound of singing, and realised the service must still be in progress. Spelman pulled out a chair and Megan sat down next to a table covered in trays of tiny glasses and bottles of communion wine.

'I'm sorry to trouble you again,' she said. 'It's about Joanna Hamilton.'

'I thought it might be.' He dropped his head, his hands clasped together in his lap.

'I know the police have already been to see you,' she went on, 'but I wanted to ask you a few more questions, if you don't mind.'

'Well, if you think it'll help.' He looked up, his blue eyes inscrutable.

'You'd never met Joanna face-to-face, had you?'

He shook his head. 'We'd only spoken on the phone. She'd called me earlier in the week to enquire about lessons. I'd said I'd call her back. I was hoping for a cancellation, but in the end the earliest I could book her in for was mid-June.'

'How did she come to choose you as a driving instructor?' Megan asked.

Spelman opened his hands, spreading them palms up. 'I don't know, Dr Rhys. I don't advertise – most of my clients come from word-of-mouth recommendation.'

'And she didn't say how she'd got your number?'

'No. She could have seen it anywhere, though – it's on a board on the roof of the car.'

Megan frowned. There was nothing in either his answers or his demeanour to make her suspicious. She decided to try a different tack. 'Last time we met you told me St. Paul's was involved in outreach work at Whiteladies prison . . .'

'Yes, we hold a service there once a month. Why?'

'Do you do that at any other prisons in the area,' Megan asked, ignoring his question, 'Featherstone, for example?'

'No,' he replied in a puzzled voice, 'just Whiteladies. What's all this about?'

Megan frowned. 'Oh, if it's only Whiteladies you deal with, I'm probably wasting your time. If any of the congregation had been involved with prisoners at Featherstone it would be a different matter. You see my worry was that if someone at the church had befriended an inmate with a record of violent offending and that person had recently been released . . .'

'He might have murdered Tessa.' Bob Spelman finished the sentence for her and gave a heavy sigh. 'Yes, I see your point,' he went on. 'But as you know, Whiteladies is not that sort of prison. We've got about half a dozen former inmates worshipping at St. Paul's now and there are a few on day-release placements who come to the midweek service.'

'I see,' Megan said. This was not what she had been hoping for. 'One last thing, if you don't mind,' she said. 'I saw Richard Ledbury running away from the church with a policewoman from the team investigating Tessa's murder.' She looked him straight in the eye. 'Can you tell me what that was about?'

'We've been having a bit of trouble from the press,' he replied, holding her gaze. 'DS O'Leary was here to provide Richard with protection.'

Oh, so that's what she told you, is it? Megan thought as she rose to leave. It seemed unlikely; one policewoman wasn't going to be much use against a determined pack of reporters.

She thought about Kate O'Leary as she made her way back to the car. Delva had been spooked enough by her behaviour towards Richard Ledbury to have her down as a murder suspect. But what possible motive could Kate have for killing Joanna Hamilton? Megan frowned. What if she'd used Joanna as a kind of cover for murdering Tessa? As a detective she'd know enough to stunt something up, make it look as if a serial killer was on the loose. But if that had been the case, Megan reasoned, it would all have backfired disastrously, because Joanna's body wasn't discovered until *after* Tessa had been murdered. It was pretty unlikely that someone using Joanna in that way would go ahead with a second murder before the first had hit the headlines.

As Megan unlocked the car her mobile rang out.

'Megan, it's Dave Todd.' He sounded excited. 'We've had

a call from a woman who saw Joanna Hamilton in Pendleton on the Wednesday afternoon. You'll never guess what . . .'

'What?' She felt a rush of adrenalin.

'She went to a dating agency – a lesbian and gay dating agency.'

'In Pendleton?' Megan couldn't quite believe this.

'I know, bizarre, isn't it? It's run by this woman from her house on the estate. Joanna called in to register and make a video recording of herself. She went there before the supermarket.'

'And have you seen this woman?'

'I'm on my way there now.'

'Can I come with you?' Megan asked, 'I'm in the precinct.'

Dave Todd was waiting in his car when she found the house.

'Why didn't she come forward before?' Megan asked as they walked down the path.

'She's just come back from a fortnight in Barbados,' Todd shrugged. 'Must be plenty of money to be made out of lonely lesbians, eh?'

The tall woman who came to the door looked about forty. She was very tanned and wore an expensive-looking cream linen suit. Her eyes were the most unusual Megan had ever seen. Lilac irises with an inner ring of pale brown around the pupil. Must be coloured contact lenses, she thought.

The woman introduced herself as Dee Lake of Lakeland Connections and showed them into a back room that had been converted into an office. There was a small television in one corner and she picked up a remote control from the table.

Megan watched in awed silence as Joanna Hamilton's face appeared on the screen. As she described her lifestyle and her interests, the camera zoomed out to a wide shot. Now Megan could see the black leather jacket, the red top and the trousers. And on her feet were the red suede shoes.

'Has this video been seen by any of the other people on your books?' Megan asked.

'No.' Dee Lake blinked and the lilac lenses shifted slightly, giving her a distinctly alien look. 'I told Joanna I wouldn't be able to do that until I got back from holiday.'

'And did Joanna tell you what sort of partner she was looking for?'

'Someone of a similar age and with similar interests to herself,' the woman said. 'She was very attractive. It wouldn't have been difficult to fix her up.'

'I assume she paid you some sort of joining fee?' Megan asked.

'Oh yes.' The lilac eyes met hers. 'Three hundred and fifty pounds, in advance. It's company policy.'

'What did you make of Madame Lake, then?' Dave asked later as they sipped coffee at a *Little Chef* a few miles down the road. 'Her alibi checks out – she went to collect her kids from school straight after Joanna left and then took them to a party.'

'She said she wasn't a lesbian herself.' Megan frowned. 'Do you think she was telling the truth?'

'Well, she's got a husband living with her and they've got two kids, so it looks like it.'

'It's an odd thing to do as a business, though, isn't it?' Megan said. 'If you're not gay yourself, I mean?'

Dave sighed. 'Doesn't get us much further, at any rate, does it? I take it you've heard the news about Sean Raven and Justin Preece?'

She nodded. 'And I've seen the piece in the *News of the World*. I assume your boss is hoping they'll dig up more along the same lines, with a bit of violence thrown in?'

'I think that's a pretty fair guess.' He looked at her and she wondered why he was so open about his dislike of Foy's methods. For most of the police officers she had encountered, loyalty to colleagues was imperative.

'Tell me something,' she frowned, 'You were the one who arrested Justin at my sister's house. Did you really believe he might be the killer?'

'I was keeping an open mind,' he replied. 'When I realised he was Sean Raven's stepson I knew the Guv'd want him hauled in. If I'm honest I was just covering my back – after all, he's nothing like that profile you gave us, is he?' He held her gaze just a fraction too long and she glanced down at the table.

'No.' She stood up, unnerved by the way his eyes had made her feel. 'I must be getting back,' she lied, 'but could you do something for me? I'd like to see that list of recently-released sex offenders – the ones you said the team had checked out.'

'Well, yes, I should be able to get hold of that for you,' he said. 'Do you mind me asking why?'

'Just curious, that's all.' This time she wasn't lying. She had to see that list for herself.

'I'll e-mail it to you if you like – should be okay if I do it from home.'

She scribbled down the e-mail address and he put it in his pocket.

As dusk fell on the ruins of Whiteladies Abbey the men and women crept through the shadows. Candles in glass jars were set on stones, incense cones lit and ceremonial ornaments laid on the wide window ledge that served as an altar.

Mariel Raven held up her arms to the night sky, the silver crescent moon on her forehead glinting in the flickering light. 'Spirits of Earth, Air, Fire and Water, we thank you for delivering our brothers Sean and Justin from those who wish them ill,' she intoned. 'Great Goddess, we thank you!'

There was a swish of cloth against bare flesh as the others held up their arms 'We thank you,' they murmured.

Mariel Raven took something from the pocket of her robe. It was a piece of newspaper, the edges ragged where it had been torn from the page. At it's centre was a photograph of Megan.

Stretching her arm towards one of the candles, Mariel Raven held the scrap of paper to the flame. 'Evil be to she who evil sees!' Her words rang out in the darkness. Megan's face was lit up for a split second. Then it blackened and crumpled to a cinder, floating up into the night sky.

Chapter 17

Megan woke with a start. She sat up in bed, her heart racing. The back of her neck was wet with perspiration. In the nightmare she had been gasping for breath as a man in a mask stuffed a white dishcloth into her mouth.

She peered at the red quartz display on her alarm clock. Six forty-five. She knew it was pointless trying to go back to sleep. Her head thumped as she swung her legs over the edge of the bed and groped around with her feet for her slippers. Today was a day she had been dreading. She was due to meet the Vice-Chancellor at nine o'clock. All that had happened over the past few days had pushed it to the back of her mind. But there was no getting away from it now. She was going to have to face the music. And it would be all the harder to bear now that she and Patrick had parted.

She made herself a coffee and took it up to her study. Last night she'd been too exhausted to check her e-mails. She wondered if Dave Todd had sent the list of sex offenders yet. As she waited for the computer to come on she reached into a drawer, bringing out a packet of cigarettes and a lighter. She put them on the desk and frowned. She hadn't touched a cigarette since before Christmas. Patrick had helped her quit. The packet had been lying in the drawer all that time. Just in case. She flipped it open and slid out a cigarette. It felt strange when she put it in her mouth. Big and clumsy. She flicked the lighter but nothing happened. She flicked it again, then she shook it. Empty.

'Oh bugger!' She spat out the cigarette and broke it in half, turning to hurl it and the packet into the bin. She swivelled her chair back round, staring hard at the computer screen. Yes, she had e-mail. Something told her before she had even clicked the mouse that there was going to be a message from Patrick.

'In *Amsterdam*!' she said aloud as she read the text. 'My God, you don't hang around, do you?'

He said that he had gone to Amsterdam to talk things over with Kristine. He had agreed to start maintenance payments as soon as the baby was born, provided she agreed to a DNA test to prove the child was his. The fact that she had agreed to this made it pretty clear to him that he wasn't being set up.

He knew that in order to meet the maintenance payments he was going to have to give up his PhD and return to his old job with the Dutch police. So he was going back to Liverpool to pack up his things and would be calling at Megan's house on Thursday at about 2pm to collect his Doc Martens and some CDs that he'd left in the cupboard under the stairs. If she didn't want to see him would she mind leaving them in the porch?

And that was it. No impassioned plea for her to take him back. Just 'With love, as always, Patrick.' What was she supposed to make of it? Grabbing the mouse she erased his message from the screen. Her hand shook from the mixture of misery and anger welling up inside. Trust Patrick to make this shitty day even worse, she thought. Desperate for distraction, she scanned her inbox. There was a message from Dave Todd. Good.

She printed out the list he had sent and took it back to bed along with a fresh mug of coffee and some toast. It made grim reading. The crimes committed by the men on the list ranged from multiple rape to unlawful intercourse with a minor. Beneath each name were details of the prison or prisons where the sentence had been served and a list of previous convictions. It also gave the current address of the offender and the length of time since his release. She was only halfway through reading it when she glanced at the clock and realised she had just forty minutes to get dressed and get to the university.

The Vice-Chancellor's office was in an old, ivy-clad mansion that had once housed the whole university. It was the only really attractive building on the campus, the rest having been added in bits and pieces from the 1950s onwards. As she walked along the red-carpeted entrance hall she had a sick feeling in her stomach. Never in her career had she been reprimanded; colleagues had commented enviously on her meteoric rise to Head of Department. At thirty-six years old she was the youngest person ever to have held the post. And the first woman. Even though she knew that technically, she'd done nothing wrong, she felt she had let down all the people who had believed in her enough to give her that chance.

She was shown into a room that smelt of beeswax and cigars. There was an ancient-looking leather-topped desk by the window and two huge reproduction leather arm-chairs facing each other in front of the fireplace. The Vice-Chancellor's head was completely obscured by the winged headrest of one of them, and when he spoke she jumped.

'Doctor Rhys.' His voice was a throaty growl; the legacy of a lifetime of smoking. 'Sit down, please.'

He quizzed her about her affair with Patrick, making her feel like a naughty schoolgirl called into the headmaster's office. She tried to explain that there had been no intimacy between them until Patrick had changed PhD supervisors; that she would never have contemplated embarking on a relationship with someone whose work she was responsible for assessing. She stopped short of telling him they had split up. She didn't want to give him the satisfaction.

'Doesn't look good though, does it?' He scowled at her from behind his black-framed spectacles. 'Not something to make a habit of.'

My God, she thought, *what does he take me for? Does he think I've slept with other students?* She opened her mouth to protest but he beat her to it.

'And this doesn't help.' He pulled a newspaper from the side of the chair. It was Saturday's local evening paper, open at the page bearing her photograph. He waved it under her nose. 'This kind of thing doesn't put the university in a very good light.'

'But I didn't . . .' she began.

'A warning, Dr Rhys,' he cut in. 'No more *fraternising* with the students. And perhaps you should think about cutting down on the police work. Stick to academia. That's what you're paid for.'

When she got back to her car she was trembling with rage and shame. The tears in her eyes and the pounding in her brain made it difficult to concentrate on driving. At the Bull Ring roundabout she nearly crashed a red light. All she wanted was to get home and hide herself away. It was a miracle she made it back in one piece.

She threw off her clothes and jumped into the shower, as if the sharp jets of water could blast away the memory of what had happened. Bundling her hair into a towel she wrapped her bathrobe tightly around her wet body and ran into her bedroom, burrowing under the duvet like a hunted animal.

In the warm darkness she tried to rationalise the Vice-Chancellor's words. She had only been given a warning. Not the sack. That was something, at least. But what really grated were his comments about her police work. The university had been only too happy to bask in the media spotlight when she'd made headlines for solving a string of rapes in Scotland and the murders of three Birmingham prostitutes.

She lifted up the covers and glanced at the clock. Beside it was the list Dave Todd had e-mailed earlier. She grabbed it, scanning the pages with renewed determination. She was damned if she was going to give up this case. Vice-Chancellor or *no* Vice-Chancellor.

She was so deep in thought the phone made her jump.

'Megan, it's Delva.' The voice sounded faint and Megan could hear traffic in the background. 'I'm in Pendleton. They've found another body – did you know?'

'What?' Megan's hand tightened on the receiver.

'It's a woman – that's all I know. Des had a call from his mate at Tipton Street nick. I'm just on my way to the flat where they found her.'

'Where is it?' Megan made a grab for her clothes, cradling the phone between her ear and her shoulder.

'It's above the electrical shop in the precinct,' Delva said. 'Number 7A'.

Dave Todd stared at the woman lying on the bed. Her chalk-white thighs were marbled with dark brown streaks where the blood vessels had begun to putrefy. Her swollen stomach was tinged green below the blackened mess that had once been her breasts. A corner of blood-stained fabric protruded from her swollen lips and on the tight, stretched skin of her forehead were the unmistakeable lines of a pentagram.

'Her name's Susan Thompson.' Steve Foy was standing by the Venetian blinds that screened the bedroom window from the curious glances of the shoppers below. 'Forty-six years old. Worked as a receptionist at the doctor's.' He nodded in the direction of the surgery. 'They came round when she didn't turn up this morning.'

'How long's she been dead?' Todd pulled a handkerchief from his pocket and held it over his mouth.

'More than thirty-six hours, the FME said. Post mortem should give us a better idea.'

Todd looked at him. 'What time were Raven and Preece released?'

'Just what I was thinking.' Foy nodded slowly. 'Five o'clock Saturday afternoon. So anything up to forty-two hours, they're still in the frame.'

'When was she last seen?'

'Half past five last Thursday afternoon. That's when she left the surgery. She didn't work Fridays, so no-one missed her until this morning.'

Todd frowned 'She lived alone, then, like Joanna Hamilton?'

'A widow,' Foy replied. 'One daughter living in America.'

'No boyfriend?'

'None that her pals from the surgery knew of.'

Megan was pulling into the precinct carpark when Dave Todd rang.

'I'm outside,' she said.

There was a pause at the other end. 'How did you know?'

'Tip-off from a friend in the media who got it from one of your lot.'

'Hmm.' Todd knew better than to ask who her friend was. 'I'll come and find you.'

Megan waited by the entrance to the supermarket. She could see a short, uniformed figure with spiky ginger hair standing with his back to her in the main square. Steve Foy. He was being interviewed by Delva, who had positioned him in front of the shop above which the body had been found.

Dave Todd appeared from the opposite direction, having come out of the flat's back entrance. In a few brief sentences he told her what he'd seen.'

'I'm going across to the surgery to talk to the colleague who found her,' he said. 'Want to come?'

Megan glanced towards the square. 'What about your boss?'

'He's off to the mortuary as soon as he's done with the TV people,' Todd said.

'Nice one, Steve,' Megan muttered as they headed for the surgery. 'Nothing like getting your priorities right.'

The colleague who had found Susan Thompson's body was a frail-looking woman with short grey hair. Her face was ashen and the her hands shook as she related the horrific experience of letting herself into the flat above the electrical shop.

'She'd given me a key in case of emergencies,' the woman said, her voice almost inaudible. 'When she didn't come in this morning I knew straight away something must be wrong. Sue was hardly ever ill, but on the odd occasion when she was, she'd always phone to let someone know.'

'I'm sorry to have to ask you these questions, Mrs Green,' Todd said, 'But can you tell me exactly what time you last saw her?'

'It was twenty to six last Thursday evening,' the woman replied. 'I remember because we were supposed to close the surgery at five-thirty. I said, "Come on, Sue, it's time we were going home."' She clasped and unclasped her hands in her lap. There were no tears in her eyes. They would come later, Megan thought.

'Did you get the impression she didn't really want to go home, then?' Todd asked. 'What I mean is, was she lonely, being on her own?'

The woman shook her head. 'She never said so. She had plenty of friends.'

Todd leaned back in his chair, folding his arms. 'And yet nobody missed her for four days?'

The woman closed her eyes, the crows' feet at their corners deepening as she tensed up. 'That was my fault,' she whispered. 'We were supposed to be going away for the weekend but I had to cancel because my son and his wife needed me to babysit.'

A uniformed WPC came into the room with a tray of tea and the woman took one, cradling it in her hands.

'Mrs Green, this might sound like an odd question,' Megan ventured, 'but can you remember exactly what your friend was wearing when you last saw her?' She caught Dave Todd's sideways glance.

'Well, yes, I *think* I can.' The woman frowned. 'It was a navy knee-length skirt and a patterned blouse. It was a nice blouse; *Marks & Spencer's*. She wore it a lot.' The woman paused, chewing on her lip. 'And she'd bought a pair of new shoes. I remember her commenting on how comfy they were, considering they were new. They were red.'

So they'd found her at last. Not such a mess as the first one, but pretty gruesome viewing, nonetheless. That black reporter had scooped the Beeb, getting an interview right outside the shop. And it was on the front page of the evening paper. **BLACK MAGIC KILLER CLAIMS THIRD VICTIM***. Another cutting to add to the collection. It was getting easier and easier. Just two more days to go and there'd be a number four. Who would she be, this star-in-waiting? One woman had already passed the audition. Wouldn't even need following home. Her address was there on the desk, in black and white.s*

Chapter 18

'Pendleton is a community living in fear.' Delva Lobelo was standing in the main square of the precinct. In the background were groups of sombre-faced shoppers and on her right was a woman in overalls. 'Joining me now is Molly Hutchins,' Delva announced. 'Molly works at Pendleton Pantry.' She turned to the woman. 'Molly, what's the atmosphere been like over the past few days?'

Megan was sitting in front of the television in her pyjamas. The coffee table in front of her was littered with the lists and charts she had spent all night compiling. Everything she knew about Tessa Ledbury, Joanna Hamilton and Susan Thompson had been fed in to the computer and cross-checked.

She stared at the image on the TV screen. The woman from Pendleton Pantry was saying how shocked she had been by the news that a body had been lying in a room just yards away from the café; that someone who, like herself, lived and worked in the precinct could be dead for four days without anyone realising.

But someone did, Megan thought grimly. Yesterday Dave Todd and the rest of the team had made endless phone calls and house-to-house visits. She had been with him to the flats on either side of the electrical shop. No-one had seen or heard anything. Nor had there been any reports of anyone suspicious hanging around outside. Hardly surprising, really, Megan thought, given that the murder had taken

202

place above a busy shopping precinct where strangers were coming and going all day long.

She picked one of the lists from the pile on the table. It showed aspects of the murders and details about the victims that were consistent across all three cases. All had been stabbed in the chest at least thirty times with a knife; all had been found with a white dishcloth of the same make and design in their mouths; all had lived in homes whose front or back doors were fitted with a Yale-type lock – the kind an experienced burglar would have no trouble picking – and all were last seen within a half-mile radius of Pendleton shopping precinct.

There were other details that differed in each case: the ages of the women spanned three decades; Tessa had blonde hair, Joanna's was dark brown and Susan's a pepper-and-salt mixture of grey and black; one woman was a married mother of young children, another a single lesbian and the third a widow with a grown-up daughter. There were far more differences between the women than there were similarities, Megan reflected.

She thought about Foy's theory of an occult connection. Nothing had been found in Susan Thompson's house to suggest an interest in anything of that nature. And her friend at the surgery had told them that Susan was the sort of woman who wouldn't even read her horoscope because she thought it was 'a load of tripe'.

She looked again at the list of similarities between the women. Although Tessa and Susan were naked and Joanna fully-clothed, all of them were barefoot when their bodies were found. Susan's clothes, like Tessa's, had been lying in a pile at the side of the bed, but – as had been the case for both Tessa and Joanna – there were no shoes or slippers on the floor. The shoes Susan's friend remembered her wearing were in a cupboard in the hall along with an assortment of other footwear. Was it significant that two of the victims had been wearing red shoes when last seen alive? Megan frowned. If only she knew what Tessa had been wearing on her feet. Although she owned a pair of red shoes, no-one had been able to recall if she'd had them on when she went to the precinct.

She thought about the style of shoes Joanna and Susan had been wearing. Joanna's were high fashion stilettos, while Susan's were low-heeled *Clark's Springers*. The red shoes Megan had seen in Tessa's house were more like Susan's than Joanna's. The only similarity between all three pairs was the colour, and the fact that they were proper shoes with covered toe sections rather than sandals.

Megan reached for the mug of lukewarm coffee that had kept her from nodding off in front of the TV. She had come across shoe fetishists during her research on sex offenders. One particular case stuck in her mind, of a man who had targeted women on buses in Wolverhampton in the 1950s. Armed with a razor blade, he would sit on the long sideways-facing seats, apparently looking at the floor, but what he was really doing was studying the feet of the women sitting opposite. If he spotted a woman wearing high-heeled ankle-strap shoes he would lean forward, as if to retrieve something he had dropped, and slash at the woman's ankles with the blade. He always waited until the bus was about to stop and he was up and away before anyone realised what he'd done. His victim was left screaming in agony, criss-crosses of blood oozing from her legs. He was eventually caught, but the reason for his bizarre obsession was never discovered because he committed suicide while awaiting trial.

She stared at the list on her lap. Was the killer a man like this? A man fixated by women in red shoes? That would certainly explain why the three victims were so different in every other way. The frenzied nature of the stabbings suggested that the victims represented a woman who aroused uncontrollable rage in the killer. Someone who, in real life, he was unable to murder. But what about the pentagram? What was the significance of that?

With a sigh she replaced the list and picked out another. This one showed the times of the last reported sightings of the three victims, together with estimates of time of death. The latest report on Susan Thompson stated that she had been dead between three and four days when her body was discovered. Joanna's time of death had been even more difficult to pinpoint. But Tessa had died within two hours of leaving Pendleton precinct. Working on the basis that the other women were killed within a similar time frame, Joanna would have been murdered on a Wednesday, early evening and Susan at the same time on a Thursday.

Megan looked at the dates. There had been a murder every week for the past three weeks, with the last sighting of each victim occurring within a twenty-four period between Wednesday and Thursday evening. A chilling thought occurred to her. Tomorrow was Wednesday. Would there be a *fourth* victim by tomorrow night?

She looked at her watch, knowing she should be in her office at the university. Since the meeting with the Vice-Chancellor she had popped in only briefly to collect a pile of exam papers, which now lay untouched in her study. She would phone in and make some excuse. *You're taking a huge gamble.* She grunted, ignoring Patrick's voice inside her head. Yes, it was a gamble. She was risking the wrath of the Vice-Chancellor, possibly her position as head of department, on solving this case. But how could she turn away now?

The sound of Delva's voice drew Megan's attention back to the television. 'Some news just in,' she announced, 'is that the team investigating the murders of the three women have re-arrested a man they were questioning at the week-end. The police haven't named the man they've taken into custody. We'll have more on the story in our next bulletin at eleven-forty-five.' Delva's face disappeared from the screen as the programme went to a commercial break.

Who was it, Megan wondered? Surely not Sean Raven? He was languishing in a police cell when Susan Thompson was murdered. It must be Justin Preece, then. She pressed Dave Todd's mobile number but his phone was switched off.

Mariel Raven stormed into the foyer of Tipton Street police station dragging a terrified-looking girl in her wake.

'Where is he?' She shouted at the man behind the glass partition. 'What have you bastards done with my son?'

The girl began to sob, her large breasts straining the fabric of her dress. A button popped open and she struggled to fasten it, her wet fingers staining the pale pink cotton.

'She'll tell you!' Mariel Raven grabbed the girl by the shoulders and pushed her towards the desk. 'Go on!' she yelled. 'Tell them what you and Justin were doing at six o'clock last Thursday night!'

Dave Todd was called to take the girl's statement. Mariel Raven had been taken off to another room and the girl seemed calmer now she had gone. Her face, streaked with mascara, looked much younger than her eighteen years.

'Here you are, take one of these.' Todd offered her a box of tissues. 'Now if you'd rather talk to a woman officer I can arrange for someone else to come and take your statement.'

'No,' the girl cut in. 'I just want to get it over with.'

'Right.' Todd picked up his pen. 'You said you were with Justin at his mother's house?'

She nodded.

'Was it just the two of you, or were there other people there?'

'There were others,' she whispered.

'And what were you doing?'

The girl bit her lip, her eyes fixed on the graffiti-etched surface of the table. 'We had sex,' she mumbled.

Todd frowned. 'You had sex with Justin? And there were other people in the house? Was it a party?'

'It was for the ritual. The others left the room while we did it.' She blinked and a tear rolled down her cheek. 'He was cross with me.'

'Why?' Todd said gently. 'Why was he cross with you?'

'Because it hurt me,' the girl sniffed. 'He didn't know I was a virgin.'

Megan was looking at the list of sex offenders Dave Todd had sent. Something had struck her as she read through the previous convictions of one of the men. Clive Birkinshaw was a rapist. He had been ruled out by Steve Foy's team because he was currently on remand in Winson Green on a charge of GBH.

Birkinshaw had been released from Durham jail just before Christmas after serving six years for attacking a woman in Derby. Before that he had done a stretch at Sudbury for handling stolen goods. It was the dates of that jail term which had caught Megan's attention. The date given for the rape offence meant it had been committed while he was still an inmate of Sudbury. How could that be?

She frowned. Sudbury was an open prison. *Like Whiteladies*. What had Bob Spelman said about prisoners on day-release work placements? She felt the hairs on the back of her neck stand up. What if the killer was someone like Birkinshaw? Someone jailed for a minor offence who had graduated to murder while in prison? *The University of Crime* – that's what some of the lifers she'd interviewed called the prison system. It wasn't hard to imagine how fantasies might fester and develop in an atmosphere like that. Birkinshaw must have raped while he was out on day-release. She had to get into Whiteladies. Find out which of the inmates were allowed to work in Pendleton.

She went to call Dave Todd but the phone rang out before she reached it.

'Meg, it's me.'

'Ceri!' It was a relief to hear her voice. She'd had her phone switched off for the past two days.

'I'm coming back tonight, but it won't be until late. I'm going to wait until the kids are ready for bed, then they'll sleep on the journey.'

'Are you all right?' Megan asked. It was a stupid question. How could her sister be all right after all that had happened in the past few days?

'I'm fine, honestly,' Ceri replied. She didn't sound it. 'Do you know what's happened to Justin? They can't still be holding him – not now they've found that other woman?'

'I don't know what's happening at the moment.' It wasn't really a lie. She didn't know for sure Justin was the one the police had re-arrested.

'Only he's still not answering his mobile,' Ceri went on. 'I wanted to try and talk to him – before I see Neil, I mean.'

Megan bit her lip. 'Do you think that's wise?'

'I have to get things clear in my head, Meg. I've been all over the place the past couple of days.' There was a pause. 'Neil's due back at lunchtime tomorrow. Jill down the road's offered to have the kids so we can talk properly.' There was a hollow laugh at the end of the line. 'She's the only one still speaking to me.'

'Ceri, you won't go anywhere near Pendleton, will you?'

'Course I won't. I should think it'll be a ghost town, anyway. Who's going to want to go shopping there after what's happened?'

'You'd be surprised,' Megan sighed. 'Some people are very ghoulish.'

Steve Foy glared at his sergeant. 'So where are these other witnesses then?' He tossed the girl's statement onto the table. 'His bloody mother's obviously put her up to this!'

Todd held Foy's gaze. There was a tell-tale trace of whisky in the peppermint blast of his boss's breath. 'We've contacted two so far,' he replied. 'Both of them back up the girl's story.'

Foy grunted. 'What a surprise! It a bloody witches' coven man! Ma Raven's got them all in her power!'

Todd cleared his throat. 'With respect, Guv, I don't think that'd stand up in court.'

Foy brought his fist down on the table. 'Bail the bastard, then!' His too-bright eyes narrowed to glittering slits. 'But you tell him I haven't finished with him yet!'

No stars out tonight. Not long to wait now, though. Soon be away from this shithole. Ride for miles, then; free as the air.

There was a time when it seemed an impossible dream. What Mum had made was an invisible prison cell.

'I want you to look like Dorothy.' Her voice whispered down the years. She had said it often. While buying party dresses in Beatties' children's department. While coaxing hair into sausage-roll ringlets with rags that itched in the night. And while choosing the shoes a boy was never meant to wear.

Yes. Freedom came at a price.

Chapter 19

Getting into Whiteladies proved almost as difficult as gaining entry to the maximum security prisons in which Megan had done so much of her research. The only way to bypass the reams of red tape it required was to get police authorisation.

It was pointless asking Steve Foy, who still seemed hellbent on pursuing his occult theory. According to Dave Todd, the re-arrest of Justin Preece had come about on the premise that he was registered at the surgery in Pendleton, *ergo* he knew Susan Thompson. 'As did the three thousand-odd other patients on the books,' Dave had said when he told her.

He had phoned last night to tell her that Justin had been bailed. After hearing her idea about Whiteladies he had contacted the governor himself. He'd got permission for the two of them to visit at nine o'clock the following morning. How he had managed it without Foy being informed Megan didn't like to ask. What mattered now was getting the names of those day-release inmates as quickly as possible.

Ceri was getting ready for the confrontation with Neil. She had dropped the children off and had run herself a bath. She needed a small oasis of calm in which to think. To plan what she was going to say when he got home.

She knew he couldn't have seen the piece in the newspaper. He had phoned her each night while he was away and it had been a real struggle, trying to pretend everything was normal. He knew she'd been to the cottage at Borth but she'd lied about the reason for her sudden trip to Wales, saying her lectures had been cancelled because of the police investigation at Pendleton. That had worried him. He had begged her to be careful when she got back, which made her feel even more guilty about what she was about to do.

Mark Westerman could have been Dave Todd's father, Megan reflected as she shook the governor's hand. Same build, same accent, same gold-rimmed glasses. The only striking difference was that Westerman's hair was completely white.

'What we need to know,' Megan said, taking the proffered cup of coffee, 'is whether any of your inmates are on day-release placements in the Pendleton area of Wolverhampton.'

The inner third of Westerman's bushy, silver-flecked eyebrows slid upwards like two exotic caterpillars sensing food. 'Can I just clarify one thing?' he said. 'We don't have sex offenders or anyone with a history of violent behaviour at Whiteladies.'

'I know that none of the inmates here has a *record* of that type of offending,' Megan said. 'The sort of man I have in mind could be someone who's slipped through the net. Someone who's been convicted of a lesser offence but has a violent past that's never been detected.'

'Well I really don't think . . .'

'Are you familiar with the Clive Birkinshaw case?' Megan cut him short.

The caterpillars jumped. He looked straight at her but said nothing.

'The rapist who attacked a woman while on day-release from Sudbury?' She had done her homework. 'He was working for a local electrical firm and managed to a rape a fellow employee because nobody supervised him during the lunch hour.'

He nodded, a wary look in his eyes.

'I'm sure the governor of Sudbury would have said the same thing as you about his inmates before that blew up in his face.' Megan's gaze was unwavering as she waited for a response.

'I can assure you the men allowed out on day-release are very carefully vetted and monitored.' Westerman glanced out of the window.

'I don't doubt that, but the man responsible for these attacks is incredibly good at covering his tracks. We're not talking about your average villain, here, Mr. Westerman. To kill three woman in the way he has without leaving a shred of forensic evidence – that takes a pretty shrewd mind, wouldn't you say?'

'Yes, but . . .'

'The kind of mind that could just as easily con people in the prison service into sending him to a place like this,' Megan went on, 'and once here, con anyone else who stood in his way. That's what Birkinshaw did.'

'I spend every day of my working life with conmen, Doctor Rhys.' His voice was little more than a loud whisper but the venom in it was unmistakeable. 'Are you suggesting I don't know my own job?'

'I'm not suggesting anything of the kind,' she said. 'But three women are dead. All them visited Pendleton shopping precinct shortly before they died. The man who organises the Christian outreach here at Whiteladies tells me there are inmates on day-release attending services at Pendleton. I *have* to know who those men are, Mr. Westerman, if only to rule them out.'

He let out a deep breath and folded his arms across his chest. 'All right,' he said grudgingly. 'But I want to make it clear I'm not happy about the way this investigation is being carried out.' He turned to Dave Todd. 'I'll be writing to your lead officer on the matter,' he said. 'You should have gone through the proper channels. Shropshire police should have been informed, for a start. Any inmate of this prison comes under their jurisdiction, not West Midlands.'

Westerman walked across to the computer terminal on the other side of the room. 'We only allow inmates out on day-release two days a week,' he said, his back to them as he stared at the computer screen. 'We don't have the resources to let them out every day.'

Megan caught her breath. 'Which days?'

'Wednesdays and Thursdays. They have a 7pm curfew.'

Megan and Todd exchanged glances. 'What time do they leave in the morning?' she asked.

'Wait a minute.' Westerman sounded irritated. They waited for what seemed like ages while he clicked away at the keyboard. Finally there was a whirring noise as the printer churned out a list of names. 'Here you are,' Westerman said, sending the piece of paper skimming across the table towards Megan so that it almost fell onto the floor.

'Thank you,' she said, grabbing it as it brushed her elbow. There were twelve names on the list. Only three of them worked at Pendleton. Two were at the supermarket; one in the bakery and another in the warehouse. The third did food preparation at Pendleton Pantry.

'The men on that list will have left here between eight o'clock and eight-thirty this morning, depending on their mode of transport. Some have their own cars; others travel into work on motorbikes or cycles.'

Megan's eyes widened. 'Can you tell me which ones have cycles?'

'Not without looking at their files.' Westerman glared at her.

'I'd like to see your files on these three, then, please.' She underlined the names and pushed them back across the table.'

'Of course.' His tone was icily polite. 'If you'll just give me a moment.'

As the door closed behind him Megan and Todd turned to each other, simultaneously letting out a breath.

'Bicycles! It's got to be one of them, hasn't it?' Todd shook his head and ran his fingers through his hair.

'We've got to get into their cells, Dave,' Megan said. 'Find something concrete.'

Westerman marched back into the room with a bundle of files under his arm.

'I've brought all twelve,' he said flatly. 'Don't want to be traipsing up and own that corridor all afternoon.' He pushed the buff-coloured folders towards Megan. She and Todd sifted through them, picking out the Pendleton men.

'This one,' Todd said, leaning across the desk to show her. 'It says he cycles to Pendleton.'

Megan looked at the photograph of a grim-faced man with close-cropped brown hair. She felt it was vaguely familiar but couldn't think why. Her eye travelled down the page. *Nicholas Stern. Age 37. Work Placement: Pendleton Pantry*. The man in the café. The one who had asked for Delva's autograph. Now she remembered.

Flicking through the pages of the file she learned that he had been convicted three years ago on five specimen charges of burglary. He had previous convictions for burglary and possessing heroin. He had been transferred to Whiteladies from Winson Green six months ago.

'He's a burglar and an ex-heroin addict?' Megan could feel her heart beginning to thud.

'Yes.' Westerman took the file from her. 'He also has a degree in Film Studies from Birmingham University.' He looked at her as if she was something on the bottom of his shoe. 'Nick is one of our most talented inmates. He's made several video recordings for us. We're planning to move him from the café next month – he's been offered a work placement at the Lighthouse Media Centre.'

'This one has a bike, too,' Todd cut in.

Megan looked at the file. It was the warehouseman at the supermarket. *Edward Fitzsimmons. Age 43*. He'd been jailed for seven counts of stealing mobile phones. His previous convictions included burglary and handling stolen goods.

Megan jumped to her feet. 'We need to check both of them out,' she said to Todd. 'Can you organise that?' Then she turned to Westerman. 'I want their cells stripped,' she said. '*Don't* under any circumstances try to contact either of them, okay?' Westerman glared at her, his eyebrows knitted. 'I can only allow you to search inmates' cells in the presence of a prison officer,' he said.

'Fine – if you can call one of your officers I'd like to start straight away.'

Westerman muttered something under his breath and picked up the phone.

Dave Todd was on his feet, frowning at his mobile. 'I'll have to go outside to get a signal,' he said to Megan. 'I'm going to head for the supermarket. I'll get another squad to go to the café.'

'Okay,' she said. 'I'll call you if I find anything.'

Ceri glanced at her watch. Neil's plane should be landing in forty minutes' time. Two hours from now he would be home. She felt a tremor run right through her body. They had been married for eight years. Eight years of her life, about to be thrown out of the window. She wondered what would have happened if she hadn't got the lecturing job; hadn't met Justin. Would she have carried on? Pretended to herself that this was a life worth living?

She slipped on the matching set of cream lace-trimmed underwear Neil had bought her last Christmas. It was pretty. Not exactly sexy. The kind of thing a good wife should wear for her husband. But she was not a good wife. And she was not intending for Neil to see it.

When Megan was shown inside Edward Fitzsimmons' cell she did a double take. It looked exactly like the rooms in the student halls of residence at Heartland. There was a single bed with a blue patterned duvet, a bedside locker with family photographs and an alarm clock and, under the window, a table and chair. But what really surprised her was the portable TV.

'They're allowed televisions in their rooms?'

'Oh, yes,' the prison officer replied. 'And they have their own key to come and go as they please. They can go pretty much anywhere they like within the prison as long as they turn up for roll calls.'

Megan glanced at the table. There were a few library books on it. One on origami and a couple on antiques. She flicked through them. Nothing fell out. She looked through the drawers in the locker. Underwear, handkerchiefs, a couple of T-shirts and a collection of Christmas and birthday cards.

'From his wife, kids and grandchildren,' the officer said. 'That's them.' He nodded at the photographs on top of the locker. In the largest of them Edward Fitzsimmons was sitting on a bench surrounded by his family. There was a baby on his lap and another child – a little boy with blonde curls – was leaning his head against his shoulder.

'Can you get someone else to strip this room?' Megan asked. 'I'd like to see the other one.'

Nick Stern's cell was almost identical to Fitzsimmons', apart from the posters on the walls. They were all promotional material for films – the kind cinemas would have on display in their foyers. They were not mainstream films – more arthouse. *Girl With a Pearl Earring*, *Tin Drum* and

The Cook, The Thief, His Wife And Her Lover were the only ones she recognised. Some bore French text and others were in German.

Alongside the portable TV was a pile of newspapers. She picked up the top one. As she moved it she caught sight of something that made her freeze. It was the local evening paper, folded open at page three, with her photograph on it. She opened the paper out. Her mouth went dry. In the top left-hand corner of page two, drawn in blue biro, was a pentagram.

Chapter 20

Megan ran out to the prison car park, punching out Dave Todd's number as soon as she got a signal. As she waited for it to answer she spread out the newspaper on the bonnet of her car. A sentence in quotation marks jumped out at her: 'All she was wearing was a pair of red stilettos and a smile.' *Red shoes.* A terrifying thought occurred to her. Ceri's address was there too. 23 Church Terrace, Stockhall.

'Dave Todd.' His voice startled her.

'Dave,' she began, her voice shaking. 'I've found something in Nick Stern's room. It's a pentagram drawn on a newspaper – next to an article about my sister.'

She heard him take a breath. 'Right,' he said, his voice even. 'I'm with Fitzsimmons at the moment, in the manager's office. I'll find out what's happening at the café and get back to you.'

As soon as he'd gone she rang Ceri's number. It was engaged. Megan jumped into the car. She had to warn her sister. Perspiration dripped down the back of her neck as she sped along the country lane that led to the Wolverhampton road. She punched the redial button on her phone. This time she got the answerphone. 'Oh God, Ceri,' she said aloud, 'why aren't you picking up?'

As she neared the turn-off for Stockhall her phone rang out. 'Ceri?' It was Dave Todd.

'Listen, Megan, Stern's not at the café.' She could hear something very like panic in his voice. 'They said he'd got an appointment with his probation officer, but we've just phoned the guy and Stern didn't show.'

Megan felt sick. What if he was at Ceri's?

'Where are you now?' Todd asked.

'I'm on my way to my sister's. She's not answering her phone, Dave – I'm really worried.'

'Okay, I'm coming,' he said. 'Whatever you do, don't go inside on your own.'

A minute later she was pulling up outside Ceri's house. Her sister's yellow Peugeot was in the drive. She looked up and down the road. No sign of Neil's Volvo. She tried Ceri's number again. Still the answerphone. Megan got out of the car. Why would she not answer when she was clearly at home? She walked up the path to the front door. Dave had told her to wait for him, but how could she? What if Stern was in there? A few more minutes could be the difference between life and death for Ceri.

She had the front door key in her hand and as she reached for the lock she caught sight of something sticking out of the bushes at the side of the house. It was the handlebar of a bike. She stared at it. Was it the one she had seen before? Could it possibly be Justin inside the house with her sister? She hovered on the doorstep, the key inches from the lock, trying to make sense of it. Would Ceri really have invited Justin to the house with Neil due back any minute? She slid the key into the lock and inched the door open. Her instinct was to call her sister's name, but she stopped herself. Instead she listened. The house was completely silent. She stepped inside, leaving the door open for ease of escape. Then she heard a sound that froze her blood. A muffled sound, like someone trying to talk with a mouthful of food. She glanced around for something to use as a weapon. There was a bronze Art Deco statuette on the hall table. She picked it up, hiding it behind her back.

As she crept up the stairs she heard the sound again. It occurred to her that her imagination might be playing tricks on her; that what she could hear was the sound of her sister and Justin making love. She paused halfway up the staircase. Her sister's bedroom was directly opposite the top step. If the door was open she would be able to see inside; creep away without them seeing if she had got it wrong.

Her hand shook as she grasped the banister rail, trying to distribute her weight in case the stairs creaked. As her eyes drew level with the top step she saw that the door was wide open. Ceri was crouching on the floor, her back to Megan. Beside her was one of the red stiletto shoes she had worn for Justin. And nearer to the bed were a pair of legs in blue jeans; someone standing by Ceri. As Megan climbed the next step she saw at a glance it was not Justin. He was shorter and stockier and his dark brown hair was cropped close to his head. He was leaning over Ceri, who was groping behind her for the red shoe. As his hand moved something glinted in the sunlight streaming through the bedroom window. It was the blade of a knife.

Megan's hand tightened on the bronze statuette. What should she do? If she stormed in there and lunged at him he would stab Ceri. She had to distract him; confuse him. Keep him talking until . . . what?

The decision was taken away from her as he wheeled round, as if sensing her presence. Their eyes locked. For a second no-one moved. *His name*, a voice inside her head whispered. *Say his name*.

'Nick?'

The blue eyes flickered with surprise, then narrowed as he recognised her. 'So you've come for your sister?' He sounded younger than thirty-seven. There was a hint of a Wolverhampton accent. He cocked his head on one side. 'Well, she's not here.'

Megan stared at the figure on the floor. 'Ceri?' The woman's head turned with a muffled grunt. Megan could see that it was her sister's profile. There was white cloth poking out between her lips. Suddenly it dawned on her. To him she was not Ceri. She had become the woman he hated; the one he wanted to kill. That was why he was making her sister put on the red shoes. To become that woman she *had* to be wearing the red shoes.

'What's her name, Nick?' Megan took a step towards the bedroom door.

'Nicky.' He brought the knife up against Ceri's throat. 'She looks like Dorothy, but her name's Nicky.'

'Nicky.' Megan nodded slowly, frantically trying to work out what was going on inside his head.

'You don't know what I'm talking about do you?' He grabbed Ceri by the hair as she tried to edge away from the knife. 'People like you – psychologists!' He grunted. 'Everyone's always needling me; trying to find out what I'm about!'

'I know you like red shoes, Nick.' Megan took another step towards him. As she did so she caught a flicker of movement out of the corner of her eye. It was Dave Todd. He was on the half-landing below her.

'Don't come any closer!' Stern's voice rang out. Megan froze. He had raised the knife above her sister's chest. 'And drop that!' He jerked his head at the statuette. Megan let it go and it landed with a thud on the pale blue carpet. 'Now get up,' he screamed at Ceri, kicking at her feet in their red shoes. 'Get on the bed!'

Megan knew she had to get further into the bedroom; do something that would lead Stern's eye away from the door so that Dave Todd could get at him without being seen. 'Nick, please,' she cried out, 'I want to help you!'

'I told you to stay where you are!' His eyes were fixed on her as he pushed Ceri onto the bed.

'Let *me* wear the red shoes,' she pleaded, stretching out her hand 'I'm Nicky, not *her*!' He stared at her, transfixed, as she moved slowly round the bed. 'Tell her to take the shoes off, Nick,' she said softly. 'I want them. They're for me.'

'Take them off!' He pressed the flat of the knife against Ceri's neck and she kicked off the shoes. Megan bent to pick them up, moving to the opposite side of the bed as she put them on. Lifting her right leg onto the bed she extended her foot, pointing her toe like a ballet dancer. 'Look at me, Nick,' she whispered. 'Doesn't my foot look beautiful in this shoe?' She looked at him. His eyes were full of horrified fascination, like a child watching snakes in a zoo. 'Does it make me look like Dorothy?' Megan taunted him, willing him to move towards her. 'Will you tell me who she is?'

With a howl of rage he lunged at her, but Todd was on him, knocking the knife from his hand as he rugby-tackled him to the floor.

The house was swarming with police officers. The place had been surrounded when Dave Todd broke the rules to go in, unarmed. Megan was glad she hadn't known that. She wasn't sure she'd have been quite so bold if she'd realised Dave didn't have a gun.

She could see him now through the open bedroom window. He and two other officers were bundling Stern into a waiting squad car. As she watched she caught sight of Neil. From the look on his face, he had just arrived. What a thing to come home to, she thought grimly.

Ceri was sobbing uncontrollably and wouldn't move from the bed. Neither Megan nor the woman police officer sitting next to her had been able to calm her. Megan stroked her sister's hair. What Ceri had been through in the past few days was enough to turn anyone into a basket case.

'I'll go and get her some tea or brandy or something,' Megan said when Dave came back into the room. He followed her downstairs.

'What about you?' he said, shutting the kitchen door behind him. 'Are *you* all right?'

'I'm fine.' Her fingers trembled as she flicked the switch on the kettle and she felt his hand on her shoulder. She wheeled round and he took his hand away. 'You were very brave up there.' She could see her eyes reflected in his glasses. For a moment neither of them spoke.

'No, you were the hero.' She broke away, reaching for mugs on the shelf above the microwave. The kitchen door opened and a man in white overalls appeared.

'Could you come and talk to the SOCOs, Dave?'

'I'll catch you later, okay?' Todd's expression made her crumple inside. It reminded her of the way Patrick had looked at her when he was a student and she was his supervisor.

As Todd went through the door Megan caught sight of Neil. He was standing in the hallway, his mouth open and a dazed expression in his eyes. He looked completely out of his depth. She left the tea and ran to help. But before she could get to him he turned towards the stairs. Ceri was stumbling down them, clinging to the banister rail for support. Before she reached the last step she fell into his arms.

There was nothing Megan could do but leave them to it. The trauma that Ceri had been through had obviously turned her feelings about Neil on their head. It was something they were going to have to talk through themselves and her presence was not going to help matters.

She blinked as she walked through the front door into the bright sunshine. The police had sealed off the road and beyond the striped tape groups of curious neighbours had gathered. She spotted a TV camera mounted on a tripod. Delva was standing close by. She looked as if she was interviewing somebody, but her height prevented Megan from seeing who it was. Moving down the path, Megan drew closer to the camera. It was Steve Foy. She could hear his voice.

'I'm very pleased it's ended without further casualties,' he was saying. 'And it certainly shows the value of good police work.'

As Megan stepped behind the camera she caught Delva's eye. Delva raised her eyebrow half an inch. Megan shook her head, a wry smile on her face.

The next morning Delva called at Megan's house, minus the cameraman.

'I just came to see how you are,' she laughed. 'I *would* like to do a background piece in a few months' time, though, when the case comes to court. And don't worry, I'll make sure you get the credit you deserve for catching the bastard.' She leaned forward in her seat as Megan poured coffee. 'Why did he do it? I heard a copper muttering something about red shoes . . .'

Megan nodded slowly. 'It's a really bizarre story.' And it was a story she was safe to tell. She knew Delva was legally bound not to report a word of it until Stern had entered his plea of guilty to all three murders.

She told Delva what Stern had told the police last night at Tipton Street station. About the mother who had wanted a girl so desperately she had made him wear dresses as a child and told people his name was Nicky. About the Christmas when she had dressed him up to look like Dorothy from *The Wizard of Oz* and told him he was going to be famous, just like Judy Garland. And about the beating he received when his father discovered the two of them, all rigged out, watching the film.

'That was where the obsession with red shoes came

from,' Megan explained. 'All through adulthood he'd tried
to cultivate a macho image. But at university he got into
drugs and ended up a heroin addict. He turned to burglary
to fund his habit and ended up in prison. That made him
worse.' She paused to take a sip of coffee. 'He was afraid
of 'turning gay', as he put it. In prison he developed a
desperate urge to crush the female persona his mother
had foisted on him as a child.' She shook her head. 'From
what I can gather the people he was mixing with in jail
encouraged him in this fantasy of attacking women. He
conned everyone in the system into believing he was a
model prisoner, but when he got out on day-release this
rage he'd been building up just boiled over.'

'Was that why the women were stabbed so many times?'
Delva's cup was perched halfway between the table and
her mouth. She had been hanging on Megan's every word.

'I think so,' Megan replied. 'There's a term for that kind
of frenzied attack. They call it overkill.'

'So by stabbing the women in red shoes he was trying to
kill the little girl his mother had tried to turn him into?'

Megan nodded.

'But all this black magic stuff,' Delva frowned. 'Where
the hell did that come from?'

'He carved a pentagram on his victim's heads.'

Delva's jaw dropped. 'My God! I knew there was something really horrible going on that no-one would talk about,
but . . .' she broke off, her hand across her mouth.

'I know.' Megan shrugged. 'It completely threw the police.
I thought it might have been done deliberately to make it
look like some kind of black magic ritual. But as it turned
out, we were both wrong.'

'What was it, then?'

'His signature,' Megan said simply. 'His surname is the
German word for 'star'. That was why his mother was con-

vinced he was going to be famous. And in a twisted kind of way I suppose he's fulfilled her prediction.'

As Delva said goodbye Megan glanced at her watch. Patrick would be arriving soon to pick up his boots and CDs. She must make herself scarce. Or should she? The doubts that had been festering in her mind since she'd ordered him out of the house came flooding back.

She could never give him a baby and he would have wanted one eventually, so wasn't this the next best thing? Yes, it would be torture, seeing him with it, but perhaps she could bring herself to accept it in time. Maybe she would even grow fond of it when it came for holidays, as it surely would.

She stood there, staring at the front door, wondering what on earth she should do. However she tried to rationalise it, there was one fact she couldn't ignore. Patrick had lied to her. He had lied about what happened in Holland last Christmas. And because of that lie he had started his relationship with her under false pretences. Maybe something like that could be forgiven when there were other reasons to keep a relationship together; when there were children, like for Ceri and Neil. But there wasn't anything like that . . .

Megan slumped back onto the stairs, her head in her hands. Glancing up, she noticed the pile of post still lying on the mat. She picked it up. On the top was a yellow envelope. She tore it open. It was a card with a print of Monet's *Waterlilies* and the words 'Thinking of You' on the front. Inside was written: 'Hope you've recovered from yesterday's drama. Be nice to talk to you about something other than serial killers. All the best, Dave.'

She smiled. Reaching for the coat rack she pulled down her jacket. It was time she was on her way.

Have you read the first Megan Rhys novel?

FROZEN

Megan has been asked to advise on two murders: young prostitutes, dumped like rubbish, seemingly the victims of two men working together. But there is something wrong with the information the police are giving her. Someone is trying to manipulate her. Or are her own prejudices colouring her judgement?

As the killings add up, Megan is being pushed harder and harder towards one solution – and someone is getting into her house.

Can she trust her instincts?

Is the killer closer than she realises?

ISBN 1-870206-60-6

£6.99